THE HUNT CLUB

Dorsh Publishing
La Jolla, California
DorshPublishing.com

ISBN: 978-0-578-14456-6

AUTHOR'S NOTE

This book is a work of fiction. The narrative sections of this book are not meant to describe anyone, living or dead. All names, events and most places are a complete figment of the author's imagination.

This book is dedicated to:

…my wife, Patty, for her continuous support and encouragement during the creation of this story.

…the Memories of Gena-Soda-Rickens-a-Furda-Minikins Parkway and all the people who played a part in my years in Mayfield Heights.

Thanks to Harry Polkinhorn, for his editorial expertise

And special thanks to Peggy Irvin of The Art of Nature for her friendship, proofreading, and cover design
TheArtofNature@gmail.com

Prologue

Water rushed furiously past overloaded storm sewers and over curbs, flooding the streets and sidewalks. It rarely rained in August, but for the past twenty-four hours it poured. Blue and red flashing lights bounced through the palm trees and off the dark, shiny, drenched pavement as the two San Diego police cruisers entered the alley. Each officer switched on his searchlight and swung a wide beam in the direction of the sopping, bloody body.

Both officers, wearing yellow, department-issued slickers, bolted from their cars, and hurried to the victim. Stooping next to him, the first officer remarked, "Another one of La Jolla's finest, huh?"

"Is he still alive?" asked the second officer.

The back of the victim's head was braced on the wall of the church. He sat slumped in a diluted pool of blood. He was unshaved, with rain-soaked, matted hair, and was clearly terrified, his swollen eyes rapidly moving from side to side.

"Hey, buddy, can you hear me? What's your name? Do you know who did this to you?"

His khaki pants were torn below the knees, and his boots were covered with mud. He wore two jackets. A dark inner jacket was zipped up to his neck. The outer was filthy and half open. Embroidered on the upper left chest area of the inside jacket was a blue and white burgee with a red star in the center, San Diego Yacht Club.

"Maybe this guy's not homeless." remarked the officer. "Maybe he was just in the wrong place at the wrong time?"

"Yeah, look at his eyes. I'll call for an ambulance."

As 126 Baker made the call, the first officer slowly rolled the victim to the left and spotted the handle of a knife protruding from his side.

"Make that 11-41 a code 3, will ya? There's a knife sticking out of his right side." Leaning close, the officer said, "Listen, sir, can you hear me? An ambulance is on the way. You might die. What's your name? Who did this to you? If you know who did this, you better tell me now."

The rain was falling harder as the ambulance backed into the alley. While paramedics placed him onto the gurney, the officer leaned closer, squeezing his hand. "Tell me, man, what's your name? Who did this to you?"

The victim's desperate eyes penetrated the policeman's. His mind was spinning as he uttered in a dreadful tone, "Finch, Finch! He, ah, he didn't..."

Chapter 1

Summer 1957

The sound of the rushing water was almost deafening as it leaped over the edge of the falls and smashed into the eroded and jagged rocks below. Cool mist filled the air with a musty fragrance. Flat, slippery moss covered stone shelves that edged their way out over the crystal-clear current as it rushed downstream from the base of the drop. The sun's rays barely penetrated through the dense wall of trees on the opposite side of the river.

Augy and Finch stood on the largest shelf. Finch was fishing. He held his pole in his right hand and extended his left arm up and out to his side while lightly pinching the fine nylon line with his left index finger and thumb. The nearly invisible line stretched out into the racing water. Once in a while, with the thought of attracting a fish, he would give it a tug. Augy, ten feet to the right of Finch, was pulling and yanking on his line as he shook his pole back and forth. His line was again tangled in a tree branch, which hung out over the moving water.

"Hey, Finch, help me, will ya?"

"Again, stupid head, are you caught again?"

"Come-on, I don't need no sermon. Just help me get this line off the tree."

Finch, sure-footed so he wouldn't slip on the slippery green moss, slowly stepped sideways toward Augy. "You hold my rod and hand me yours."

As Augy switched places with Finch he said, "Don't break my line again. I don't wanna lose the hook."

"Hey, if it breaks, too bad. We been here all day, and all you do is get caught in trees or tangle up your line in the reel. Why do you fish, anyway?" He started to laugh as he pulled a cherry bomb out of his pocket and held it up toward Finch. Teasingly, rolling it back and forth between his thumb and forefinger. "I fish 'cause I like to put this in their mouths and watch 'em blow up, same as you."

Finch, laughing back, replied, "Someday I would like to know how a fish tastes, instead of, all the time, wearing parts of its head all over my clothes."

***

The summer of 1957 was an adventurous time for the two twelve-year-olds. They often rode their bikes down the worn, smooth, brick-surfaced Old Mill Road into Gates Mills. Finch, as usual, daydreamed of a fantasy life as they coasted past walls of giant trees surrounding the ivy-covered stone mansions.

The Chagrin River wound for miles and through several communities. It was mostly shallow with an occasional deep rocky bottom. Certain edges of the river looked like pools where the current slowed and the water almost stood still. It was beautiful. The falls were located across the street from the kennels at the Hunt Club, a private gathering spot for the wealthy.

No fishing trip was complete without blowing up at least a half dozen fish and then, of course, sneaking into the dog kennels and harassing the hunting dogs until they wailed and howled. The boys were always chased away by the groundskeepers. The falls were the favorite fishing spot for the boys. Suddenly, after one of many strong tugs, Augy's line came loose, and Finch reeled it in as fast as he could. At the same time, Augy started to reel in Finch's line.

"Hey, Finch, we gotta go. It's gonna take forever to pedal up the hill."

"Okay, Aug, but first let's go visit the dogs."

"Aw, come on, not today. I gotta get home."

"How come all of a sudden, you gotta go home?"

"I just do; that's all. My sister is coming over for a barbeque and stuff."

"What kinda stuff?" Finch snickered.

"Just a barbeque, that's all, you dick. No other stuff."

The boys gathered their gear and began the strenuous trip for home. They zoomed by the Hunt Club and pedaled past the stately Red Fox Inn. Small, quaint shops were clustered on both sides of the road. The two-block long, late eighteenth-century wooded village took Finch into another world. He often visualized how great it would be to obtain the affluence and the lifestyle associated with living and growing up in the community of Gates Mills. He pedaled faster, in order to catch up with Augy, who was almost in a standing position and peddling furiously.

"Wait up!"

"What do you want?" shouted Augy, as he looked over his shoulder at Finch, then sat and started coasting to slow down.

"It would be nice to be rich and live down here, ha?"

"Heck no, asshole! Who wants to live down here, anyway? I don't know nobody here and school would be too far to go to."

"You shit-head, if you lived here you would go to Hawkins or Gilmore, and your mom and dad would buy you a red sports car when you turn sixteen. You could wear one of those big winter coats with the wood and rope buttons. The ones with the big hood. I bet they wouldn't chase you out of the kennels anymore, either, because you could be a member of the place and everyone would know you."

"Finch, you're dreaming again. You're nuts."

"Yeah, some day, you'll see. When you come visit me, you're gonna have to pay to see me."

"Sure, people are gonna come pay to watch you blow up fish. An' you think I'm dumb? You're the stupid head."

"Aw, eat shit, asshole!"

"Yeah Finch, what should I do with your clothes?"

"Never mind. I'll beat you up the hill."

Chapter 2

"Hey, Ma, I'm home." Augy shouted as he burst through the side door.

"Shush, she replied. "That's $200.00 in the fourth on Mayberry. I got it, thanks. Later, bye."

"What's for supper, Ma?" Scribbling on her note pad, she said, "Augostino, you know better than to come barging in here wit a louda voice. Go wash up, your father will be home soon. Get the barbeque ready."

"Is Donna comin'?"

"Yes." Then the phone rang again. "Yeah", she answered. "You got no more credit wit' me. Don't call here no more!"

Augy's family was somewhat different from the majority of blue-collar families in Mayfield, a small suburb 20 miles east of Cleveland. His parents were much older than most of the other kids' parents in the neighborhood. His father owned his own business and spent much of his time away from home. He always drove a new Ninety-Eight Oldsmobile while his neighbors could hardly afford more than their Chevys and Fords.

Felicia, Augy's mother, practically lived in her kitchen, wearing old, faded house dresses. Augy always thought she looked like she was wearing a tablecloth from an Italian restaurant. Her days consisted of cooking and talking on the phone. She pulled and stretched the long red phone cord behind her as she paced, back and forth, from the sink to the stove to the oven to the refrigerator and then back to the sink again. Her spaghetti and lasagna were masterpieces. The tough, old Italian lady was a bookie and spent most of her daytime hours doing business as she cooked.

Living in another world, she had already raised one family and paid little attention to Augy, who was the youngest of seven children with almost ten years between him and his older sister. His real name was Augostino Joseph Romano. Augy suited him just fine. His family would always joke about how he was the true "mistake by the lake" and not the Cleveland Stadium, as it was referred to by many comedians.

His father, in order to make up for not being home much, always bought Augy inappropriate toys and gifts. Augy was the first one in the neighborhood to have a motorbike, and the first one to have his own .22 caliber rifle. Before Augy became a teenager, his father thought nothing of buying him steel-strapped, wooden kegs of gunpowder so he could experiment making rockets in his garage. Werner Von Braun was his idol.

This year the brick barbeque was new because the year before Augy had blown up the old one while attempting to launch an eighteen-inch pipe bomb, which, to date, was the closest he had ever gotten to actually making a rocket.

***

Finch arrived home by cutting through the hedges, which separated his back yard from Augy's. His pants were muddy, and the front of his white tee shirt was covered with splotches of fish blood. His right arm held his bicycle high over his head, while his other arm was pressed tightly against his side bracing the rod and reel, which were tucked into his armpit. His left hand extended down awkwardly gripping his pants at the waist so they wouldn't slip down. The old, thin, white leather belt, a hand-me-down from his brother, was a fad in the late 50s. Augy always teased him about the belt and would want to use it as a stringer if he caught any fish. Finch dropped his bike on the grass, ran by the side of the small, one-car, wooden garage, and tossed his fishing pole through the open door into the corner.

Anna, his mother, was standing in the kitchen waiting for him. The screen door slammed behind him as he shot thru the narrow stairway into the kitchen.

"Jakela, where have you been? I have been worried sick. Were you with that Augy boy again?"

Edging past, Finch said, "Yea, we went fishing down by the river." He spotted the fresh chopped liver and onion sitting in a bowl on the counter. His favorite.

"Did you catch anything?"

Scooping with his forefinger, then licking, he said with his mouth stuffed, "No, we never catch anything."

Sternly, she replied, "Don't put your finger in there! I don't understand. If you never catch anything, how come you go? Your brother never went fishing, and I always knew where he was." Stretching her arms from her sides in frustration, she said. "I never know where you are or where you are going to be from one minute to the next."

"Come on, Ma, give me a break." His arms reached out in front of him, mimicking in his way, as if he were begging for mercy, "I can't sit and read all day, every day, like he did."

"He still does, you know. That's why he will be a successful rich man, and you won't be."

Turning, Finch walked toward the stairs and thought to himself, not again, I don't need to hear this again. Why couldn't my brother be an asshole like everyone else's? "Furthermore, keep your feet off the wall up there. You're making marks all over."

***

Finch's family represented a minority of transplanted Jewish immigrants found within the community of Mayfield. His real name was Jacob Richard Nubaum. When his family moved to Mayfield in 1953, he had just turned eight years old. A name like Jacob or a nickname like Jake, Richy, or Dicky would certainly have caused undue peer pressure within the mostly Italian community. His only sibling was his brother. Myron was seven years older and gave Jake the nickname of Finch because when he whistled he sounded like a bird. Jake liked the name Finch, especially around the neighborhood boys.

Shortly after moving to Mayfield, his mother got a job at Charky's. This was a fast-food restaurant with a mouth-watering menu of greasy burgers, crisp fries, and thick chocolate malts. In the summers, Myron was responsible for Finch but would just lie around all day and read. His idea of being in charge of his kid brother was to have Finch peddle his bike to the restaurant at least twice a day, first for lunch and then later for an afternoon snack of malts and fries. Pudgy was a good description of Finch until he hit twelve in 1957.

That year, Myron went off to Ohio State, and his mother switched jobs and became a clerk at a drugstore in downtown Cleveland. Finch's extra weight soon dropped off.

His father was in his late forties. He was a fairly passive, short, balding man, who felt self-conscious because of his deep Yiddish accent. He was a taxi driver. The ninety-nine dollar monthly house payment wasn't as easy to gather as some would think. His father would leave for work at 5 a.m. and usually arrive home by 4:30 in the afternoon.

Anna, Finch's mother, would start her walk to the corner at 7:15 sharp, so she could catch the 7:30 Redifer bus to downtown. The bus ride usually lasted an hour, but on some winter days it took as much as two hours, each way.

Every evening, Finch's father would go to bed early, and his mother would sit at the kitchen table, smoking cigarettes, drinking coffee, and stressing the importance of Finch's future with education. "A doctor, you have to be a doctor, maybe a lawyer," she repeated endlessly. His brother graduated high school early and had numerous awards and scholarships. Every time Finch received poor grades, his mother would lecture him and shove his brother's success down his throat. As Finch grew older, he manipulated his average grades on his report card to As and Bs, thereby easing any verbal confrontation with his mother. Now that she was working downtown, he had more unsupervised time. He rebelled by spending most of it inciting mischievous activities with the neighborhood boys.

Most of the other boys had nicknames as well: Pock Face, Suey, RJ, Puckey Deenis, Tubless Screwdriver, and Birdseed, also known as Chocolate Charley, or Chung Wah Charlie. There was The Lush and one tiny little girl named Bone, to mention a few. Augy was just Augy.

Chapter 3

Aside from all the foolishness, the neighborhood boys had a solemn, unspoken code of honor between them. If you got caught doing something wrong, you never squealed. Finch was smart and the only one who consistently got away without getting nabbed.

The fact that Finch and Augy were always together gave some people the impression that they were related. They had known each other for almost five years and considered themselves brothers. It didn't seem to matter that Augy had straight black hair, black eyes, with an olive complexion, and stood five-feet seven inches at the age of twelve. He was a tough kid, strong as an ox, built like a brick wall, as some would say. Finch, at twelve, was five inches shorter than Augy. He had short, sandy-blond hair, blue eyes, and a light complexion. He wasn't tough but was solid. Getting rid of the chocolate malts really helped.

***

In the summer months the boys were virtually inseparable. During the daytime they hiked and fished. They spent many nights camped out in one or the other's back yards. Confirming that their parents were asleep, they wandered around the neighborhood looking for something corrupt to get into.

One late August night, the two of them were walking the neighborhood streets and couldn't help but notice several for sale signs.

"Hey, Finch, I got a good idea. Let's take all the for-sale signs we can find and put them in Pock Face's front yard."

"Good idea, Aug, but I don't want to be around when his old man wakes up. He'll kill us."

"Screw him. I wish I could see Pock's face when he sees them."

The boys worked for hours, rushing up and down the neighborhood streets quietly yanking and carrying every for-sale sign they could find. At five a.m. there were about thirty-five signs stuck in Pock Face's front yard. They ran back to Augy's, crawled into their tent, and soon fell asleep.

At 7:30 the canvas flap tore open.

"What the hell is going on here?" demanded Augy's father. "Where the hell were you two last night? I want you to get out here and put them back right now." Augy and Finch sprung up in a daze.

"What are you talkin' about? We didn't do nothin'" Augy spurted, as he yanked on his pants.

"Don't give me that, you little shit. Get up. Get out front and put them back. Finch, if you don't want your parents to find out about this, you better get your butt up and out front with Augy." Holding a firm grip on the back of their necks, he forcibly escorted the boys to the front of the house.

Both mouths dropped simultaneously, and their eyes opened wide. There, firmly planted in Augy's front lawn, stood all the for-sale signs. Finch, smiling as he clinched his teeth, looked at Augy and said, "He won again."

"Take them back!"

"Okay, okay," said Augy. "We'll take them back where they came from." The boys started yanking the signs out of the ground. Augy's father slowly backed his white '57 Olds out of the driveway. Emphasizing his disgust, he shook his head from side to side, but he was laughing to himself as he pulled away.

They spent most of the day hauling the signs down to Ridgebury Woods, where they hurled them, one at a time, into a large, stagnant, scum-ridden pond.

Chapter 4

1958

The neighborhood was well aware of the pranks and mischief the boys seemed to be consistently involved in. Most situations were simply laughed off and considered petty. A few incidents, however, seemed to get under the skin of some rigid old-timers.

Finch was thirteen years old when he got his first real job as a newspaper delivery boy for the Sun Press, a local neighborhood weekly. The route consisted of transporting papers to the seventy-five homes on his street and part of the next. Finch's biggest challenge during his newspaper career was collecting and making change for the monthly fee of $1.50.

Giant arched oaks and buckeye trees towered over and covered the street and sidewalks. Being outside was like living in a never-ending tunnel. The fully dressed trees in the summer allowed spiraling rays of light to penetrate to the street and concrete sidewalks below. In the fall, a beautiful spectrum of colored leaves set the stage for Halloween and then Thanksgiving. The winter months were captured as a gigantic, snowy white, heavenly arch. Spring was like a rebirthing of fresh new growth joined by the melodious sounds of busy birds setting up their new homes.

Most homes were simple, mid-1940s, brick and wood, two-story, colonial-style affairs and were situated about 20 feet from the sidewalk. There was, however, an occasional old, wood farmhouse set well back from the street occupied by mostly older residents who had sold their land off to the developers who had subdivided and built the neighborhood.

***

Chester, the sixteen-year-old grandson of Mr. Concherto, would visit every summer. Mr. Concherto was an eighty-three-year-old, slouching, white-haired, wrinkled man. Most noticeable were the globs of hair growing out of his ears and nose. To Finch, Chester resembled some kind of monster he had once seen at a movie. He was big, mean, and, unlike his grandpa, he didn't look white. After all, everyone in Mayfield looked the same to him. Finch was afraid of Chester. His hair grew out of his head in short stalks, giving the impression that he was wild and untamed. He was tall and solid like Augy. He had a scar on his lip, which ran right up into his wide flat nose. None of the neighborhood kids wanted to play with him because he was habitually much too rough with them. It was rumored that Chester was living in a reformatory somewhere in Iowa, except when he came to visit his grandfather in the summers.

Finch would fold and pack his papers in a canvas bag, which he then draped around the rear fender of his old hand-me-down Schwinn. Chester always picked on Finch when he was delivering his papers. Chester thought nothing of standing in front of Finch, blocking him, as he pedaled to deliver the paper. Chester would knock the bike over, grab all the papers, and start throwing them in a 360-degree circle. Finch really hated going up the long brick walkway to collect at Mr. Concherto's house. The doorbell seemed to ring a million times before the old man answered. Every time Finch came to collect, Mr. Concherto would try to introduce his grandson to him by asking him to invite the terror out to play with him and the other boys. Did the old guy actually think Finch didn't remember him? Meanwhile, Chester would always stand right behind his grandpa, making funny faces at Finch, tossing him the finger, holding his breath, until his face turned red, and clasping his fists with rage. Finch was always nervous when he saw the big kid. He just knew that one day, Chester would jump over his grandpa and fly through the screen door and kill him.

Old man Concherto couldn't hear very well. Finch was convinced that it was because of all the hair in his ears. One early evening, after nervously preparing himself for the imminent confrontation, he rang the bell and the door opened.

"Collecting," said Finch. Old Man Concherto looked at Finch, pulled a wad of money from his pocket, which was tied with a rubber band, and handed him a fifty-dollar bill. Finch stared at it like it was something from outer space.

"Umm," hesitating. *What the Fuck am I supposed to do with this?* he thought.

"I want to pay the paper a year ahead." Finch was confused; he wrinkled his forehead and squinted his eyes. He could barely collect for part of a month, yet an entire year. "I would like you to meet my Grandson; his name..."

Just then, Finch's fear became reality. Chester swung open the screen door, jumped from behind the old man, and stood with his back arched and his arms high over his head, like the wings of a condor. He was laughing as he looked directly into Finch's face. Then, with his mouth wide open, he roared like the MGM lion, which was rumored to have killed its trainer.

Chester's eyes were big red firebombs. Some of his teeth were missing, and others were bent. Finch, traumatized and in a state of panic, dropped the fifty-dollar bill and tripped, face first, over his bicycle onto the bricks. He sprang up from the brick walkway, grabbed his bike by the handlebars, pushing, running, and stumbling out toward the street. He leaped onto the seat and began frantically peddling away. Chester sprinted out the walkway and into the street chasing after him.

"You people are crazy. I am never coming back here." Barely able to keep his feet on the pedals, he kept twisting his head around and saw Chester getting closer and closer. The bicycle, weaving back and forth, hit the curb and flung Finch into the bushes by the vacant lot next to Tubless Screwdriver's house. Chester leaped over the bicycle and sidewalk onto Finch as he scrambled to get away. Finch started to cry.

"You little fuck. What did you call me back there?"

"Leave me alone. I didn't mean anything."

"I'm gonna kick your little ass, once and for all, you little fucker." Spit oozed from his mouth as he slapped Finch's face. "Say Uncle you little mother fucker!"

"Uncle, Uncle, Cousin, Brother! You're hurting me! What else do you want me to say?!"

"Wise ass! Call me all the dirty words you know. Come on, call me some names." He started tugging on Finch's ears.

"Ow, that hurts!"

"Come on you little fuck, call me names! I wanna hear all the dirty words you know!"

"Shit, fuck, damn, hell, darn!"

"No, come on, real dirty stuff like motherfucker and cocksucker." He smacked him again.

"Motherfucker, cocksucker, prick, damn, shit, fuck, cock, dick! Let me go!"

"Next time, you little fuck head, I'm gonna kill you." He dismounted, stood up, and brushed the dirt off of his clothes. "Now get the fuck outta here. Don't you be tellin' anyone about this, you understand?"

"Yeah, Yeah, I understand."

"Not a word to anyone, you little dick. I'm on probation. You won't be ridin' no bike. I'll come back and break your fuckin' legs. Got it?"

Finch sniffled, "Yeah, yeah, I got it." Chester turned and started walking home.

You're gonna pay for this, you bastard. Wait till I tell Augy.

***

When he got home he was still shaking. His parents were watching television in the living room and didn't see him as he came in.

"I'm home," he yelled as he ran up the stairs to his room. He grabbed the phone and called Augy. "Get over here. I gotta talk to you. This is a fuckin' emergency." In less than a minute, Augy had jumped over the hedged rhododendrons separating the two backyards, swerved around the ragged crabapple trees, and torn through the back door of Finch's house. Then he bolted up the stairs to see Finch sprawled out on an old steel-framed cot at the top of the landing.

When the home was originally built, the attic was not finished as living area. The original owner, however, converted the space into two rooms. Instead of plaster walls, rough-finished paper-board along with raw knotty pine tongue-and-groove boards made up the walls and ceilings. This area was definitely a do-it-yourself project. There were two closets without doors. Wood dowels were nailed into the sides of the closets to hold clothes hangers. Worn green and purple carpeting ran from wall to wall. There in the main room sat a picnic table, two benches, and the steel roll-away. There were dozens of games, books, and boxes piled three feet high around the perimeter of the room. At the opposite side of the big room was an arched door, which led to Finch's bedroom. When his brother was home, they shared the area.

Out of breath, Augy, leaped down onto the floor next to the cot, shuffling his feet high up on the wall in front of him. "What happened to your face, Finchy? It's all red. What's the big fuckin' emergency?"

"Don't call me Finchy." He then proceeded to tell Augy the story of old man Concherto, his collecting adventure, and Chester.

"You know, asshole, you always complain about that kid. Let's get him." Augy exclaimed.

"What do you mean, 'let's get him'? You got a frog in your pocket?" Finch knew exactly what Augy meant; that's why he had called him.

"Don't be funny, asshole. We gotta get even with that shithead. He can't get away with that stuff."

"How do we get even with him? He is as big as you are and a lot more crazy."

He continued to shuffle his shoes up and down on the wall.

"I'm not crazy for wanting to help my friend, Finchy."

"Stop the Finchy shit and tell me what you're going to do."

"Okay, I'm not doing this alone. We need a plan, a plan to get his ass once and for all. He's only here for the summer, right?"

"Right," replied Finch. "Then he goes back to the reform school in Iowa somewhere. He even told me he is on probation. He told me he would break my legs if I told."

"Well, Dicky, get your casts ready. You're telling me, aren't you? Does he ever leave his grandfather's house?"

"No. I don't think so. He is always hanging around the yard someplace. But his grandpa wants him to go make friends and hang around with us. I don't want this asshole around me. He'll kill me."

"He won't screw with you as long as I'm here. Maybe we ought to pretend to make friends with him and then kill him."

"Bullshit, man! This guy is a mean mother. He'd just as soon kick your ass as mine. In fact, he even said he would kick your ass." He didn't say that but Finch knew it would really piss Augy off.

"He doesn't even know who the fuck I am. How could he say he would kick my ass?"

"He just did. That's all."

"Hold on!" said Augy. "I think I am getting' an idea."

"Oh, shit, not another one of your asshole ideas. We always get in trouble because of you."

"What are you complaining about, Dicko? You never get in trouble, and you never have to take the blame for nothing. I always do."

"Okay, you're right, so what are we going do to him?"

"You come over to my house tonight. Tell your mom and dad that you're sleepin' over."

"What are you going to do?"

"Not me! We are gonna do it. Just come over after supper, and I will tell you about it later. I gotta go now. See ya."

***

At 11:30 p.m. the boys quietly exited Augy's back door. They hung around a few minutes to see if Augy's parents' bedroom light went on. Once the coast was clear, Augy went into his garage and grabbed a small paper bag. Finch whispered sarcastically, "Sandwiches?"

Augy didn't answer. Then they cut through Finch's back yard and started up the street toward old man Concherto's house.

"Okay, here's the plan. You go up to the door and ring the bell. When the old guy comes to the door..."

"Wait a minute!" Finch said. "Are you nuts? I'm not going up to any door in the middle of the night."

"Why not?" replied Augy. "People are always knocking at the door in the middle of the night."

"Yeah, not at my house. What kind of crazy people knock on doors in the middle of the night? Who comes over your house in the middle of the night?"

"My sister, that's who. Whenever she gets in a fight with Frankie, she comes over. She always stays in my room, well, sometimes."

"It's a good thing she doesn't come over to my house because my father would have a heart attack."

Augy ran his fingers through his hair. "Okay, then, I have another idea."

"I can't wait to hear."

"We'll sneak into the back yard. He still has a stink-house, right?"

"So?"

"Okay, okay, we push the stink-house over a few feet from the stink-pit. Then we make noise in it, and when monster face comes running outside to see what the noise is, he falls into it."

"That's really stupid. Who says Chester is going to hear the noise and not the old man? Who says he is gonna come outside? What if he has a gun? What if he calls the cops? If he sees me, then he will know who it is. Good plan, stupid head."

"Okay Finchy, let's go check out the stink-pot."

"Don't call me that!"

"Then don't call me names, neither."

The boys stooped and sidled like crabs, 65 feet, next to the hedges which bordered the back property line on the south side of the yard. When they finally reached the old house, their legs were aching and beginning to cramp.

"Oh, shit, my legs are killing me," moaned Finch as he fell backwards on the grass. The cramping was agonizing.

"Come on, you little puss; let's go. We gotta get Chester into the stink-house."

"How are we gonna do that? What are you going do?" Finch asked.

"We can just wait for him to come out and take a dump."

"That's another fucking smart idea. Here we go again. Shit for brains! How many times do you wake up in the middle of the night to take a dump?"

Augy, rubbing his calves and kneeling next to Finch, looked puzzled as he offhandedly replied, "Oh, I didn't think of that. You got any good ideas?"

"That's good. Now it's my turn. This whole hare-brained thing was your idea, and now you want me to think of something? What's in the bag?"

"A little boomer. I made it after I left your house."

"Great, let's blow the fucker up. Man, you are really crazy."

They weren't as quiet as they thought they were. As the boys edged their way around the back of the house, a light came on in the kitchen. The wood screen door squeaked as it opened slowly. The boys watched as Chester stepped out onto the brick stoop. "Somebody out here?" The monster stood naked, except for his boxer shorts. He looked around and carefully stepped into the yard. As he opened the door to the outhouse with his right hand, he flipped a cigarette into his mouth with his left hand. The door closed.

"Now what, fuck head?" whispered Finch.

"Watch this." Augy picked up a small stone and tossed it at the worn wood siding on the stink-house.

"Who's there? Somebody out there? Don't fuck with me. I'll kick your ass," Chester said sternly.

"Fuck off, you asshole," replied Augy in a voice loud enough for Chester to hear.

"Oh, shit, here we go," blurted Finch.

Chester tugged on his boxer shorts, and leaped out the door into the yard. Augy, with a running start, plowed right into Chester's side and knocked him down. Chester was stunned from the solid impact. Augy quickly got up and started kicking Chester in the ribs. He pounced down upon Chester's face with his right knee. Chester's nose bled like a faucet. Finch, following Augy, grabbed Chester's arms and held them over his bleeding head. Chester squirmed from side to side as Augy slapped him, first with his palm and then with the back of his hand. Then Augy's powerful hand grabbed Chester's throat.

"Fuck with my friend, will ya?" Augy's temper raged.

Chester was choking and gurgling blood. Augy bent his head forward just above Chester's face. "You hare lip motherfucker. Who the fuck do you think you are? This is my fucking neighborhood.

There ain't no room for you here. Got it, cow-fuckin' boy? Think you can kick my ass, huh? How do you like this shit?"

Chester coughed as he spit blood into Augy's face. He tried to free his arms from Finch's hold. Finch quickly sat back and put his feet on Chester's shoulders as he held tight and stretched the monster's arms toward him. Chester squirmed in pain. He continued to kick his feet, but both boys held him firmly.

With his free hand, Augy snatched a handful of dirt and grass. He waited until Chester attempted to breathe through his mouth, then he shoved the filthy mixture into his mouth and ground the rest into his bloody face.

"Okay, fuck face, it's your turn. I wanna hear all the dirty words you know. Come on, you prick. Talk to me before I bust you in the face again. Oh, yeah, I almost forgot. Say fuckin' uncle. Uncle. Uncle. I wanna hear you say fuckin' uncle. Then you need to say you're fuckin' sorry to my friend here. Got it, asshole? Come on, you dumb hare-lipped, bow-legged juvenile delinquent. Fuckin' talk to me!"

Just then Finch felt Chester's right arm pop and loosen. Chester let out a muffled agonizing cry. He pulled his legs up to his waist and began to shake from the excruciating pain. Finch had dislocated Chester's shoulder.

Augy grabbed the paper bag from his back pocket. He reached inside and pulled out the small two-inch pipe, capped at both ends and full of gunpowder. The fuse protruded from the center of the pipe. Augy grabbed and held Chester's racking face tightly as he forcefully shoved the pipe deep into his mouth, past his lips and teeth.

"Now it's your turn not to tell. Fuck with me and next time I'll light this son of a bitch and blow your goddamned brains out. Got it, jailbird?"

Chester nodded rapidly, acknowledging Augy.

As the boys stood up, Augy provided one last fervent kick into Chester's groin.

Chester moaned and whimpered.

Finch turned to run, but Augy stood fixated and proud, taking a deep breath. He held it and then slowly let it out as he flexed his chest and smirked. "I promise he won't fuck with us anymore. Let's go."

Chapter 5

Finch was the dreamer. He was always thinking of ways to make money. He thought of writing a series of books for children. He would call them "How-to books."

"How to steal money from the new kids at school."

"How to make your parents believe everything you say."

"How to skip school and not get caught."

"How to fudge your grades."

And "How to sneak out of the house at night."

He decided not to write them because it dawned upon him that it would be hard to distribute or sell them without his parents finding out. He did, however, decide to get into the newspaper business for himself. He sat, for hours at a time, upstairs by the picnic table. He tinkered with an old toy printing press that his brother used to have. It didn't take long to figure out how to place each letter in a metal channel, composing words and sentences.

The name of his street was Genesee Avenue so he called his creation "The Genesee Journal." It was a one-page, one-edition newspaper. He decided he would circulate it by sliding it into the fold of each of his regular papers on his normal delivery day.

He was fired from his paper route. The phone didn't stop ringing at his house for days. Neighbors were threatening to sue his family. His mother and father were furious with him. The police visited his house, twice.

The Genesee Journal ...volume 1

Mr. Concherto has a kid living with him who is out of juvenile jail for the summer. Lock your doors and watch for foam in his mouth. He has bent teeth. His grandpa has lots of fifty-dollar bills.

Jimmy Jantz has a mother who works all night and a sister who also works all night but doing different stuff with Jonny Garvin's dad in the alley by the first crossroad. I saw them. So did Billy Balls. Captain Woods sits in his police car with her every Tuesday, behind the Mayland Theater.

Marty Collier said his dad comes home and hits him and his mom a lot. He said he hides in the closet sometimes. His mom always wears sunglasses. His dad steals trees from the old nursery on River Road. Marty said he would shoot him someday. Screwdriver's mom gets a lot of beer from Berry Tavern. My mom says she even smells like beer.

My dad said that Captain Woods is a dirty police guy. He gave him a ticket once, asked for money, and he kept the money.

Mrs. Glasson has a cat named Pussy. Pock Face tried to tie it up and burn it, but it got away. Mr. Glasson punched Dave Sopperel because he cut through his yard. The police came and Mr. Glasson gave them money. Cops make a lot of money.

the end

Needless to say, the printing press went into the trash, along with Finch's first business venture.

Chapter 6

1960

A real-estate developer had purchased the obsolete Mayfield Golf Course and was building homes. A giant billboard faced Mayfield Road and read "Welcome to Golden Gate Estates." The boys spent hours, in this, their fifteenth year, playing and watching as giant land movers rolled back and forth.

One evening in late May, after dinner, the boys ventured over a few blocks from their homes, past the first crossroad to Golden Gate. There, sitting and waiting, in all its magnificence, sat a giant yellow Caterpillar tractor. Finch dared Augy to climb on board.

Soon afterward the engine roared, and thick dark smoke poured out of the black hinge-topped exhaust pipe. Finch turned and ran.

Augy, in all of his glory, smiled assertively. The loud roaring engine was deafening, especially in the stillness of the quiet early evening. Augy stood and stepped, with authority, up onto the large metal seat. He smiled and pounded his chest like King Kong. His white teeth glistened as the rays of the setting sun beaconed through the alley onto his proud physique standing high above the ground.

Aware that no one was watching him, he plopped down onto the seat and started pushing in one pedal after another while simultaneously stroking, back and forth, two long handles, which protruded up from the floor. The big earth-mover jerked, then zig-zagged through the dirt as it made its way toward the first crossroad. Augy, realizing he didn't know how to control it, panicked and leaped off the right side. He barely missed the rolling steel treads as he fell into the rock-laden dirt. He got up and started running in the same direction as Finch. The boys were almost out of sight when the tractor took a sharp turn to the left and smashed into the side of a brick house on Orchard Avenue. The family inside was having dinner at the time. No one was hurt, but, more important to the boys, no one got caught for that fiasco. They got away again.

***

One afternoon, in mid-July weeks after the tractor incident, Finch and Augy were stretched out atop a large mound of dirt, which at one time had been a golf-course bunker, on the site of Golden Gate Estates, where it backed to Orchard. Augy, with his tee shirt off, was on his belly. Finch was spread-eagled on his back. The summer sun was hot, the sky a powder-blue.

Augy seemed to be in a trance as he gazed at a young housewife, sunbathing nude, in her backyard. Finch was daydreaming and staring into the cloudless sky.

Suddenly, Finch rolled to his side, facing Augy. Reaching into his pocket, he pulled out a Zagnut bar, his favorite candy. While peeling off the wrapper he said. "Hey, man, I been thinking. You know, Golden Gate can make us rich."

"All you do is eat those Zagnut bars. I don't s'pose you brought one for me, huh? Anyway, screw Golden Gate."

Leering, Augy said, "Think she would like to teach me a thing or two? She can make me rich."

Finch turned his head in the direction of the housewife. "Hey, man, all you think about is girls and sex stuff." "Nice tits, huh?" Finch remarked so Augy would think he cared.

"That's better than thinking about you," Augy replied.

As he finished his last chew of the candy bar, he turned toward Augy and sat up. "Yeah, that's true. Think she has any daughters?"

"Who cares about daughters, man? She's just right. Look at her bonjollies."

"You know," Finch said with authority, "it's a fact, that if she likes to be naked, her daughters like it, too. Anyway, she's old enough to be your sister."

For a second, Augy's face lost expression. He looked at Finch and said, "Yeah, you should see what my sister does to me, or used to do to me before she moved out..." Then he looked questionably at Finch and said, "What kind of fact?"

"It's a fact. I read it somewhere." Finch said confidently, "If the mom is sexy and likes to put out, then the daughters do it also. Anyway, tell me about Donna. What did she do? You never told me about that."

"Yeah, well, kiss off, Dicky." Augy swiftly changed the subject. "What about Golden Gate is making us rich?"

Finch tried again. "Aw, come on. Tell me about your sister. Does this have anything to do with when you dropped your rocks with Betty Anne, and the Doctor called it Stonies? You said your balls felt like weights, and when I was leaving your house that night, Donna was coming in the bedroom, smiling. She told me you were going to be fine. What did she have to do with anything? Did she do something to you?"

"Never mind, Fucko. I'm not talkin' about it anymore. What about making money from Golden Gate?"

Finch was quiet for a few seconds, while reorganizing his plan. "Okay, sex-brains, you know how they finish some of these houses before the others?"

"Yeah, so?" Augy picked up where he left off, staring at the housewife.

"Well, asshole, the keys are in the doors." Then he reached over and shoved Augy, "Pay attention."

Rotating and looking at him, Augy said, "Okay, now I am paying attention. What in the name of heck are you talking about?"

"The keys, man, the keys. Didn't you notice that after the door guy puts on the doors, the lock guy comes and puts in the locks and leaves the keys right in the dumb locks?"

"So?" he said, with a furrowed and confused look on his face.

"So shit head..."

"Don't call me shit head. You're the shit head!"

"Okay, okay, I'm sorry. Can I finish now?"

"Will you hurry up, please! She's gonna go inside pretty soon."

"Goddamn it, will you listen to me?" scolded Finch. "We could take the keys to the corner and get another set made for us. Then we could put the original ones back. No one would ever know."

"So what good is another set of keys gonna do for us?"

"Think about it, you dim-wit. We could get into all of the houses after people buy 'em."

Augy thought about it for a second, sat up and said, "That's a great fuckin' idea."

Within two weeks the boys had all of the keys to two streets of homes in Golden Gate. Late in the fall, after families had settled in to their new neighborhood, the boys would occasionally sneak into various homes. They always broke a window. This way they thought no one would ever suspect them of having keys. One night they broke into the house of the school track coach. They ransacked everything while looking for money, guns, and fishing gear. They stole his starter pistol and two boxes of blanks. Sometimes they even leased the keys to a few choice friends for money. Augy was the official keeper of the keys.

Chapter 7

Augy and Finch got bolder each year. Their perception of innocent fun turned into some serious crimes.

At the beginning of the school year they extorted lunch money from the new kids. They poured acid on some of the teachers' cars in the parking lot. In the evenings they broke into the school, ransacked the school offices, and destroyed important papers. One Friday afternoon they unlocked the outside basement storage room doors, and on Sunday morning they found a car with the keys in the ignition at the Uncle Bill's store, in The Golden Gate shopping center. They quickly drove to the school, broke into the visual aids department, and took hundreds of dollars of equipment, such as projectors and tape recorders. Then they drove to the Chagrin River and dumped them in the water. Then they abandoned the car by the woods on Ridgebury.

It was always just the two of them. They knew that if they included someone else in the robberies, they would be taking a chance of being caught. They could have included Chocolate Charley, Suey, and Pock Face, but they knew if it was just the two of them, their confidences were sacred. In fact, they often joked and called themselves the light-fingered five minus three. They lived by the code.

Every Thursday afternoon the police chief stopped at Augy's house to place a few bets. One day he happened to mention the burglaries to Augy's mother. That night at dinner the discussion at the table centered on how proud they were of Augy for not being involved in those crimes. Augy and Finch decided it was time to take a breather from the robberies.

***

While still fifteen, they became proficient with their arsenal of toys. The BB guns, knives, and bows with arrows became part of their daily playthings. As the boys experimented, .22 caliber

Winchester rifles entered the scene. On occasion, they would play Russian roulette with the starter pistol. Finch always stored his stolen rifles at Augy's house because he knew his father and his mother would not understand how someone could have fun with a gun. The rest of the summer and much of the fall and winter were spent at Ridgebury Woods, shooting at cans and bottles, not to mention birds, rabbits, and squirrels. Oftentimes, Augy would load Finch's gun with blanks. Finch couldn't figure out how he would then miss his targets. After all, he hit them most of the time.

The boys measured and mapped out their own special territories in this wooded wonderland. They constructed an A-frame treehouse, about 20 feet up in an old maple tree, where Augy often came to hide and Finch came to daydream of wealth. In order to protect their hideout, they constructed a trap next to the path, which sided up to the tree. Fishing line spanned the opening, which when triggered would flip an old wood bucket and send a mixture of rock, dirt, and gravel down onto the intruder. Augy was bombarded twice.

Augy, the incisive outdoorsman, hunted with steel-jawed traps baited with peanut butter, which he tied off at the base of large trees. When captured, without their legs being torn off, some of the critters would make their way back to the neighborhood and be given to Pock Face, who would use them to further his study of taxidermy. When he failed, as he frequently did, he would end up preparing a barbecue banquet for the hunters and their friends.

In the woods, next to the pond, natural gas came up out of the ground. The boys would light the gas and watch it burn. It would burn for weeks at a time. They cleared the brush from around the flame so it wouldn't start a fire in the woods. All the kids knew about the flame, and sometimes they roasted marshmallows and cooked hot dogs on it.

One afternoon The Lush, RJ, Suey, and Pock Face were camped by the flame when Pock Face started to burn some twigs. The wind picked up, and soon the fire spread to the surrounding brush. They spent a few minutes attempting to put the fire out. Then when they thought it was out of control, Augy, RJ, and Suey decided to run away. Pock Face was left to extinguish the fire. He took off his jacket and tried to smother the flames. His jacket was burned, and his eyelashes were singed. Some of his hair burned as well. After fifteen minutes he decided to run away. As he sprinted down Ridgebury, he heard the sirens coming to save the day.

When he got home his mother asked him what happened to his hair and eyebrows. He lied about the fire and said he was at Augy's house when one of Augy's rockets exploded in the brick barbeque. She told him to stay away from that Augy boy. He nodded and went on his way.

***

The boys got into bodybuilding. Augy's father had provided a full set of weights, benches and other necessary equipment so Augy and his friends could work on becoming Mr. America. This was also a fruitless attempt to keep Augy around the house. He was now six feet tall, solid as a rock, and strong as an ox. He grew like a hearty beanstalk.

He and Finch were so close they became blood brothers that year. One afternoon while playing their version of mumblety-peg, they were tossing their pocket knives at each other's feet when Finch, while reaching for his knife, cut his hand between his forefinger and his thumb with the razor-sharp blade. It didn't seem to hurt him so Augy thought it would be a good time for them to forever bond. He quickly slashed himself in the same place, reached out, grabbed Finch's hand, and pressed his bloody laceration against Finch's. Putting his face directly into Finch's face with his eyes penetrating deep into Finch's, he repeated, "The Code, Finch, we can never forget The Code. Swear on it, Finch. Brothers forever. Swear on it."

This bloody ritual comforted Augy in two ways. First, he felt this bonding would seal their loyalty to each other, and second, this assured him that Finch would never rat on him or bear witness against him.

Chapter 8

1961

One afternoon Augy, Finch, Pucky Deenis, Tubless Screwdriver, and The Lush met at McDonald's on the corner of Worton and Mayfield Road. The store was built in the summer of 1961, with no inside seating. Large round tables and curved benches were located at the front of the restaurant on a paved patio surrounded by parking spaces. A sign spanned the huge golden arches and read "Over 250,000 served." This was the first fast-food facility in the neighborhood.

The cheap burgers were a hit with the neighborhood boys, because they could stuff themselves on less than a dollar. Most times when they were hungry and broke, they would scavenge the parking lot for pennies, nickels, dimes, and an occasional quarter. Once bankrolled, they would walk up to the window, order their food, plop down at an unoccupied table, and feast to their hearts' content.

Augy always bragged that he had an allowance, which was the reason he had more money than the rest of the group. He would typically buy three or four hamburgers, a couple of orders of fries, and a vanilla shake. Finch bought two cheeseburgers, fries, and a chocolate shake. The Deenis bought a Big Mac and a Coke. Tubless Screwdriver had his usual fish sandwich, a cheeseburger, and an order of fries as well. He didn't order a drink. Lush ordered two shakes and a fry. They all grabbed handfuls of ketchup packets from a bin sitting just outside the pick-up window. Then they crammed together around the table.

While consuming their afternoon snack, as they liked to call it, Augy said, "You guys remember when this place was an apple orchard? A lot of times me and Finch would cut branches off the trees, trim them with our knives, and stick apples on the ends. When a car or bus drove by, we would flick our sticks and bombard them with crab apples. A couple a times we got some windows to break."

Laughing, he went on, "I once got a windshield, and the guy almost smashed his car."

Obviously amused, the other boys were laughing, fidgeting, and cramming food into their mouths as if this was the last meal they were ever going to have. "Remember, Finch? The guy turned around and chased us down the street, but we got away when we ran through the lot next to Chung Wah's house. Pucky, we hid in your back yard for an hour."

"Yeah, that was a lot of fun," replied Finch.

Deenis said, "You guys could get into a lot of trouble doing that stuff. Heck, you should've knocked on the door. I would've hid you."

Augy shot back," Shit, man, that's nothing. I used to trap Cathy Marker in the woods across the street and feel her up. She liked it, too. You never seen tits as big as hers. One time I was in her house, and we were alone on the couch, and her dad came home, and I had to jump out the window before he could see me. Mrs. Sabatino saw me flying out the window and told her husband, and then she called my parents."

"Holy shit!" said the Lush. "What happened then?"

"Aw, nothing. They just told me to stay away from her."

Finch, was becoming irritated with Augy's recitation and interjected, "You know, man, you need to keep that shit to yourself. One day your ass is gonna be grass. The Code, man, remember The Code?"

"Yeah, I know, but these guys are our friends. They won't tell anybody." The boys, all but Finch, shook their heads in agreement.

Finch, gesturing with a pointed finger said, "You better just watch what you say."

They sat quietly for a minute and then Pucky, who didn't order any fries, reached across the table and started to grab some of Finch's fries. Without warning, Finch rose from the bench and latched onto Pucky's wrist.

"Drop 'em!" he said." Pucky, still holding onto the fries and thinking Finch was just kidding, started to pull his arm away. Finch got up on the table and leaped onto Pucky, knocking him backwards onto the pavement. "Don't touch my fuckin' food," Finch hollered. Pucky hit his head on the pavement and almost started to cry. The other boys jumped up off the benches and stepped back to give them room. Finch and Pucky wrestled as Finch kept repeating, "Keep your hands off my food. No one touches my food. You understand?"

Just then, The Lush grabbed and tore open ketchup packets and started throwing ketchup on everybody. "Don't touch my food!" he mimicked. He was laughing, and the other boys began to join in.

"Food fight! Food fight!" hawked the boys, all the while tossing ketchup, fries, and splattering milk shakes on one another.

Pucky said, "Okay, okay, I'm sorry. I didn't mean nothing. I won't do that again. Don't be so darn sensitive. Jesus Christ, man!"

Augy interrupted and announced," My friend Finch here doesn't like to share his food. He won't share with me neither. I made the same mistake once. I don't touch his food never."

Finch got up, reached out to Pucky and helped pull him to his feet.

The boys watched intently as Pucky nodded, assumingly accepting Finch's apology. Finch turned and started to walk away when Augy, covered with ketchup and splotches of milk shake, walked up close to Pucky and whispered, "I know you think by helping you up that he apologized, but he really didn't."

***

It was a Saturday in late fall of 1961. Word had spread throughout the previous weeks that Augy was going to launch his biggest, most powerful rocket of them all. The exact location and time were a mystery. The neighborhood boys and girls were anxious to observe what they believed would be another thrilling, disastrous attempt by the neighborhood troublemaker. References to him included, crazy, stupid, uncontrollable, and freakish. Most parents warned their kids to just stay away from him.

There were, of course, his loyal circle of friends, like Chung Wah Charlie, The Lush, and Suey. Most of the others were starting to drift away from him.

Finch, over the past year, had become a less frequent companion to Augy. He spent his free time working at the Mayfield Heights Pool and at the Eastgate Coliseum, an indoor sports center containing a bowling alley, swimming pool, and a billiard room.

It seemed as if everyone was awaiting the news of the launch. They knew Augy was crude and daring. His few old friends were his allies. They grew up knowing that when they needed someone to stand up for them or to protect them, they could always count on Augy. His friends would never betray him.

Augy had worked feverishly over the past ten days researching and building his dream. During school hours he visited the library for hours at a time, and when he got home he secluded himself in the workshop of his garage. He cut pipes, soldered metal supports, made fuses, and built a compressed reservoir for his fuel.

His two-stage, three-foot-high rocket was appropriately named 271. The State of Ohio and the County of Cuyahoga were in the process of extending the newest freeway, Highway 271, directly through the center of Augy's much-treasured, Ridgebury Woods.

Standing tall on each side of the tree-scraped right of way stood tall, majestic trees with multicolored foliage. Autumn was Augy's favorite time of the year. He loved the early morning frosts and the spectrum of colored lights as the sun's rays shined through the trees. He was disappointed with the construction of the new road as his stalking grounds were being destroyed by bulldozers and cement trucks. Sprawling ranch homes at the opposite side of the woods lined the edges of the clearing and could now be seen in the distance. Augy had heard his parents talking about how the homeowners had complained about the loss of privacy and the upcoming noise from the cars and trucks that would pass by twenty-four hours a day.

Construction equipment sat idle this day as Saturday was typically a day off for the crews.

Augy called Finch, The Lush, and Tubless Screwdriver to spread the word that the launch was to be at three p.m. Word got around quickly throughout Mayfield, and by two p.m. there were small groups of kids standing at the edges of the woods near the launch site.

Augy, Finch, and Screwdriver carried two boxes and a burlap bag full of paraphernalia, including 271. They trudged up the crossroad, past Ridgebury Boulevard to where the freeway pavement ended. Steel rods and mesh protruded from under the cement where Monday's pour would begin.

Augy had Finch help him assemble and set up the support cage for his rocket. The structure was strapped to the steel rods, and the silo-shaped stand was ready for the missile attachment. Augy worked carefully for the next ten minutes, aiming and aligning 271 for its maiden voyage.

Onlookers edged closer to watch the final preparation. Augy attached three sets of fuses to the bottom of the lower stage. He rolled the fuses out from the platform in three different directions. He knew he had only three tries, otherwise, he would be the laughing stock of the neighborhood. He stood and motioned for everyone to move back. He waited until the calm breeze stopped and then bent over near the end of the first fuse. Nervously, he looked up and saw everyone staring at him.

This better work, he thought. Then he asked Finch if he wanted to light the fuse.

"No fuckin' way," replied Finch, as he edged his way back from Augy.

Augy took out his Zippo and flipped the top open. He lit the fuse and quickly stepped back from the launch pad. The sizzle of the burning fuse could be heard 20 feet away. Some bystanders put their fingers in their ears while others just gritted their teeth and watched intently. He listened as Tubless counted aloud, "…nine, eight, seven." Then the fuse stopped burning. Augy looked around as his audience started to quietly boo him. He motioned to them to stay back as he approached the rocket from another angle and stooped again. He lit the second fuse, sidled up to the third fuse, and lit it as well. He jumped back and landed on his butt. The fuses were burning quickly and then they seemed to fizzle where they attached to the bottom of the fuselage. He watched carefully and started to crawl toward his malfunctioning creation. As he approached he heard the crowd booing and laughing.

Just then a scorching spray erupted from the fuel cell. He could feel his eyebrows burning as the loud detonation lifted 271 into the air. The stand fell as planned and the rocket shot up at an angle toward the woods' edge. He lay back on the dirt watching as the first stage broke away, and the rocket soared 200 feet into the cosmos. Kids were cheering. Finch and the other boys smiled with pride and exuberance knowing how important this day of reckoning was to Augy.

The rocket disappeared over the treetops. Silence engulfed the onlookers. All eyes shot towards the treetops. Suddenly a muted blast could be heard in the distance. Everyone started to run through the woods toward the noise. Before they reached the other side of the woods' edge, they saw flames soaring from the rooftop of an old, white, ranch-style home.

Soon the entire area was inundated with fire engines and police cars. Local residents heard multiple explosions and came out to watch as the home burned.

Augy was taken to the Mayfield jail. On Monday, after a short hearing in the local courthouse, he was released to his father. A November court date was assigned. Until then, he was to remain home and have no contact with his friends.

Chapter 9

The advent of driving legally allowed the boys to become more independent. While awaiting his court date, and certainly when his father was not home, Augy often snuck out during the day.

Having his own car increased his boundaries to neighboring suburbs.

Augy started to hunt and trap near the old covered bridge in Chardon, a small farming community east of Mayfield. Chardon was located in Geauga County and was named after Peter Chardon Brooks, a wealthy Bostonian, who had been the area's first landowner. The township was organized in 1816, and the village was carved out of the township, later becoming the county seat.

One mid-October afternoon in 1961, Augy drove to Chardon. He parked his car off the road and near the old covered bridge. Then he started wandering around looking for some of his traps that he had so cautiously set a few days before. Soothed by the peacefulness of the wooded fantasyland, he stepped softly. He perked up when he heard the noise of a girl singing as she peddled her bicycle down the path covered with yellow, brown, and red leaves. He could see her in the distance approaching his territory.

Thoughts of his sister's sensations and emotions flashed in his mind; her long fingers gently touching him, her hard nipples and warm wet lips and tongue moving over his naked body, her final groan of satisfaction as he exploded within her.

Augy hated all females because he was convinced that they had power over him. He rejoiced in the power of sexual termination believing it was his way of getting even for his weakness. He had often wondered what it would be like to kill someone.

Augy hid in a thicket, enthralled while watching and contemplating. His mind became charged with thoughts of an assault. *No one knew where he was, and no one would ever suspect him of doing anything to her.* He made his way closer to the path, and when she came upon him, he leaped from the bushes like a mountain lion attacking its prey. She fell fast and hard onto the ground.

Swiftly grabbing the bicycle, he flung it away from her. Plunging down on top of her, he straddled her torso. Holding her arms down with his knees, he maliciously positioned his powerful hands over her nose and mouth. His eyes blinked rapidly, and his head jolted back and forth as if he was experiencing an electrical charge. The girl cried and attempted to scream as she wrestled with her captor. Her tortured body twisted and bounced as she tried to free herself. He could feel her saliva between his fingers. Augy's eyes grew large; his forehead was soaked with perspiration. His skin was tingling. His blood bubbled as it raced through his shaking body.

It felt as if a nuclear weapon had gone off. He released one hand and began unfastening his belt, tears bolted from his cavernous black eyes. He increased the pressure on her wet face. He felt the cartilage in her nose crack as it pushed up and back into her brain. He stared at the warm blood oozing down the side of her face.

"I've got you now, bitch. You like it? You can't touch me anymore. I've got you now."

The twelve-year-old uttered a final whimper as her body became unbound and forever limp.

It took an hour for the gratification to disappear. He finished burying her next to the clearing by the woods' edge. Augy, still wet from sweating, gathered his traps, and rolled her bicycle alongside him as he walked to the road by the bridge. With intentions of dumping it miles away, he loaded her bicycle into the trunk and drove away.

The tranquil, late-afternoon breeze peacefully moved through the tall trees sending a steady stream of leaves to the ground.

***

The next day, the girl's disappearance in rural Chardon Township had become the topic of every news broadcast and newspaper in northeastern Ohio. Television broadcasts aired the agonizing appeal of the girl's parents pleading for her return. Her family had recently moved to this rural wooded Chardon community from the crowded, crime-ridden streets of Cleveland. Eastern Ohio communities, like Chardon, were presumed to be safe and unthreatening.

Three days later, the bloody body of twelve-year-old Denise Crayson was found in a crude shallow grave next to the clearing in Crawford's Valley.

In due time, the priority investigation by local law-enforcement agencies subsided. The sheriff's department in Chardon, Ohio, marked the file as unsolved. Neighboring jurisdictions left the investigation in much the same way, but not before placing some degree of incompetence upon the local officials.

Chapter 10

1962

Finch, at seventeen, was 5 foot 9, somewhat solid, and now smoked ceaselessly. He was handsome, with his blond hair, blue eyes and a smile that could melt away the heart of any teenage princess. Many adults as well, after having a conversation with Finch, walked away bewildered, believing everything he said. This provided a sense of accomplishment and security for him. Sometimes he was so convincing that he even believed his own lies and exaggerations. Finch knew that the truth was anything he could get people to believe. His family said he was destined for success as a lawyer or a politician.

One Friday night in late October, Finch was on his way home from work when he cruised into McDonald's parking lot. Augy was sitting alone at a table.

Before he could get out of his father's Chevy to say hello, Augy approached and began to tell Finch a story about some friend of his who was drag racing his father's car, lost control, and smashed into a telephone pole. He and his friends left the car at the scene of the accident and got a ride home from one of the other boys. Before they left the scene, they tore the ignition wires out of the switch.

Finch had pulled away from Augy over the past several months as he realized that he and Augy were living in different worlds. Finch was busy working most of the time and was starting to get more serious about his studies. His mother's constant harping finally made an impression on him, and he was planning on going to Ohio State after he graduated. His brother was now in medical school, and he encouraged Finch. The thought of making something of his life was becoming a reality.

In July of that year, Tubless Screwdriver was heading back from Chesterland where he and a new friend, both supposedly with fake IDs, were drinking at a local beer bar. Tubless in his souped up '57 Chevy was doing about 95 miles an hour when he lost control and veered across a double yellow line on Mayfield Road. The red convertible virtually disintegrated when it smashed head-on into a tree. Both boys were ejected from the car and died. Tubless was found a hundred feet away hanging from a tree branch. The tragedy was an eye-opening, life-changing event for Finch because earlier that day Tubless had asked Finch to go along. He began to think of his own destiny.

Augy was going on with his story, telling Finch in detail how the friend snuck home, quietly scurried to his room, and went to bed. Augy was enjoying himself, and Finch was getting tired of the same old boring story. "Wake up! Wake up!" the kid's father cried.

After listening for fifteen minutes to Augy's rambling, Finch interrupted. "What's the point of this story?"

Augy stopped rattling, sat quiet for a moment, and then began motioning with his arms. "I just wanted you to know what's been going on in my life, ya know? I haven't seen you in a while. There's no real point or anything. Just the same old shit." Augy sat down quietly and stared at the Ford dealership across the street where the woods used to be. Finch stood, looking at him with pity.

Augy, discounting embarrassment, sat straight up and looked at Finch. "You been workin, ha Finch? When you gonna buy your own car?" He pointed with pride at his rusted '59 Oldsmobile.

"I can't afford a car. My brother has this old shit Triumph. He said he might give it to me when he gets outta med school."

"A motorcycle?"

"No, it's a sports car."

Uncomfortably laughing, Augy said, "Yeah, one of those college boy cars, ha?"

"I guess so." Finch sighed. Unclenching his arms, so as to not look judgmental, he said sympathetically, "What are you going to do, Aug? I mean like after school. What do you want to do?"

With no hesitation, Augy shot right back. "I'm gonna take up rocket science. I want to build rockets. I've always been good at making boomers, right?"

Finch knew that Augy would be lucky to graduate from high school, much less go to college.

"So what ever happened with the court thing? Did you get off, or what? You kind of disappeared for a while."

Augy stood up, repositioning himself on the top of the table. He sat again with his feet on the concrete bench and said. "I got my ass kicked. The judge was a nice guy by not sending me to reform school and that. But he said if I did anything bad or got caught for something I would be sent away for a year. He told us that when I graduate I should go into the service."

Sliding closer, Finch said, "I wouldn't call that getting your ass kicked. He's probably doing you a favor. If you go into the service you can learn a trade or something, maybe go to school on the GI Bill."

"Yeah, I know." Brushing his fingers back through his thick black hair. "My old man wants me to get into the trades." He hesitated for a second and started to outwardly giggle. "Think they have rocket trades?"

Finch, attempting to mimic the laugh, said. "I doubt it, but you would be a heck of an electrician or something."

Brooding, Augy went on, "Yeah, I guess you're right." Then he turned his head and looked at Finch. "What are you gonna do? Go to college and become some rich guy, I suppose?"

Finch nodded, "I sure hope so." Finch stood up from the table to shake Augy's hand. "Hey, man, I have to go." He said in a soft, friendly tone.

Augy got up, ignoring the handshake gesture. His strong arms embraced Finch. He squeezed him twice and then patted him on the back. "Not everybody can go to college, right?"

Slowly nodding in agreement, Finch placed his hand on Augy's shoulder. "You'll be okay, Aug. I know you will. Keep in touch. I gotta go."

Chapter 11

Later that year, and continuing through most of 1963, Augy started hanging out with some of the tough Italian kids in the Cleveland area. Some of their families were rumored to be connected to the Mafia. They spent many evenings stealing 8-track tape players and radios from cars.

Once in a while, Augy was given the opportunity to assist in collecting money from people who owed money to his newfound friends. His size and strong hands became an asset to his new pals. Instead of holding a gun to someone's head, like his friends did, he would simply grip their throats and choke them to near death. He soon became known as "The Grip." He liked the name and was always compensated for his help. Other times, when he needed quick cash, he arranged to lease a couple of Golden Gate keys for an evening.

***

One rainy Saturday, in the fall of 1963, Augy was given instructions, by his new friends, to make a collection for them. He had learned that if you take something from someone who took something from someone else, then that someone won't go to the police. He may come after you, but he isn't going to the cops. If he fears you enough, he won't come after you. "But if you're an asshole and steal from innocent people, you're going to jail."

Augy approached Shaker Lakes cautiously. Shaker Lakes was a section of parkland designated as natural green space for people wanting to escape the industrial growth of Cleveland in the late ninteenth century. Trails, fields, and recreation areas were transformed from the land that had been farmed by the North Union Shaker community of years past.

Augy circled the area slowly, while keeping his eyes on a parked car by the bridge. He cautiously pulled up behind the red Pontiac. He reached into the glove compartment and retrieved a snub-nosed pistol. Walking slowly, his rigid arms hung down at his side while firmly gripping the pistol in his hand.

The door of the Pontiac swung open and a man, dressed in a black leather jacket and noticeably smaller and older than Augy, stepped out onto the wet road "Is this some kind of joke?! You're just a kid!" he exclaimed.

Augy was silent. His arm was rigid as he raised the pistol pointing it directly onto the guy's forehead. The man began shaking as tears rolled from his eyes. Augy calmly pulled back the hammer of the gun with his thumb.

Just as Augy was contemplating pulling the trigger, the man reached into his pants pocket and pulled out a wad of bills, banded together in a roll, and handed it to Augy. Glancing at the money, he motioned to the guy to take off his leather jacket. The jacket immediately switched owners. The guy got back into his car, started the engine, and quickly disappeared down the road. Augy slipped on the undersized jacket, sauntered back to his car, and drove away.

Chapter 12

9 a.m. Thursday, January 2, 1964

The worn-out, red '59 TR-3 roadster seemed to be floating down Old River Road. A trail of powdered snow spewed, like a rooster's tail, fifteen feet up and out from the rear. Finch was meticulously guiding his beauty through curves, pretending it was a concourse. "Worn out" was a compliment. The black canvas top was torn and weathered. The once beautiful, leather seats were severely torn, scratched, and cracked. There were no side curtains. The windshield resembled an assemblage of spider webs. Dark, rotting pine two by fours ran from side to side where the floor used to be. The rocker panels were rusted through, and the wire wheels were heavily spray-painted with silver-gray Rustoleum. The only things that worked were the heater and the radio. The radio dial was corroded so badly it could only receive one station, located about forty miles west, "WHK" from downtown Cleveland.

Augy had called Finch earlier in the week and begged for this last get-together. Finch was apprehensive and no longer had anything in common with Augy. They had gone their separate ways, but Finch felt sorry for Augy and decided to spend one last afternoon with him.

As they journeyed east, both boys were shivering from the cold. They bounced with each bump while singing to "The Wanderer," which was playing on the radio. Neither knew all the words, but they sang out loud anyway, making up their own versions of the song as they drove along.

"Well, I am the type of guy who likes to mess around...who likes to find a chick... and take her to the ground" They call me a wanderer and a wonderer... I go around and around and around..."

As the song ended Finch looked over at Augy and said, "Great song, huh?"

"Yeah, man, some day they will call me the wonderer or wanderer."

"Augy, you're so dumb you don't even know the difference between a wonderer and a wanderer."

"Hey, how come you always pick on me? You're not so damn smart yourself. I bet you don't even know the difference."

"Yeah, I do, too," replied Finch as he almost bounced over the door, laughing. "A wonderer is a kind of bread with little colored balloons on it, and a wanderer is a guy who walks around and eats it. He wanders while he wonders, or maybe wonders while he wanders."

"Kiss-off, asshole. What are you going to do with this piece of shit car, anyway?"

"Don't call this a piece of shit. It's art. Art in motion. I'm going to restore it someday."

"Okay, your piece of shit art? You takin' it to Columbus?"

"No, my old man won't let me take it. It probably wouldn't make it anyway."

"Who's gonna watch it, or where you gonna leave it while you're in school?"

"My brother said I could store it in his garage while I'm gone. He's got that big old house down in Shaker Heights. It has a brick carriage house in back. I have to bring it there tonight. Then my parents are going drive me to Columbus tomorrow morning."

"What time do you leave tomorrow?" asked Finch.

"Around 8:30. My old man is gonna take me and Suey to the airport. I don't know why we joined on the buddy plan. I don't even like him. You shoulda joined with me."

"Yeah right, and not go to college. My parents would have disowned me. I didn't want to go to Ohio State, but my old man said that because my brother went there, I have to go there. I couldn't even get in last September. I could have started in June or in January, so I picked January."

"College man! You gonna be a big college man! Are you gonna join one of them frat-in-aries?"

"It's fraternities, asshole, and I doubt it, because my brother never joined one. How long is basic training?"

"I'm not sure. It's either eight or twelve weeks. I should be home by Easter. Will you be home then?"

Swerving away from the snow bank on the side of the road, Finch said, "I should be home around then. That's if I don't flunk out first."

"You won't flunk out, man. You're smart. No one can do a con like my buddy Finch can. I bet you could buy your grades and shit, like in high school."

"I wish. So what do they teach you in basic training? How to kill and shoot and other shit?"

"I hope so. I can't wait to get over there and blow away those little slopes. I already know how to shoot. What other shit do I need to know? They oughta just give me one of those machine guns an' a uniform an' send me there. I could end the fuckin' war by myself."

"Yeah, you're a really tough guy. Where the hell is Parris Island, anyway? It sounds like some island paradise where Gilligan and Mary-Anne screw around all day. Maybe you'll get laid."

"No shit! I wish. It's somewhere in South Carolina, and according to what I hear it ain't no paradise. Guys get the shit beat outta them for no reason. It's like Pock Face's old man. When he comes home from the bar, he beats the shit out of Pock Face and his mom. For no reason! Pock Face always says he's gonna hit his old man with a bat if he does it again. Then he always does it again, and the asshole never does nothing. I'd kill the bastard. You know me. I get even for everything. If they try to screw with me I will kick their ass. My brother-in-law, Donna's husband, was in the Marines, and he told me that it's the best place I could be. He thinks it will make me a man. Where the hell has he been? I already am a man. I just wanna go over there and blow shit up."

"You're just talking tough because you're scared. I wouldn't want to go over there, either."

"I'm not scared. You are."

"Yeah, I would be if I was going over there. Lightner's brother went over there and got killed. He was only there for a couple weeks, and he was bigger than you. I don't wanna get killed. Maybe I'll join the Peace Corps."

Augy, becoming irate said, "Yeah, fuckin' Kennedy started his Pussy Corps. It doesn't help anybody teaching people how to build things or teaching them how to read. You want to help people, then you gotta kill the bad guys. Castro, my old man used to say, we gotta get Castro, and that we were headin' for World War III."

Finch listened and didn't want to argue with him. He knew this would probably be the last time he saw his old friend.

"What are you gonna become in college, a doctor or something like your brother?"

"I don't know, man. But it's going have something to do with money, and it's not going to be here in Ohio."

"Where then?"

"My brother keeps telling me that Cleveland stinks and that I should move someplace else, like Hawaii or California. He keeps telling me that after school I should move away and not make the same mistake as him, by moving back. Maybe I will."

"Where would you go?"

"I don't know, someplace warm maybe, like California." Finch, squirming, looked from side to side admiring the snow-covered fields and woods. "Shit, I don't think I have ever been out here before."

Augy sat rigidly bracing himself between the dash and the floor. "The bridge is comin' up pretty soon. You better slow down."

"Hang on." The small car jerked and fishtailed as he down-shifted from third gear to second. Slowing to five miles per hour, it rounded the last curve, next to the Chagrin River, near the old wood walking bridge.

"Watch out, man. There's a ditch around here," said Augy as he turned off the radio and hung over the door looking into the snow.

Turning the car to the right, Finch said, "I got it, man. There's only about three inches of new snow. Aug, you seem to know this place really well. When was the last time you were here?"

Reminiscing, with no intent to tell Finch the truth, Augy said, "Ah, it's been a while. It's certainly been awhile." As they crawled to a stop, the only audible sounds were the purring of the engine and the sound of the tires crushing the fresh snow. "I'll open the gate. Then you pull past it, I'll close it again, and we can head on in."

Augy hoisted himself up through the torn top, over the frozen door, and stepped into the snow. He looked in both directions to see if anyone was coming. Satisfied that they were alone, he walked up to the wood and wire fence. He untwisted the wire, which held the gate closed, and pushed it forward. The wood base of the gate frame slid across the snow like a razor blade creating a small mound at the end of the open arc.

After Finch pulled through, Augy pulled the gate back to its closed position and retied the wire. He got back in, and they continued on the last quarter mile of their journey. In a few minutes they stopped at the woods' edge, making sure the car could not be seen from the road. Augy jumped out and quickly reached for his rifle bag, which was located behind the seats.

"In a hurry, Aug?" Finch asked in a humorous tone. "Grab mine, will ya?" Augy reached behind the seat again and pulled out Finch's rifle bag. He handed it to Finch, and both boys unzipped the bags and removed their .22-caliber semi-automatic rifles. They tossed the bags onto the seats and walked to the rear of the car. Finch opened the trunk, and Augy grabbed two boxes of shells. He stared at the boxes for a second and then handed Finch his box. They removed the shells from the boxes and stuffed them in their coat pockets.

"I already loaded them at home, said Augy, as he laughed.

"What's so funny?"

"Aw, nothing, man, just thinking of something I used to do."

Finch ignored the remark and watched as Augy sidestepped from the car, reflectively gazing from side to side, reliving his last visit to these woods in Crawford's Valley.

Finch shuffled through the snow behind him, attempting to mask the footprints. In about ten minutes the boys were deep into the dark woods. Although the sun was bright, the trees were compressed, and little light penetrated into the grove. Their mood was tranquil and calm as the boys stalked circuitously, looking for something alive to shoot at. Finch pulled a Zagnut Bar from his pocket, dropped the wrapper onto the snow, and shoved the candy bar into his mouth like a cigar. After separating for 25 minutes, which resulted in no luck, they got back together again where the trees began to thin out closer to the clearing.

Augy spotted a small squirrel dashing over the snow. It suddenly stopped. It sat up as if it could sense their presence. Its heart was beating a thousand times a second as it sat motionless, facing him at a four-degree angle. He motioned to Finch, and they both planted themselves. They simultaneously removed their gloves and carefully took aim. The squirrel turned abruptly with its back then facing toward the two hunters. Augy had the squirrel's low back in his crosshairs while Finch was trying to hold his rifle steady.

Just as the duo started to squeeze off their first round of the day, a distant rumbling sound entered the peaceful rural winter wonderland. They looked at each other, then instantly looked back at the squirrel. Both boys shot at the same time, creating a series of multiple and noisy blasts. The squirrel was gone. They both missed.

Augy yelled out, "You dick-head, you made me miss! Damn you, Finch! Damn it!"

Finch was looking across the clearing where the snow-covered road stopped, and the noise was getting louder. The Triumph was parked in that direction. He grabbed onto Augy's sleeve and lifted him into a standing position.

"Be quiet. Listen," he motioned as he pointed to his ear.

Augy responded, "Someone is coming!"

Shoving Augy at the shoulders, Finch said, "Oh, shit, we're not supposed to be in here. This is private property. You said no one ever comes in here. We're finally gonna get caught. Our last fuckin' day in town."

Stumbling, Augy scolded, "Shut up, Finch. Just follow me." He led Finch into the thicket next to the clearing. He took off his red and black hunting jacket and propped it up behind a snow-covered bush. Then he and Finch ran around a half circle through the woods to the other side of the clearing. Augy pushed Finch down into a prone position. Then he got down next to him.

As the sound grew louder the boys could hear voices. They became motionless, like the squirrel.

"Who's in here? This is private property. Come out now, and you won't get hurt. We heard your gun go off. You're not fooling anybody."

Finch looked at Augy and motioned with two spread fingers. Augy nodded in agreement. Indeed, there were two men in the truck.

It was obvious that the two boys were worried. Finch and Augy were watching and listening for an imminent confrontation. They were both in a trance. They listening intently with their heads slightly cocked to the side.

"Get under the seat. Cover yourself!" exclaimed one of the voices. "Who's out there? If you know what's good for ya all, you better come out now." The chocolate-brown, open-back International Scout crept forward toward the clearing.

The boys spotted two men, both wearing hunting jackets and fur-lined caps. One had his earflaps tied on top of the black leather dome, and the other one wore his hat untied with the flaps and ties dangling on both sides of his head. The man in the passenger seat was holding a rifle. The long barrel pointed down between his feet toward the floor. The wood rifle butt rested in his lap. With his right hand, he raised and slid the shiny steel bolt back toward his chest. Then he reached into the left pocket of his coat and pulled out a long shiny shell. He placed the casing into the slide by the firing chamber. With a quick forward and downward motion he planted the bolt back into place. He was ready and loaded for action.

Augy, looking at Finch, whispered, "No one knows we're here." Finch shrugged and said nothing. Then Finch pulled his rifle from his side and carefully took aim. Augy stared at him for a second, assuming Finch's approval for what was about to happen.

"We know you're in here. We heard your shots. Come on out now!"

As the vehicle made its way into the clearing, the driver said, "Hey, Tom. What's that over there? It looks like someone is hiding over there, on the left, behind that bush. I can see his coat." Augy's distraction had worked.

The weighty passenger groped as he twisted his body and looked off to his left, over the driver's shoulder. Then he shouted, "I see you in the bushes. Come on out, or we'll blow you out!"

The sounds of repeating blasts echoed through the trees for only seconds, yet it seemed like hours. Finch and Augy got up only when they were convinced that their pursuers posed no harm. They walked up to the open Scout. Both boys seemed tranquilized. The driver was slumped over the steering wheel with his eyes wide open. Blood was seeping from one small hole above his left temple. His arms drooped at his sides. The obese passenger was crouched over the long floor-shift lever. Partially clotted blood oozed down his face, from the two holes in his forehead and the one in his eye. Blood covered the dark, wooden rifle butt, which rested on the floor between the seats. His mouth and one remaining eye were wide open.

The boys were dazed. They didn't touch a thing. Augy rushed to the other side of the clearing and gathered his jacket. They slowly walked around the vehicle staring at what they had done.

Suddenly, Finch squinted with a sickening look on his face. Augy blinked rapidly.

As he looked at Finch for his reaction, he quietly voiced, "Hey, Finch, I woulda never thought you had it in ya." Then his voice got louder. "I'da bet you couldn't do this."

Finch was still and somewhat dazed. He couldn't hear Augy. Repeating quickly, Finch said, "Oh, shit! Look what we did! Oh, shit! We killed them. Our ass is fuckin' grass. Goddamn it."

"Hey, Finch, no one knows who we are here. Listen, Finch, just keep your cool! Finch, pay attention to me! No one knows about this. Just you and me, Finch. We can go on our way tomorrow, and no one will know. Believe me when I tell you that no one will ever know. I've been through something like this before. No one will ever know, Finch. The Code, Finch, remember The Code. No one ever fuckin' talks, right?"

Finch, in somewhat disbelief, looked into Augy's bulging black eyes and spoke slowly.

"Right, fuck-head! I knew I shouldn't have come with you today. Let's go. We've got to get the hell out of here."

***

Glancing over his shoulder, back into the woods from where he had come, he left a path of erratic snow-packed footsteps. His hands were bright red where the saturated blood had frozen and dried. Blood-stained tears sat like ice shavings on his cheeks. His red and green checkered jacket was covered with spots of white clotted snowpack gathered from where he had fallen and rolled. Mittens dangled from their tiny suspenders on his sleeves. His hat was gone. Thick blond hair lay matted and still upon his head. Both arms appeared frozen at his sides.

As he walked deliriously in shock, a repeated mumbling sound could be heard from his semi-frozen lips "French, Frynch, Fininch ... French, Frynch, Fininch." The seven-year-old had no idea where he was.

***

Fred Masters was just taking his time, enjoying the white peaceful afternoon scenery as he slowly tooled down Old River Road. Fred had lived in Chardon all of his forty-seven years. Fred was an only child of farming parents. Throughout most of his life he explored, fished, and hunted practically every inch of this thirty-three-mile square of wooded paradise. He quit high school at sixteen and worked a few years as a mechanic at the local service station.

Fred never married, and after both of his parents died in 1959 he inherited the farm, left his job, and lived what many people would consider the life of a hermit. He was a big man of 250 pounds, supporting a bushy beard with no mustache.

Fred always wore black, resembling his Amish neighbors. He enjoyed his afternoon rides up and down the snowy back-country roads in his gently worn 1949 Ford pick-up. His driver's-side window was usually rolled down because he couldn't control the old junkyard heater. It was either on or off, too hot or too cold.

He first spotted the boy as he passed him wandering near a side road at the edge of the old Crawford ranch. As he traveled further he began thinking to himself that it was strange for someone that young to be roving around in the freezing cold, especially alone.

Crawford's Ranch consisted of an old, burned out homestead containing fifty acres of forest and rolling open meadows. Barbed wire fencing surrounded the entire property. Red, worn, and weathered no-trespassing signs hung every fifty to a hundred feet along the fence line. This location became somewhat famous a few years ago when a local girl had been found buried in a shallow grave. She had been raped and murdered. Her killer was never found.

Hunters from the city, especially in the fall and winter months, ignored the signs and ventured onto the land, hoping to shoot squirrels and rabbits. Locals thought nothing of a few echoing rifle shots now and then. After all, the property was deserted, and the nearest home was out of firing range.

"Maybe his folks were with him and I didn't see 'em," Fred thought. *"It's awfully cold out there. Why didn't he have a hat on?"*

Slowing to a crawl, he made a U-turn and headed back toward the boy, who was walking in the same direction as the creeping truck. Fred managed to roll the passenger window down, keeping his left hand on the wheel. He scooted over the torn, brown-leather bench seat. His coat fell to the floor. He spoke toward the boy's back. "Hey, boy! Hey, there! Hold on a second."

The boy continued walking. Fred pulled off the road next to the fence and stopped the truck. As Fred got out of the truck, the boy turned and started to walk away from the road and back into the valley. Fred lifted his heavy coat from the passenger foot well and threw it over his shoulder. He stepped over the fence and walked after the boy. "Hey, kid! Are you okay? Hold up a minute!"

Slowly approaching the boy, he noticed frozen blood covering the boy's hands and face. He kneeled beside him, placed his coat over the boy's back, and said, "Everything will be alright."

The boy was in shock, blindly staring into Fred's face. His head and body trembled as he repeatedly mumbled, "French, Frynch, Fininch."

"My name is Fred. Let's walk over to the truck." He tried again. "What's your name?"

The boy did not respond. "What are you doing out here alone?" Still, no response! He coaxed the boy toward the road.

When they reached the barbed-wire fence, Fred lifted the rigid torso of the boy over the top and set him down. He was standing stiff, facing the front of the truck. The boy had stopped his mumbling, but couldn't stop shaking. Fred helped the boy up onto the seat, got into the truck, started the engine, and turned on the heater.

"My name is Fred. What's your name?"

No answer.

The boy stared toward the woods at the end of the meadow. He sat, sporadically mumbling again, but Fred couldn't make out what he was trying to say. The boy was shivering, even with the heat blowing and the heavy coat draped over his body.

"Boy, we are going to take a ride into town and see if we can find your folks, okay?"

***

Fred pulled into the slushy, gravel-covered parking lot of the Chardon Township Sheriff's Office. It was four miles east of where he had discovered the boy. The old, grubby, brick single-story building was at least a hundred years old. The round, steel chimney pipe from the wood stove inside protruded through the angled, corrugated-metal roof and poured white smoke into the crisp air. A bright, yellowish-red reflection onto the chimney pipe was caused by the sun setting lower in the sky. Large, wood-framed window panes were glazed over with frost.

"It's gonna be okay, kid. Sheriff Murphy will help us find your folks."

The door opened in, and a small cowbell fastened on the inside top of the door clanged. The wood-planked floors creaked as they stepped inside. Six feet in from the door stood a five-foot-high, dark mahogany counter running from one side of the room to another. This separated the makeshift lobby and the approach to the four desks in the middle of the room, which were arranged in a square and facing one another. Tattered wood file cabinets covered the length of the back wall. Several drawers were partially open with files and papers bulging from within. Wood paddles from the two old ceiling fans circulated the air and heat from the pot-belly stove, which rested against the brick wall to the left.

The sheriff, leaning back in an old wood office chair, was talking on the phone. His legs were supported by his boots, which were propped up on the desk. Doris, an older, white-haired woman wearing a blue and white flannel shirt, jeans, and a white vest sat across from him and looked over to see who had come in the door.

She stood, tucked her shirt in, and started over to the counter. "Well, look who's here." She said, "Freddy Masters. I haven't seen you in ages. Who is that with you?"

Before Fred could answer, she noticed the crusted blood covering the boy's face and hands. "Oh, my God," she expelled. "Sheriff, Sheriff, come quick!"

They sat the boy in a chair. He was terrified and said nothing. Fred had explained how he found the boy wondering around and how he thought it best to bring him to the station. Both Sheriff Murphy and his assistant, Doris, knelt down in front of the boy. He appeared to be six or seven years old. Murphy continued to drill Fred, while Doris looked through the child's pockets for some clue as to who he was. The boy sat trembling.

As she lifted the collar on his jacket she noticed a cloth patch, sewn onto the jacket's label. "Sheriff," she interrupted, "his name is Andy Fowler."

The sheriff looked into the boy's hollow eyes and said, "Andy, Andy, snap out of it."

Nothing! Gripping Andy's shoulders with both hands, he squeezed tightly while gently shaking him. The sheriff's voice grew louder, "Andy Fowler, Andy, snap out of it. What happened to you? Talk to me!"

Just then, Andy's mouth opened wide, both eyes came alive, and his hands rose from his sides. A torrid river of tears formed and gushed down his face. Crying uncontrollably, he screeched, "they're dead! They killed them! They were shot!"

Chapter 13

1966

In the spring of 1966 Private Augy Romano was being processed for a dishonorable discharge from the Marine Corps. He was accused of shooting his sergeant and then blowing him up with a grenade during a nighttime firefight in the jungles of Vietnam.

While awaiting his hearing at Camp Lejeune, Augy stalked Captain Jack Lyons' beautiful young blonde wife for two weeks before his careless invasion. Jack Lyons was the young attorney attempting to prosecute him for his alleged criminal activity in Vietnam.

Augy beat her so badly she almost died. He would have killed her if it weren't for the little girl on the stairs screaming as she interrupted his sacrament. He successfully fled the scene. The hearing was ultimately dismissed, and he was processed through a General Court Martial, which deemed him as a disgrace and unsound for military service.

Five weeks later, Captain Jack Lyons died suspiciously in a car crash.

1978

Twelve years later, in 1978, Augy was sentenced to ten years in prison at the Ohio State Penitentiary for attempted rape, robbery, and aggravated assault of two co-workers at a private munitions plant near Wright Patterson Air Force Base in Dayton, Ohio.

***

Andy Fowler's mother never remarried after the tragic incident in Chardon. Andy's grandparents were compassionate, and the farm provided sustenance for many years. On occasion, the church would provide varying sums of money from an undisclosed contributor.

Living in his father's home was the only way Andy and his mother could survive financially. As a child, Andy was shy, a good student, and a member of a very close, loving family. Many evenings were spent sitting beside his grandfather in front of the old stone fireplace listening to stories about his father and uncle. Although his grandfather devoted his life to him, he missed his father. His room had been his father's room and his bed his father's as well. Andy was sure his father watched over him as he faithfully said his prayers each night before crawling under the covers.

There were times, when darkness consumed his room and the air became still, that Andy actually heard his father speak to him. *"Find them,"* he would say. *"Don't let them get away. You're the only one who can help."*

As he grew older, Andy continued to be plagued with the nightmares of his youth, spending summers gathering information and interviewing anyone who could remember the murders. His journal noted a small red car, a candy wrapper, gunshots, and voices shouting at each other.

After graduating from Cleveland State University with a degree in education, Andy began teaching social studies to junior-high-school students in the Mayfield school system. With his summers free, he continued his incessant but deadlocked investigation of the murders.

Andy was now thirty-two years old and nearly six feet tall. His thin frame, brown hair, full beard, and wire-rimmed glasses contributed to his John Lennon appearance.

Years ago, Andy had remembered a small red car sitting aside the clearing in the woods. The original police investigation confirmed that there were two possible shooters, although ballistics could only confirm one. They did find a candy wrapper and some spent shell casings near the scene as well. The worn tire treads confirmed the presence of a small car, but they had been unable to determine what kind of car it was.

Summer

1989

After nine years of having his summer's free and playing amateur detective, Andy decided to accept a summer position as an assistant to a high-school science teacher. Two weeks into the four-week nature program and while classifying birds at Squires Castle in Metropolitan Park, a young student was causing commotion by teasing and calling the other kids names.

As Andy approached the boy, he heard him squawking at another student. "Hey, Finch, come here. What's matter? Don't you like the name Finch?" he bellowed. Andy's mind flashed; his heart pounded anxiously as he re-experienced the words he heard while hiding under the blanket in the back of his father's truck.

"My God!" he shouted spontaneously, "Finch, I bet that's it. Finch!"

***

Intermittently scraping bottom as it sped up the long driveway, the old Volvo wagon sent a trailing cloud of fine dirt and dust up into the air. Andy was blowing his horn as he rocked and bounced, nearly hitting his head on the roof.

Fred Masters, the passer-by who had first spotted him, was now a much older man. Andy visited him every summer. The curvy, narrow dirt road leading to the Masters place was worn and trenched. The old dilapidated farmhouse sat back about a half mile from the main road.

In past visits the two would trade the same information back and forth. Fred could only recollect Andy deliriously wandering around the old Crawford place repeating the words French or Frynch.

Andy parked next to what, at one time, had been a barn, then quickly walked up onto the leaning porch and knocked on the screen door. "Hello, Mr. Masters, it's me, Andy. Andy Fowler. Are you home? I figured it out." The last of the trailing dust blew past the front door as Fred Masters hurried to greet Andy.

"Slow down, Andy, slow down. Come in here and sit down."

"Mr. Masters, I figured it out!" Andy said exuberantly. "One of the guys was named Finch, not Frynch or French. He went to Mayfield High School and drove a red sports car."

"Hold on there. How did you find that out?"

Andy explained that his co-teacher in the summer nature program heard him exclaiming the words Finch, Finch. The other teacher remarked that he went to high school back in the mid-sixties with a kid nick-named Finch. Andy was convinced he had solved the puzzle. A fabricated call to Finch's brother gave Andy the location of the killer. Everything seemed to fit into place, the name, the car, and the time frame.

Fred cautioned Andy about his discovery. He told him to speak with the police before doing anything on his own. Andy wished his grandfather was still alive, because he had always given him wholesome advice, which he now so desperately needed. Fred was certainly not a substitute for his grandfather, but Andy did respect him and his opinions. Fred told him not to give his family any false hopes and to be positive he was correct before incriminating someone.

***

Old sheriff Murphy had long since retired. The current body of law enforcement in Chardon was much different than it had been 25 years ago. Andy's recurrent visits to the police, every summer, became predictable and were fruitless endeavors to rekindle an old sleeping case. His latest attempt to convince the police chief how he learned of his father's killer restored some attention. However, the chief stated that they were occupied with current investigations, and it would be a while before they could assign anyone to the case.

"Oh, come on!" Andy exclaimed. "I finally get the clue of a lifetime, and you guys are too busy? Give me a break! I demand to know when you are going to put someone on this."

"Look, Andy," the chief replied, "I'll see what I can do. We'll get back with you as soon as we can." As always, Andy left frustrated. He knew that they would never get back with him.

He didn't tell his mother and grandmother the real reason he was going to southern California. He told them he was attending a teachers' workshop.

Chapter 14

July 1989

August Romano served his ten years in The Ohio State Penitentiary. He spent the past two years, while on parole, working in a machine shop and saved most of his money. His large frame, dark complexion, pearl-white teeth, and jet-black ponytail supported his intimidating and commanding presence.

Augy still hated women, especially beautiful women. He felt they had mysterious sexual powers. Years prior, while on leave from the Marine Corp, Romano's sister, Donna, had been choked to death in the back seat of her car just three miles from her home in a suburb of Cleveland. Augy's Atlanta alibi was never disputed. Her killer was never found. Soon thereafter, he became estranged from his remaining family.

When probation ended, Augy felt he was a free man. It was time for Finch to pay the piper. He decided to look up his old friend by visiting the alumni association at The Ohio State University.

The old, stone, ivy-covered two-story building housed post-graduation records of donors and past member graduates, many of whom had contributed large sums to their alma mater. Information, however, is not readily available to the public.

Augy, a master in the art of seduction, flirted, with the young co-ed clerk who was sitting on a stool behind the counter. "Wow, if I knew Miss Ohio worked here I'da come in a long time ago," he said smiling while flashing a fake badge and private investigator's ID.

She looked up at him and said, "Can I help you sir?"

"My name is John, and please don't call me sir. I used to be not that much older than you are," he laughed.

Grinning, she said, "I'm sorry."

"You know, you really are very attractive. You could definitely win a beauty contest. Hands down, no competition! I'm not kidding, either."

"Thank you." She replied smiling. "You're old enough to be my father. How can I help you today?"

"What's your name, pretty lady?"

"Michelle."

Augy glanced at her breasts. Her tiny nipples pushed into her scarlet and grey Ohio State tee shirt. *"No bra,"* he said to himself. *"A sign of self-sexual gratification. Bet her little nips rubbing against that cotton shirt turns her on."*

She laughed. "Your kind of nice. Strange but nice."

Augy smiled as he ran his hand through his ponytail. "Michelle, I was hired by an old friend's family to help locate him. His grandfather is on his death-bed. His parents died many years ago, and he has had no contact with his relatives at all."

Although somewhat cautious, she liked his flattering style. She also admired his firm muscular build, dark tan skin, and bright white teeth. *Not bad looking for an old guy!*

After extensive pleading and a $200 donation to Michelle's education fund, Romano was able to learn that his long lost friend, Jacob Nubaum, had made several contributions to the university during the late 1970s. His last known address was a post office box in La Jolla, California.

Two weeks later, Romano quit his job, emptied his bank accounts, and booked a first-class, one-way airline ticket to San Diego.

Wednesday, August 9, 1989

The early morning, short commuter flight from Columbus to Hopkins airport in Cleveland was uneventful for August Romano. He had dressed comfortably for his trip with a black polo shirt, black slacks, and low-cut boots. At the American Airlines counter he confirmed his seat assignments and then walked to the departure gate of flight 632 to Dallas/Ft. Worth, where he was to switch planes and arrive in San Diego at 2:20 p.m. Pacific time. His luggage consisted of one brown leather-trimmed duffel bag, which he carried at his side.

With forty minutes to spare, Augy sat patiently near the gate, watching people pass by. Internal conversations were going on in his head. He liked to pretend that he could figure out what travelers did for a living, how much money they made, where they lived, what they drove, and where they were going. When he spotted an attractive girl or woman, his thoughts turned to punishment. He pictured himself as godlike with the responsibility of making them pay for their sexual sins.

He was anxious to get to California. The purpose of the trip was two-fold: one, to find and see what his old friend Finch was up to; and two, to experience first-hand the uninhibited sexual fantasies of beautiful southern California females, which he heard so much about while in prison.

***

Andy Fowler leaned over and gave his mother a kiss on the cheek. "I love you, Mom," he said, then edged over and opened the passenger door. He got out, closed the door, and walked to the back of the Volvo station wagon. He opened the tailgate and removed his two suitcases.

"Are you sure you don't want me to come in with you?" she asked, mothering him as always.

"No, no, Mom, I'm fine. Thanks for the ride. Go home, I'll call you from San Diego."

"Have a good time."

Andy hesitated for a second, "I will. I'm sure I will. Give Grandma a kiss for me. See you in a few weeks." He intermingled with the crowd and made his way through the line by the American

Airlines check-in area. Internally, he felt nervous and frightened. His stomach churned. He knew he had to resolve the past. He had to get even for the murders. He thought about his useless visit to the authorities in Chardon. *"If they won't do anything, I will. Who is this guy Finch? What does he do now? How will I get him alone? Maybe it really wasn't him, after all. No one knows me. They won't be able to trace who I am. I can get in and out of there before anyone suspects anything. He'll pay, that son of a bitch. He'll pay for what he did."*

"Next!" The voice came from a ticket agent on the far side of the counter. Andy walked over and handed his package of tickets to the young woman behind the counter.

"Good morning," she said. He returned the greeting and placed his bags on the scale next to the counter. "Final destination San Diego, California. Just the two bags?" she confirmed as she leaned over and placed the baggage ties on the luggage.

"That's enough for me," he replied.

She stood, stapled his tickets together and handed them back to him. "Have you been San Diego before?"

"No, first time."

"You'll love San Diego. I was there on my honeymoon last year."

"That's nice," he replied avoiding eye contact. He didn't want to carry on a conversation with her for fear that she might remember him.

"If you get a chance, don't miss Old Town. It is really unique, lots of shops and restaurants and Mexican music. Oh, and their zoo is world-famous."

"Christ, he thought, *every other ticket agent I ever met was a bore and this one won't shut up."*

"Your plane is on time, Mr. Holmes. It will be boarding in a few minutes, at gate 34. Have a nice trip."

Andy turned and grinned. "Yep, that's me. Sherlock Holmes."

***

Romano was one of the first to board the plane. Aisle three, seat A. He placed his bag in the overhead compartment and sat with his legs crossed in the wide leather seat. A flight attendant immediately approached. "Good morning, sir. Can I get you coffee, champagne, maybe a cocktail?"

His eyes traveled up and down as he rated her on a scale of one to ten. "Eight," he replied aloud.

"Pardon me sir?"

"Oh, I'm sorry. Champagne sounds good to me, thank you." His shiny black ponytail hung onto his shoulder. Many passengers glanced at him as he sat comfortably smiling at them while they passed by on their way to the back of the plane. Romano sat, internally rating most of the women. That one, the blonde bitch, he thought, I could have her screaming for mercy.

"Here's your champagne, sir. Can I get you anything else right now?"

"No, no, this is fine for now, thanks."

Andy boarded the plane, and as he was about to pass Romano he glanced at him, sitting with his champagne and smiling like a peacock. Their eyes made contact, although it was only for a second. Andy experienced a strange hint of familiarity. He walked slowly down the aisle to his seat at the back of the plane. He forgot about Augy. He sat pensively in his seat, staring out of the window for most of the flight to Dallas/Ft. Worth.

***

The pilot announced that it was sunny and ninety-seven degrees in Dallas. After deplaning, and with 55 minutes until his next flight, Romano made his way out of the terminal in order to have a smoke. Andy took the shuttle to gate 44, checked in, and waited to board the plane to San Diego.

It was too hot outside for Romano so he reentered the terminal with a lit cigarette in his mouth. He stopped and looked for a restroom sign. Dozens of people passed as they made their way through the terminal. A policeman approached him.

"Excuse me, sir. There is no smoking in here. You can smoke outside if you'd like."

"Hey, fuck off, asshole," he said to himself. *"It's a million degrees out there."*

The police officer reiterated, "Sir, could you please put out your cigarette."

"Sure, sorry!" he said as he turned and walked back to the exit door. He pushed the door open, flicked the cigarette onto the sidewalk, turned, and started walking toward gate 44. Romano finally found a restroom by gate 40. He barely had enough time to use the facilities and get to his gate before departure. He was the second to last person to board the plane. Still in first class, he sat by the aisle and next to an older man who wore a white shirt and tie. *"Oh shit, I gotta sit next to a fuckin' suit."*

"Good afternoon, ladies and gentlemen. My name is Captain Marshall, and I would like to welcome you aboard American Airlines flight 223 A to San Diego. Sorry for the delay. We've been asked to wait here at the gate for a few minutes. Hopefully it won't be too long."

***

"Yes sir, I understand. I have his profile. We just arrived in Dallas. I will call you when I get there."

The private Lear jet taxied on the tarmac next to the American Airlines terminal and stopped. The hydraulic stairway opened from the top and dropped slowly to the ground. A medium-height, slim, young, sandy-haired woman wearing a white blouse, navy pantsuit, and low heels carefully stepped off the plane. She held a tattered leather briefcase in one hand and a suitcase with her blazer draped over the top in the other. An airport police vehicle arrived and stopped at the end of the wing. She carefully stepped off the plane and walked to the car. She was transported to the terminal where she took an elevator to the second floor and boarded flight 223 A to San Diego. Upon entering the plane, she stopped and spoke briefly with one of the flight attendants.

The entry door closed behind her. Romano's eyes followed as she was escorted to one of the two vacant seats in the rear of first class. *"Now that might just be a ten in disguise,"* he thought as he watched her place her bag on the inside seat next to her. He stared at her Maidenform through the thin wrinkled white blouse. *"Nice firm ones,"* he said to himself. *"A little on the small side but doable."*

"Ladies and gentlemen," in his southern drawl, "this is Captain Marshall again. We have been cleared for departure. Sorry for the delay. Relax, buckle up, and enjoy the ride. I'll check back with ya' all in a while. Flight attendants, prepare for departure."

***

Upon his arrival in San Diego Romano rented a white corvette, drove to La Jolla, and checked in at a seaside motel in the Bird Rock area. Within three hours, he located Anna Nubaum, living in a retirement home near San Diego State University.

The phone rang seven times until the elderly widow answered.

"Hello," she said.

"Hello, is this Mrs. Nubaum?"

"Who is this?" she replied suspiciously, thinking it was a telemarketer.

"Mrs. Nubaum, my name is Robert Grossman." Augy figured by using a Jewish-sounding name, it might put the old woman more at ease. It worked. "I am calling from Mayfield Heights, Ohio. I am the alumni chairman for Mayfield High School."

"What kind of chairman?"

"The alumni chairman. It's my job to locate the graduates from Mayfield High School. We are trying to put together a newspaper or newsletter for all of the people who graduated." Augy was convincing, as he first learned of Finch's successful older brother, the doctor, then, secondly, of Jake's name change, divorce, and prospering business.

***

Gazing through the windows as his taxi crowned the top of Ardath Road and started down into the village of La Jolla, Andy Fowler was amazed by the sight of huge sprawling homes imbedded into the lush hillsides. Looking forward through the windshield, he could see the ocean approaching in the distance. As he entered the old community, homes seemed to get closer together. Many large, estate-type homes sat on small lots, sometimes next to hundred-year-old, tiny cottages. Gated driveways, red-tiled roofs, and manicured lawns surrounded him. The older and newer wood-sided and stucco houses were meticulously maintained. Mercedes, Jaguars, Ferraris, and Porsches seemed to line the streets.

"This is really a different world," he thought. As he reached into his wallet to pay his driver, he asked, "What do these people do for a living?"

Leaning over the seat, the old, white-haired taxi driver smiled and said, "These people think they own the world and everything in it. But in reality, my boy, everything owns them."

Andy checked in at the Sea Lodge Inn on Prospect Street. After unpacking, he grabbed his old briefcase, opened the French doors, and walked out to the balcony. He placed the briefcase onto the table and walked over to the railing. A late afternoon breeze blew through the majestic palms next to the sandy beach below. Staring north, over Coast Boulevard, up the coast line, he watched pensively as surfers paddled through small whitecaps into the sea.

Andy had never seen a palm tree or an ocean before, much less a surfer. He sat at the table, slowly opened his case, and began to study vast pages of notes, which he had compiled over years of researching and investigating the deaths of his father and uncle.

Chapter 15

Thursday, August 10th

Jay Newman slowly reached over to his nightstand and patted the snooze lever on his Bose radio. It was seven a.m. The music stopped as he rolled back into a cuddled sleeping position. He put his arm around Serena's waist and squeezed. She was soft and warm. Jay had always been enthralled by her smooth skin and fit body. Serena was thirty-four years old, petite, and weighed 110 pounds. Jay was forty-four. He gently ran his fingertips over her flat belly, then up under her red silk teddy onto her small firm breasts.

The music sounded for the second time. He leaned over, stretched out his arm, and turned it off, then rolled back over to Serena, and with his foot, pushed the comforter toward the bottom of the bed. Serena was lying flat on her back. Her long natural blond hair was spread over two silk pillows. Her ruby lips were moist. Jay placed his fingertips on her right thigh. While barely touching the surface of her skin, he moved his hand in a circular motion. Smiling, as she opened her passionate blue eyes, she said, "Don't stop, darling! That feels so good."

"I'll never stop," said Jay. "I could just lie here next to you all day. You know, you're just as beautiful while you sleep as you are when you're awake."

Serena smiled. "That's why I married you, because you make me feel so special."

"You are special," he whispered.

He moved his hand over to the top of her panties and then under the elastic waist band.

"Ooh," she moaned. "That's nice!" She began raising and lowering her hips as she gently grabbed his erection and squeezed. "I need you now," she gasped. "Please, I can't wait."

As Jay pulled off her panties and straddled her, Serena spread her beautiful tan legs, wrapped her arms around Jay's neck and slowly pulled him down on top of her.

***

While sitting on the side of the bed, Jay placed one foot on the floor. Then he chuckled as he remembered the old Jack Lemon movie, *Hold That Tiger*. Lemon referred to the $200 a day he had to clear in order to make ends meet. Jay said aloud, "Well, that's a grand." Then the other foot went down. "Here's another one."

He picked up the remote control and aimed it at the wall in front of him. Jay loved electronic gadgets. The drapes opened. Then he pushed another button and the sliding door slid silently in its channel as it also opened. Sounds of gulls and the gently rolling surf penetrated into the master suite of the ocean-front estate.

Jay was handsome and in good shape. After putting on his bathing suit, he walked out onto the expansive teak deck and uncovered the spa. He watched as the steam rose into the air, then stepped in and turned on the jets. "Ah, this is nice," he said aloud.

He adored his beautiful young wife and six-year-old daughter, Carlie. For a moment, he thought about how his ex-wife disliked children and how she secretly had her tubes tied a month before their wedding.

Minutes later, Serena and Carlie walked out onto the deck. Serena sported a red silk blouse, white shorts, and red flats. Her hair was in a ponytail and pulled through the back of her black, silk baseball cap. Carlie wore a yellow sun-dress and white sandals. While holding onto her mother's hand, she leaned over and gave Jay a kiss.

"Morning, Daddy," she said.

"Morning, Pumpkin," he returned the kiss. "How are my little princesses this morning?"

"Good, Daddy, I'm going shopping with Mommy today."

Jay kissed her again. "Make sure Mommy gets you something really special, okay?"

Serena looked into Jay's eyes, smiled, and said, "little princesses, huh?" Then she leaned over and whispered, "For a dirty old man you were pretty good this morning."

Jay laughed. "I'm sorry. I didn't mean it that way."

"Ah, ha," she replied with a teasing smile on her face. Then she handed him the morning paper and placed his coffee next to him on the deck.

"Were off, darling," she said. "We have many things to do today."

Jay winked, "you girls have a good day. I'll see you tonight at the club."

"Oh, darling," she said as she remembered," I have karate at 4:00, so I won't be down until about 6:00 or 6:30."

"No problem," replied Jay. "I'll meet you on board."

"Bye, Daddy."

***

Bobbie, or Roberta as she liked to be called, was his ex-wife and ex-partner. When Jay married Bobbie, her aging father brought him into the clothing business. The old man owned one schlock clothing store in the Hillcrest area of San Diego. The business was hardly worth anything, but the half an acre of land and buildings were situated in a prime commercial redevelopment area. A short time after his father-in-law's death, the buildings were destroyed by an electrical fire.

Jay sold the property to a developer for three quarters of a million dollars. With this newfound capital, he restructured the business and turned it into a multi-million dollar enterprise. Jay now owned a chain of men's clothing stores, twenty-seven stores in all, from Santa Rosa to San Diego, all located just a short distance from college campuses. He was convinced that his success was a result of his scantily dressed, bikini-clad, all-female sales force. His models, as he called them, were generally co-eds from the local universities.

He was well liked by most people and disliked by a few. Religious groups and some politicians usually made negative comments about his business profile, even though many of them wore his line of suits and sport clothes. A portion of his profits went to various charities.

Bobbie was the same age as Jay but looked ten years older. As part of the divorce in 1980, he gave her $500,000, assuming she signed over her half of the business to him. She, according to Jay's attorney, signed the papers, kept the money, and then changed her mind after he married Serena.

Bobbie became crude and embarrassing to be around. She threatened Jay about the cause of the fire and wanted an additional $250,000 to keep quiet.

Prior to the divorce, Jay started taking Serena to meetings and on business trips. She was hired as his marketing director. Opening more stores caused Jay to spend more time away from home. Bobbie became suspicious and hired a private detective to follow them. Nothing was reported to her as unusual or him being unfaithful. However, she started accusing Jay of having an affair.

The affair didn't take place until after the accusations by Bobbie. Jay didn't deny his desire for Serena. Although Serena was much younger than Jay, she was extremely mature for her age, soft-spoken, and sophisticated, mixing well with his clients and peers. She had a natural gift when it came to public relations and advertising.

***

After reading the paper and finishing his coffee, Jay got up and walked out to the edge of the deck. Looking out at the beautiful Pacific, he scanned the shoreline in both directions. He took a deep breath of fresh salt air. While running his fingers through his thin, wet, light-brown hair, he noticed a big man stepping out from under the deck.

"Hey, what the hell are you doing down there?" Jay shouted.

The vagrant scurried out over the ice plant toward the sandy beach. He didn't say anything nor did he look back at Jay.

***

Although necessary, most of the time, Jay hated wearing suits and ties. He decided today would be a casual day. After dressing, he walked into the kitchen putting on impeccably pressed blue jeans, a white golf shirt, white socks, and loafers. He sported a lightweight hounds-tooth blazer over his right shoulder.

"Good morning, buenos días," he repeated, as he spoke to Martha the housekeeper.

"Good morning, Mr. Jay," she replied. "Would you like something for breakfast?"

"No, thank you. I will get something at the coffee shop."

"Which car this morning, Señor Jay?" asked Jaime, Martha's husband.

"The black Porsche will be just fine," responded Jay.

"Mrs. Serena took that one already."

"Okay, then the blue one." He laughed.

Jaime scurried out into the garage to lower the top of the cabriolet. Jay followed, and as he stepped inside the car, he made it a point to show Jaime the sandy shoe prints on the highly varnished hardwood floor of the garage.

"Jaime, have you been walking around in here with wet sand on your shoes again?

"No, sir, that's not from my shoes," replied Jaime.

"I don't want this floor scratched. Please clean it up."

"Yes, sir, right away," Jaime answered.

***

Many homes on the ocean side of the street were large, two- or three-story mansions terracing down to the beach below. Most homes were old and stately, but new homes like Jay and Serena's were beginning to pop up throughout the area. The neighborhood reeked of money. Gated driveways and secluded entries were hints that the neighbors really desired privacy. Many homes passed from one generation to another. It was rumored that Robert Kennedy had played on the beach down the street as a boy.

Jay knew that his neighbor on the north side of his home owned a media company consisting of newspapers, radio stations, and television stations throughout the country. He had never met him and on occasion saw his Bentley enter or leave the property.

Jay's neighbor to the south, a bachelor, on the other side of the paved, public-beach access walkway, owned a stately, newer, two-story, 9,800-square-foot home. Jay had met him while the home was under construction. His name was Dominic Ferruccio. Jay could never actually figure out what he did, specifically, for a living, but he suspected he had close ties to the Italian Mafia in Los Angeles or Nevada, certainly not in San Diego. There were stories about some judge in Los Angeles having to resign because Dominic did some favors for him. They weren't what Jay would consider good friends; however, Jay had been entrusted with the keys and the alarm code to Dom's house. Sometimes Dom would be gone for long periods of time, especially, as Jay often joked, when he was serving time.

About twice a year, early, before sunrise, usually on a fog-covered morning, there would be an assemblage of special agents from the FBI and the DEA along with the local police, waiting to converge on Palacio de Ferruccio. As soon as daybreak peaked over the Muirlands, the raid would begin.

Dominic often complained that the cost of replacing his doors, after they had been smashed, was more than his attorneys' fees. He told the FBI that they could have a set of keys to his home if they promised to only use them when they were raiding him. That didn't go over very well. One brazen agent told him he had more fun breaking and smashing things than arresting him.

On occasion, when Jay heard the noise and turmoil, he would step out onto the street and watch the commotion. If Dominic spotted Jay, he would nod, giving silent permission for Jay to watch over the estate while he was gone. This was usually as he was escorted, hands behind his back, out into the courtyard and guided into the back seat of an unmarked government vehicle.

Sometimes he returned the same day, and at other times not for weeks or months.

***

Jay backed out onto the imported limestone, tiled drive and then drove north. He accelerated up the small hill and then coasted down past the tall palm trees that lined the curbs on both sides of Camino de La Costa, or better known to locals as "The Street of Dreams." He turned left onto Palomar Street and then a right onto Neptune Place. As he drove past Wind n Sea beach, he scanned the surfers, joggers, and a few unrelenting fishermen sitting on the rocks with their lines stretched out into the shallow surf.

***

Jay parked in front of the original 1950s-style Coffee Cup Cafe on Wall Street. It was now 9 o'clock, and most of the morning regulars were still there. Jay stopped for coffee at least three or four times a week. The group consisted of mostly old-time La Jolla businessmen, including a doctor nearing retirement age and a local San Diego police detective. Old stories, the daily joke, gossip, gold-mine scams, and how to make a quick million bucks were just part of the everyday conversations.

He walked inside and pulled his favorite chair up to the table. Doc Matthews said, "Morning, Jay." This was followed by three other greetings, from Carl Salis, a local real-estate broker, Frank Mobley, a stockbroker, and Alis Brooks, a detective.

This morning's discussion, or scam of the day, as it was referred to, was how to place a second mortgage on a neighbor's house without him knowing about it. Mobley was unraveling his scheme, and the others were adding their wisecracks and laughing.

"I heard about this before. It's really true, dangerous but true. They do it all the time in L.A."

Jay remarked, "Sure, you heard about it before. This is the tenth time he brought it up. I'll bet he's pulling the scam on you right now, Doc."

Doc replied, "You can have my house any time you want it."

Lilly, the always smiling sixty-eight-year-old owner of the Coffee Cup, brought Jay his coffee and refilled the others for the fifth time. Jay looked cautiously into his cup.

"Where's the soap today?" The others laughed. Lilly shook her head as she turned her back and walked from the table, smiling.

"Don't complain to me," she said, looking back over her shoulder. "Quanny washes the dishes." Quanny had worked in the coffee shop for fifteen years. She was born and raised in La Jolla, nearing the end of an era when numerous wealthy bluebloods employed Blacks as housekeepers, caretakers, and chauffeurs. Many domestics and their families were provided with small, wood-frame homes near the village and beaches to live in. Back then, living up the hill in the Muirlands was prestigious; living near the village was not. After Jonas Salk moved to La Jolla, strict covenants and restrictions banning Blacks and Jews from owning property in La Jolla were removed, and families such as Quanny's typically inherited or purchased their homes from their employers.

Quanny flung a dishtowel over her shoulder, swung open the counter, and walked up to Jay. She was laughing as she rested her hand on his arm.

"Honey," she said, "I wash and rinse 'em all. 'Cept yours."

Cheery laughs grew louder, and Jay replied, "Drinking that stuff is like taking an enema."

Laughing, as she extended her arms out toward Jay.

"Sweetpie, you finally got it."

The others laughed. Quanny shook her head as she walked from the table, smiling.

Alis said, "Hey, maybe it wasn't rinsed, but at least you know it got washed."

The laughing continued, then Carl remarked about Jay's casual dress for the day. "What's this, Levi day?"

Jay struck back, "Give me a break. Look at you, the only real-estate broker in La Jolla who goes to work with cowboy boots."

"That's because I specialize in ranches and groves."

Doc remarked sarcastically, "Yeah, right here in La Jolla. There's lots a ranches and groves."

Carl said, "Who's got today's joke?"

"I do," said Frank. You guys ready?"

"Go on. Let's hear it," someone replied. "Alright, here it is. What's the difference between a duck?"

Everyone sat silent for a few seconds waiting for the rest of the joke. Frank said. "That's it, the whole thing."

"What's the difference between a duck?" said Carl. "What a stupid joke."

Doc said, "I'm getting too old for this shit."

Carl said, "Okay smart-ass, what's the difference?"

Mobley smiled, "I'm not going to tell you guys. Think about it for a while. It's really not that hard."

"Mobley, you need some serious help," remarked Lilly, from behind the counter.

All laughed as Doc rose and said, "Well, boys, it's time to go home, put on my cowboy boots, and hit the trail. My first patient is due at ten."

Carl and Frank stood as well. "We're outta here as well. See you guys in the morning."

***

Jay and Alis were sitting at the table by themselves. Alis's wife, Francesca, and Bobbie, Jay's ex-wife, were good friends. They had belonged to the same charity organizations and were both members of Las Patrones, an upscale women's charity organization in La Jolla.

Francesca came from a very wealthy, politically powerful family in Argentina. Her unlimited funds allowed them to live in La Jolla, drive expensive cars, maintain a membership in the La Jolla Beach & Tennis Club, and send their children to Ivy League schools. This difference in lifestyle from most others on the force created some animosity between Alis and his working peers. Resembling and certainly relating more as an equal, rather than some ordinary cop, was likely the reason he fit in so well with the locals at the coffee shop. Alis and Jay had remained good friends in spite of the divorce.

"Alis, I need to ask you a question," Jay said.

"Sure," replied Alis. "Shoot."

"I'd like to, now that you mention it."

"Jay, what are you talking about?"

"You said shoot," replied Jay.

"Shoot what? I still don't understand. Start over again."

"Okay, forget the shoot part. How do I get rid of this homeless guy who is sleeping under my deck?" Alis laughed, "Oh I see, you want to shoot him. Well, sorry to say, you can't do that."

"I don't want to shoot him. I just want him to go someplace else."

"You and everybody else. There's probably twenty to thirty homeless wandering around La Jolla at any given time."

"Christ," remarked Jay, "that's a lot of people for La Jolla, isn't it?"

Ignoring Jay's question, Alis remarked, "It's probably Jeffrey."

"Who's Jeffrey?"

"He's another of what we term La Jolla's Finest. He's an ex-con who hangs around Bank of America all day, harassing people and begging for money. Last Friday, he spit in some teller's face."

"Is he dangerous?"

"He might be. The beat guys are watching him."

"That still doesn't tell me how to get rid of him, if he's the guy under my deck."

"Best way to get rid of him is to move inland," Alis laughed.

"You're a big help," said Jay.

Alis's pager sounded. "I gotta go."

"One more question, then you can go."

"Hurry up."

Laughing, Jay asked, "Where did the name Alis come from?"

Laughing as well, Brooks replied, "The story goes like this. After my mother delivered me, the nurse cleaned me up and brought me to her. Now understand, I was the sixth kid in the family. My mother had five boys before me and always wanted a girl. She counted my fingers and toes, missed my pecker, and named me frickin' Alice. When she found out I was a boy, she dropped the C-E and added an S. Got it? Alis!"

Jay shook his head in dismay and Alis laughed. "I really gotta go. See you tomorrow."

Jay finished his last sip of cold coffee and tossed five dollars on the table next to the rest of the morning crew's money. He got up, kissed Lilly on the cheek, and said goodbye to Quanny.

Chapter 16

Jay rarely arrived at the office before ten. As he walked into the reception room, the phones were ringing and members of his staff were scurrying about. The walls were decorated with life-size photographs of him and his sexy models. In one corner next to the reception counter stood a life-size cardboard cut-out of him dressed in a tuxedo, smiling, and holding a sign with the slogan, "You really are what you wear."

Whenever Jay entered his business environment, he became very stringent and demanded perfection from all who surrounded him. "Morning, people," he uttered as he grabbed his phone messages from the rack on the counter. He barely heard the responses as he walked past the mirrored glass walls leading down the hall to his office. Time spent doing business was well planned and precisely executed in order to achieve the maximum results from his efforts. Since he had married Serena, he rarely teased or indulged in small talk. Once Serena left, he streamlined the operation. No one had a private office or secretary, except him. Jay had surrounded himself with extremely well qualified personnel. He was a master at delegating, which allowed him the freedom to come and go as he wished.

Tossing his sport jacket over the black leather sofa, he sat down at his massive glass desk. Swiveling his chair around so he could see the ocean and the Cove, he began thumbing through his messages: one from Ralph Forester at KFMB radio; another from David Goldman, his attorney; a third from Mel Blakely, the dock master at the San Diego Yacht Club; and two messages marked personal, will call back.

Jay swung the chair around, picked up the phone, and called the receptionist.

"Marna, have Brian call Forester at KFMB and take care of whatever he wants." Then he dialed his attorney's private line.

"David Goldman."

"David, this is Jay. What's the problem?"

"Good morning, Jay." Nervously getting right to the point, Goldman said, "I got a call from Roberta's lawyer this morning."

Jay said, "Better you than me! What does she want now?"

"She said you're ripping her client off. She wants more money."

"Jesus, you're my lawyer. Can't you make them go away?"

"It's not that easy. She's threatening to take you back to court again and to have you audited. She said she knows what you did."

"Who said that, her attorney? Look, I don't want to talk about this on the phone. Can you meet me at the yacht club for lunch? I'll be there at one."

David said, "Okay, but be on time this time. I can't wait all day."

Jay hung up the phone, and thought, *"I'm always on time, what the hell is he talking about?"*

Marna's voice came through the intercom. "Mr. Newman, there's a call on line three for you."

"Who is it, Marna?"

"I'm not sure sir, but I think it's the same person who wouldn't leave his name when he called before."

"Give him to Carl."

"I did that already. Then he called back and said he's not a customer and that he needs to talk to you personally."

"Okay, I'll take it."

Jay placed his left hand on the phone, wondered for a second as his forehead wrinkled, then picked up the handset.

"Hello, this is Jay Newman. How can I help you?"

No response.

"Who's there? Who is this?" He could hear someone breathing in the background.

"Okay, last chance. Who's this?"

"Not so fast, *Mr. Newman*," a voice replied.

Jay sat perplexed for a moment. *Who was he was talking to?* "Okay, wise ass, who are you?"

There was a moment of silence, then, "Let's just say a voice from your past, Nubaum."

Few people knew him as Jacob Nubaum. Rapid thoughts of the blaze flashed through his mind. *"No way,"* he thought. *"That was done professionally."* He squinted, wrinkling his brow, and thought, *"I was already Jay Newman when that happened."*

"Who is this?" Jay said forcibly.

The next sound was a dial tone. Jay placed the handset back in the cradle. He crumpled his messages, threw them in the wastebasket, leaned back in his chair, and stared at the ceiling.

***

Jay turned off Anchorage Way and into the driveway at the San Diego Yacht Club. The security guard, dressed in blue slacks, a white shirt, and top-siders, stopped him. Jay thought this was somewhat unusual because the guard always waived him through.

"Hello, Mr. Newman. Nice day, sir."

"What's the problem, Roger?" asked Jay.

"Some guy was asking about your boat the other day. He said he had to do some work on the electronics. Normally this is no big deal, except he first asked if you were a member here."

"Who is he?" asked Jay.

"I don't know sir, but I thought it was a little strange."

"That is strange. Marine Services is supposed to do some work on the autopilot, but they're not supposed to be here until next week. What did you tell him?"

"I didn't tell him anything, except that I couldn't let him in unless I had authorization from you or from Mel. I usually recognize most of the regular repairman, but I never saw this guy before."

"Good. If he comes back, find out who he is and what he wants." Jay pulled out a business card and wrote his private office line and home number on it. As he was handing it to Roger, he opened the ashtray and removed a new, folded, one-hundred-dollar bill.

Jay had a strange habit of keeping two of these bills in each of his vehicles. Several years earlier, when the timing chain broke on his SL, he was caught stranded in a small desert town without any cash on him. The mechanic wouldn't take a check or credit card. Jay swore that would never happen again. He placed the crisp bill under his card and handed it to Roger.

"Here's my card. Call me if you find out anything."

"That's not necessary, sir." Roger said, attempting to hand back the money.

"Don't tell me what's necessary. Just take it and remember to call me."

"Okay. Thanks, Mr. Newman. I will."

"By the way, David Goldman is my lunch guest today. He'll be here around one o'clock. Make sure you let him in, but make him park on the other side of the tennis courts so he has to walk a long way."

"I got it," he laughed. "Thanks again, Mr. Newman."

As Jay pulled away from the guardhouse, he wondered who was asking about him. He passed the tennis courts and drove to the front of the main lot. His reserved space, which was a result of a generous donation at the club's Christmas auction, was occupied by a silver Jaguar.

"This is not my day," he thought. He parked near the pool, put on his sport coat, and walked up to the clubhouse.

Jay had always been impressed by the building's unique architecture. The dramatic hip roof extended up into the sky and was topped with a matching hip-roofed cupola. The cupola and its encompassing widow's walk could be seen for miles and was a joyous sight when returning to port, especially after a long sail.

Jay crossed the entry porch, which led to the tall, varnished, teakwood entry doors encased in a smoked glass wall. He grasped one of the polished brass handles and walked into the large, wood-paneled, lobby. Several sofas and chairs were clustered along with showcases displaying many embroidered articles of clothing. For sale were goods including hats, tee shirts, sweatshirts, and jackets bearing the yacht club burgee and club name. A white, waist-length jacket caught his eye. He walked over to the counter and asked the clerk to set one aside for him. He told her he would pick it up after lunch.

Continuing down the hall toward the bar on his right, Jay passed many trophy cases displaying hundreds of awards won by members throughout the years. He especially liked the plaque honoring him for winning the San Diego to Ensenada race five years ago. At the end of the hallway, double doors stood open allowing access to the expansive, teak-decked patio dining areas.

Stepping onto the patio, he inhaled the fresh smell of a gentle sea breeze. Umbrella tables sat with blue, canvas-backed director chairs bearing the white embroidered names of members' yachts. Looking south over the deck provided views of the main channel, which lead to the club's guest dock. Lining each side of the wide waterway sat dozens of boats tied to their slips.

***

Jaime moved three of the remaining four cars onto the street. He was ordered never to touch the one covered car in the far corner. The most difficult car to move was the Ferrari. Although it was his favorite, Mr. Jay wouldn't allow him to change the seat position, so he sat like a dwarf behind the wheel as his foot stretched to reach the clutch pedal. Smiling as he revved the engine, he shifted into first gear. The car jerked and leaped out on to the driveway like a grasshopper, then stalled. The Mercedes and the Jaguar were much easier to move.

His morning consisted of sweeping, washing, and polishing the wood flooring. He was puzzled by the extent of dried footprints and sand, which appeared to have been tracked in through the side door. When examining the door, he realized it was unlocked. Surely the door was closed and locked, he thought. As part of his duties he always checked both security systems before going to bed. At least one of the panels would have displayed a red light if the door had been left ajar. For fear of repercussion, he decided to be more watchful and not tell Señor Jay.

***

Jay was sipping his "Signature Salad," which consisted of a double gin martini, two olives, two onions, and a twist, while sitting and waiting on the patio for David to arrive. Several members and their guests walked past, greeting him with smiles, friendly words, and an occasional pat on the shoulder. He thought about earlier events of the day: the mysterious phone call; the unknown workman who presented himself to the guard at the gate; and why David Goldman was concerned about him being on time.

He watched David speak with Maurice, the maître d', who cordially escorted him to Jay's table. David wore a tan linen suit, a white shirt, with a dark brown and white striped silk tie, which was pulled loose from the unbuttoned collar. David was also divorced and forty-four years old. He had graduated from Stanford and attended Yale Law School. After returning to California, he started working in a family law practice owned by his future father-in-law. He was first introduced to Jay, many years before, when they had both attended a luncheon honoring the mayor of San Diego.

Having similar political convictions, they soon became friendly. Jay often thought how it was easy for David. His wife ran off with a wealthy surgeon and asked for nothing but her freedom. Jay envied David's arrangement: no children, no alimony, and the ability to retain his home in Del Mar, a coastal community north of La Jolla. Jay had to give his last house to Bobbie. He stayed off the title on his present house because multiple business loans required personal guarantees. Serena was the legal owner. If he got into financial trouble, he didn't want her to lose it. Even though the guys in the coffee shop called ex-wives The House Keepers, he was okay with that.

Jay stood and while shaking David's hand, David said, "I would have been here five minutes earlier if I didn't have to park a block away. That's really a long walk."

Jay smiled and said, "I can't control where guests park." Then Jay thought, *"Keep fucking with me and I'll have you park in Wyoming."* The two men sat. Jay ordered another martini and one for David. Then he said, "And what's this shit about me not being on time?"

Adjusting his deck chair, David replied, "You know damn well what I mean. I waited and waited for you."

"David, I don't know what you are talking about."

"The other night, when some guy from your office called and told me to be on board at 8 sharp, I sat there for an hour and a half."

"Who called you from my office?"

"I don't know, but he said that you insisted it was very important and not to say anything to anyone."

"I never called you, and I never instructed anyone from my office to call you."

"All I know is that I sat there, damp and uncomfortable, for a long time."

"Didn't the guard stop and question you as to why you were here at 8 at night?"

"There was no guard. I just drove in."

Looking perplexed, Jay said," I don't know what you're talking about."

"Forget it," said David. "Let's talk about your ex-wife."

"I'd rather talk about your ex-wife," said Jay, raising his eyebrows.

"Jay, this is serious."

Ignoring David, Jay motioned for the waiter. He ordered another round of drinks. Then each man ordered lunch.

Jay asked. "So why is she contacting you?"

"She is concerned that you are hiding profits."

"I am, but that's between you and me, not you and her."

"Roberta knows that I am a direct connection to you. She asked her lawyer to call me to talk to you."

"For Christ's sake, David, did her lawyer call you or did Bobby contact you directly? I'm the one who pays her attorney fees. Every time she talks to her lawyer, it costs me $200."

"Maybe she is trying to save you some money."

"Bull. I don't believe that. If it wasn't for that bitch lawyer of hers always wearing a low-cut blouse and shoving her tits in the judge's face, I might have gotten a fair shake in that deal. Her damn attorney was being tutored by the judge during the whole thing."

David shrugged, ignored the remarks, and said, "Roberta knows that she can't reason with you, and she wants me to talk to you."

"Why are you talking to Roberta? When did she become your client? I pay you a lot of money to be my lawyer, not hers. I don't want you talking to her anymore." He hesitated for a moment, then said, "Furthermore, why is she threatening me? What's this stuff about having me audited? She can't prove anything."

David smirked. He couldn't tolerate when Jay went off on one of his tangents.

"Jay, she wants you to buy her out."

"I already gave her $500,000."

"She wants more."

"Where the hell am I supposed to get more?" He pushed his chair back from the table. "She signed off, remember?"

"I know she did." David began to squirm. "She is referring to the fire."

"She knows more about that fire than I do. How much does she want?"

David clasped his hands, leaned forward, and put them down on the table in front of him. He lowered his voice, stared at Jay, and said, "She'll get out of your life if you give her two million."

Jay pretended to choke on his water. "That's a nice fantasy. I thought she wanted another $250,000. Where the hell am I supposed to get two million dollars? You want me to burn down my house and my boat?"

The waiter placed their drinks and lunch plates in front of them. "Can I get you gentlemen anything else right now?" Nervously, David sat back and crossed his arms over his chest. Jay looked down at his fish and chips, then moved his right hand back and forth toward the waiter, gesturing for him to go away.

David took a bite out of his ahi as Jay inched back toward the table and with his fork poked a fry and ate it. Jay looked back into David's eyes and said, "How come there was no guard at the gate?"

"What are you talking about?" responded David. He then reached over and grabbed a French fry off of Jay's plate.

"Don't touch my food!"

David started to reach for another fry, and Jay grabbed his wrist, squeezing firmly. "David" he said, "I really have a problem with people touching my food." Releasing his grip, he said, "Please, I'll get you ten orders of fries if you want them. Just don't touch mine." He hesitated for a second, "It's just something left over from my childhood."

"I'm sorry. I understand. Some people have memory flashbacks to when they were young when food was scarce. It won't happen again."

"It has nothing to do with not having enough to eat when I was young. On the contrary, if there is one thing we had plenty of, it was food." He chose not to go any further with the discussion and said, "You eat your germs, and I'll eat mine."

Changing the subject, Jay went on, "So tell me again; the other night, when you were here, there's always supposed to be someone at the gate."

Sternly, David replied, "There was no one at the gate. I told you I just drove right through. What difference does it make?"

Jay asked, "What did the person sound like, who called you?"

"I don't know. He sounded like it was urgent. He said, that you said I need to meet with you at 8 o'clock sharp."

David finished his meal and kept silent as Jay sat staring sightlessly into the distance. Sounds of halyards clapping against aluminum masts filled the air as the wind caused the boats in their slips to sway. Club burgees waved upon tall masts, which shot up into the sky. Dinghies hung attached to their sterns. Blue, white, tan, and red canvas sail covers draped many of the vessels. The waiter broke the silence when he presented Jay with the bill. As Jay initialed it, he looked up at David, who was standing and ready to leave.

"Is she still fat?" he queried.

"Is who still fat?" answered David.

"Bobby, Roberta, that's who. Is she still fat?"

"No," he said, quickly defending her. "I think she looks pretty good."

Jay snapped back, "I'll bet you do.

***

After David left the club, Jay walked into the bar, sat at a stool, and ordered a brandy. "Tough day, huh, Mr. Newman," said Craig, the bartender.

"You know, Craig, sometimes you wish you could just get on board and sail away."

"Yes sir, Mr. Newman. I've heard that one a few times before." Jay sipped his drink, remembering how she was embarrassing to be with. She thought she was an authority on everything. He remembered the pain. He had been repeatedly humiliated by Bobbie. Her need to be accepted in La Jolla's society circles became an obsession. Once accepted into the elite assembly, she decided to call herself Roberta instead of Bobbie. To her, Roberta sounded more blue blood. "*Bitch*" he thought.

Jay finished his drink, left the bar, and walked down the hall to Mel's office. The dock master was sitting at his desk as Jay poked his head in the door.

"Mel, you called me this morning. Any news on a slip?"

"Afternoon, Mr. Newman. Yes sir, I'll have an available slip on F dock later this afternoon. Are you interested?"

"How far down?" Jay asked.

"It's next to the end tie. It's a good slip for you. Go take a look at it. There is a Mason there now, but I want to move her to your slip this afternoon."

"Can I ask you a question, Mel?"

"Sure what can I help you with?"

"Is there ever a time when there is no guard at the gate?"

"Sure, in the evenings and at night sometimes, the guards make rounds and, well, sometimes nature calls, and they have to go to the head. Why do you ask?"

"I was just curious. You answered my question. Thanks."

After the short visit to the slip, Jay boarded "SHMATTEH," his recently restored Cheoy Lee 48. Club policy allowed him to "float" from dock to dock until a permanent slip could be assigned. He lost his last slip when he sold his forty-footer two years prior.

Jay had taken delivery of his current yacht shortly after it turned four years old in 1985. The previous owner had put 10,000 miles on her by cruising long offshore passages to Bermuda, the Virgin Islands, and Argentina. Jay made contact with associates of Bob Kerry, the boat's designer, and the Cheoy Lee Seattle Rig Center Cockpit Ketch was completely restored and delivered to San Diego in 1987. Jay's attraction to the yacht began with the desire for a king-size bed in the owner's aft cabin. The spacious Vee berth was a perfect place for Carlie.

The hull was fiberglass, as opposed to wood, thus easing the continuous maintenance costs. The teak decking and spectacular wood cabinetry throughout the interior resembled a true classic. During retrofitting, Jay had a secret safe and gun cabinet installed under the navigation station table. Like many sailors, Jay often dreamt of sailing away to the South Pacific, situating himself and his family on some island and operating a small yacht charter business.

"Mel," he said, as he returned to the dock master's office, "I want to show the slip to Serena before I make up my mind. She will be here later. Is that okay with you?"

"Sure, Mr. Newman, but you can't keep her too much longer on H dock. If I don't hear from you then, we will move her for you."

Jay liked F dock because it was fairly secluded and out of the way from most other boats in the club. The wide fairway made it easy to maneuver his boat, and the view of the homes in bordering La Playa was spectacular.

"I know. Thanks. I'll let you know as soon as I can." Jay walked back into the lobby, picked up his new jacket, walked to his car, and tossed the garment in the trunk. He glanced at his watch. Four o'clock. He didn't want to go back to the office so he went back to the boat.

***

Having consumed two of Jay's "salads" at lunch, David Goldman drove carefully down Harbor Drive to his office downtown. He didn't need another 502. Upon entering the parking garage, he noticed Roberta's white BMW parked in the corner next to his reserved space. As he turned sharply and made his way closer, he spotted her standing by the wall behind her car. She was wearing tight slacks and a tee shirt as if she had just come from the gym. Her short blonde hair was mussed, and she had a navy-blue elastic band around her forehead, confirming to himself what he had said earlier: *"Looks pretty good to me."*

David parked the Eldorado and started to get out. She immediately approached and started quizzing him.

"What did he say?" she asked impatiently.

"Hold it a second, Roberta. Let me get out of the car."

Roberta was so energized she wouldn't stop fidgeting. "I'm sorry, David. Did you talk to him?"

"Yes, I did talk to him."

"What did he say?"

"Relax for a second, please! He didn't say anything."

"What do you mean he didn't say anything? All he has to say is yes."

"I don't think he has two million dollars."

"Bullshit! I bet he has more than that at home in some hidden room. I know for a fact that at one time he had almost a million in our house."

"Jesus, that's a lot of money to keep at home. Did he ever think of what a fire could do to him?" It immediately dawned upon him what he had said. They both looked at each other.

Roberta shrugged her shoulders, threw out her arms, and with palms up, said, "So, what else's new? Look, I don't want to talk about fires. I just want to talk about two million dollars. Did he say anything at all?"

David thought for a second. "Yeah, actually he did."

"What?" she asked. "What exactly did he say after you mentioned the money?"

"He said he wanted to know where the guard was."

"What guard? What are you talking about?" Roberta asked. "Never mind. I'll call him in a few days and bring it up again. Let's give him a little while to stew it over."

She moved closer to David and placed her hands on each side of his chest. Her right hand gently moved upward, wrapping around his neck and the back of his head. She pulled him toward her. As she stood on her tiptoes she tilted her head and planted her hard tongue in his mouth. Placing his hands on her tight buttocks, he squeezed his fingers as he returned the passionate kiss.

Chapter 17

The Porsche was a present to Serena on her last birthday. Jay already had one of his own but liked switching vehicles once in a while, just for the novelty. The vanity plates on Serena's black beauty read, RAGS 2. Jay's plates read, RAGMAN. His boat's name was Shmatteh; in Yiddish it meant rags. He often recollected the stories, from his father, about many of the old-time Jews, who settled on the Lower East Side of New York and would sell their goods from pushcarts. The quality of these goods wasn't always considered the best, hence the word Shmatteh, for clothing.

***

Serena kept the Porsche at 65 miles per hour and in the right lane as she exited from north highway 5 to Ardath Road. The long, double-lane, half-circle off ramp merged into another lane at the far end of the freeway overpass. Serena was familiar with this access and always kept to the right in order to allow faster traffic to pass. The top was down. She enjoyed the wind in her hair as her ponytail blew from side to side.

Carlie was strapped into the passenger seat. Her new, tiny sunglasses sat crooked upon her nose as she squirmed to right herself after the long turn. "Mommy, you are going too fast," she cried.

"No, honey, I'm not. It just seems that way because of the wind." Down-shifting into forth gear, she let the clutch out too fast, and the Porsche jerked. As she glanced in her rear-view mirror, she saw a white car on her tail.

"Where did he come from? I didn't cut him off," she said aloud. The driver suddenly leaned on the horn causing her to panic. He pulled within inches of her bumper. "Hold on tight," she shouted to Carlie.

Serena sped up, but the white car stayed in place. The horn continued to blast as it moved from one side of its lane to the other. With seconds to make a decision, she made a heel-toe shift into third gear and veered sharply to the right, exiting onto North La Jolla Scenic Road. The Porsche fishtailed, propelling dirt and loose gravel into the air behind her. The white car raced after her.

Regaining command, she down-shifted again, this time into second gear. The Porsche reacted as it should and seemed to launch itself. Carlie screamed with fright. "Mommy, Mommy."

Serena's rigid hands tightly gripped the leather-wrapped steering wheel. She trembled with fear and anxiety. The yellow lines on the road disappeared and the eucalyptus trees, which lined the sides of the road, became nothing more than a blur. The speedometer climbed to ninety, 110, and finally 125 miles per hour. Terrorized, her blue eyes glanced back into the mirror again. The white car had vanished.

***

Once home, Serena began to search for Jay. She called his office, and they told her he was at the Yacht Club. She called the clubhouse, and they told her he was there earlier for lunch but that they hadn't seen him recently. She finally called the boat. Jay answered and learned of her incident with the white car. After confirming that she and Carlie were not hurt, he anxiously hurried home.

***

Serena and Carlie comforted each other as they sat in the living room, looking out over the ocean. Martha sat in a rocking chair on the opposite side of the room. Jay hurried in and sat hugging them. "It's okay. It's all right. I'm here now."

Serena was composed, but visibly shaken by the experience. Carlie said, "Daddy, some bad man was chasing us."

"It's okay, sweetheart. He's gone now," reassured Jay.

"Mommy drove real fast, and she was crying. I was scared, too."

"I know you were, honey. You were really brave. I'm proud of you."

Jay motioned to Martha, "Take Carlie for a while. I need to be alone with Serena."

As Carlie scooted off of the sofa, she leaned over to Serena and gave her a kiss. Serena said, "I love you, sweetie pie. Thanks for being Mommy's helper today." Looking into Jay's eyes, she said, "For a moment there, I was really scared to death. I thought he was going to ram us. I don't know where he came from."

"Did you get a look at the driver? Do you know if it was a man or a woman?"

"No, I just actually assumed it was a man. Women don't drive like that. Once I realized he wouldn't go away, my mind flashed to what they taught us in the Porsche driving school."

"What happened? What do you mean?"

"I almost lost control. Well actually I did lose control for a few seconds as I turned off of Ardath onto La Jolla Scenic. I think the back end was starting to come around to the front so I took my foot off the accelerator for a second and the car straightened out. Then I put it into second and it responded and snapped back into place, just like it had in class. I almost red-lined. Then I shifted again, gripped the wheel, put my foot on the floor, and took off."

"Jesus, you must have been scared to death."

"Actually, I don't think I was frightened until it was over. I was so worried about Carlie."

"Thank God you're both okay." Jay got up from the sofa and walked over to the bar.

"Would you like something?" he asked.

"Just some water, thanks." Jay placed ice cubes in two glasses. He opened the small refrigerator under the sink, removed a bottle of Perrier, and filled her glass. He then filled his with gin. As he walked back to her, he asked if she thought they should call Alis and report it to the police.

Serena said, "It was probably some crazy kid. What are the police going to do, watch for a white car?"

"It might not be a bad idea to report it. That's what we pay these people for."

"Look, if you want to call Alis, go ahead, but I don't want a bunch of policemen walking through the house, gawking at everything."

She hesitated for a second and said, "Don't worry, Jay. Everything is okay now. I'm fine."

He sat with her, holding her hand and said, "Serena, some strange things have been happening lately."

Her forehead wrinkled, and her eyes looked directly into his. "What do you mean?"

"Well, it may be nothing, but someone has been calling the office and leaving weird messages. Someone has been asking about me at the club, and now this, with the car. I don't know if any of this is coincidental..."

Serena interrupted, "What could they want? Did we do anything that we should be worried about?"

"Then someone on the phone, this morning, used my old name and hung up."

"There aren't too many people here that know you as Jake Nubaum, right?"

"Right," he replied, "unless my mother has been talking to someone."

"Why don't you call her and ask her?"

"No, no, I'm sure it's nothing, but I just want you to be careful."

She sat quietly for a second, then responded with a puzzled look, "Who could it be? Why?"

"I don't know, dear. Just rest a while. We'll stay home tonight and go to the boat tomorrow. By the way, the boat is now at the end of F dock. I'm going down to my den. Buzz me when dinner is ready." Jay leaned over and kissed Serena on the cheek.

"I love you. Don't worry about anything," he said.

"I love you too."

***

Jay walked over by the elevator, stood, and contemplated riding or walking. His doctor wanted him to walk more, so he made his way down the stairs. The lower level of the home contained three bedrooms, the bath suites, a playroom for Carlie, an auxiliary kitchen, and a small twelve-seat theatre with a bar. He walked a short way down the hall and into the cherry-stained, mahogany wood-paneled theatre. He made his way over to the bar. Centered above the bar on the wall was a painting of his yacht. Jay slid his fingers on the bottom right side of the frame and pressed a hidden button. Adjacent to the bar, a wood panel silently slid sideways exposing a large stainless steel, bank-size vault door. Jay placed this right thumb on a laser pad. A red light flashed, and the heavy door disengaged and swung inward.

The room was fifteen feet wide and twenty feet long. It had no windows and smelled of rich leather and wood. A separate water and ventilation system could be activated in case of emergency. The hand-carved wood-coffered ceiling merged with the dark mahogany crown molding, paneled walls, built-in shelving, and bookcases.

Unlike his last home, which had had a fireproof safe, this secret room was in itself fireproof and self-sustaining. A secondary exit led to a hidden panel in one of the bedroom closets.

An oriental rug sat atop of the marble floor. As Jay entered the room, he glanced at the portrait of Serena hanging above the leather sofa. Sunglasses were raised to the top of her head, fitting snugly into her tightly pulled golden hair as it wrapped into a ponytail. Her lips were pink and moist. A tiny gold anchor necklace sparkled. Embroidered onto the left pocket of her white cotton blouse sat the yacht club burgee. Her navy pleated shorts and white boat shoes accented her bronze tan. White puffy clouds sat amongst the light blue sky background accentuating the highly varnished, pegged, wooden steering wheel and warm teakwood trim in the cockpit.

"God, she's beautiful," thought Jay, as her blue eyes seemed to follow him as he walked past the painting.

Lighting was aesthetically subtle, and the quiet sound of fresh filtered air pushed through the invisible vents. Two matching antique maroon leather armchairs faced the fireplace and reminded him of the first trip he and Serena had taken to England. On a bookshelf next to the door sat many cast models and photos of older cars. His favorite photo was of a red 1959 Triumph TR-3 roadster.

At the rear and to the left side of the room, Jay sat in his high-backed, tucked leather chair. The restored banker's desk with its roll top and small compartments was purchased at an auction dispersing the assets of one of San Diego's disgraced bankers. He slid open the top drawer of his desk, pressed the red button in the drawer, and a wall panel to his right slid out of the way, revealing multiple control panels, some with video screens, and others with cassette tape machines.

Jay was paranoid when it came to security. He had a difficult time trusting people, especially his employees. The video screens permitted Jay to eavesdrop on any store at any time. With a simple flick of a switch he could watch, hear, and record almost anything in any location. The system also provided the ability to monitor the perimeter as well as the interior of his home and garage.

He reached onto the panel and pressed another button. The wall behind him opened, exposing six large stainless steel drawers, two on the top, two in the middle and two on the bottom. Jay turned in his chair and while still seated, leaned over and opened the two bottom drawers. Each drawer was filled with one-hundred-dollar bills, banded in $10,000 stacks. Each drawer contained 25 stacks equaling a total of $500,000. The middle drawers held $50 bills totaling $250,000.

Then he removed his stainless steel, five-shot, .38 caliber Smith and Wesson revolver. He held it for a moment, flipped it open, and confirmed to himself that it was loaded. He swiveled the chair around, stretched out his arms, and took aim at the door in front of him. Then he slowly moved his arms to the right, aiming at the Triumph model. Pretending to pull the trigger he jerked his arms upward as if he felt the recoil from the discharge. At the same time he voiced the explosion with a "POOF" sound. He turned around again, placed the gun back in the drawer.

"I hope it's not him," he said to himself. *"All I need now is Augy Romano."*

Jay opened the top drawers. The drawer on the right contained various legal documents including wills, passports, life-insurance policies, and trusts for Serena and Carlie. The last drawer contained his personal documents. Amid these records were ledgers containing jumbled codes, passwords, and account numbers, which authorized access to several South American bank accounts. Lying flat on the bottom of the drawer was a portfolio with newspaper clippings dating back to Jay's childhood days in Ohio. One honored him as junior lifeguard of the year, when he was a teen and working at the municipal pool. Another was for helping physically and mentally challenged children learn to swim.

Jay's most secret clippings, however, referred to an unsolved murder, which had taken place 25 years earlier in Chardon, Ohio. Jay didn't need to read them. He knew first-hand what had happened that cold winter morning.

A small, leather-bound phone directory contained the names and phone numbers of parties who provided various services to the highest bidder, services with which Jay was quite familiar. Swiveling his chair with the book in hand, he placed it flat on the top of his desk. Then he flipped through the pages until he found the name Mac O'Donnell. O'Donnell was a burly old ex-Marine who specialized in locating people who had particular talents—talents for services that could not be located in any published phone directory.

Jay picked up his outdated, bulky, Motorola Dyna TAC 8000X brick-shaped cell phone and dialed. "Hello, hello, you've reached O'Donnell and Associates. Please leave your name, the number you can be reached at within the next 5 minutes, and the name of the person who referred you to us."

"Mac, this is client number 87. I will be in the garden for the next five minutes." All clients of O'Donnell and Associates were given confidential caller numbers. The numbers were associated with assigned locations. If Jay had given his number and said he was at home or in office, the call would not be returned.

Jay was startled and jerked as the intercom at the side of the desk buzzed. "Darling, dinner is in five minutes."

"I'll be right up. Just give me a few more minutes." Jay sat staring at the cell phone. He looked at his watch. Three minutes more. He placed the palms of his hands on his forehead and exhaled heavily. He looked back at his watch. Two minutes more.

The intercom buzzed again. "Jay, would you bring up a bottle of Chardonnay from the cellar?"

"Yes, dear, I'll be right up."

The cell phone rang. Jay picked it up. It rang again, and Jay knew he had to answer it before the third ring or the caller would hang up. He pushed the button activating the phone and said, "This is 87."

"I, I haven't talked to you in a long time, 87. How's the new family?"

"What is this, Get Smart?" said Jay, referring to an old television show, which had run from 1965 to 1970, staring Don Adams as agent 86. "What do you know about my family?" Jay said.

"Just, just like to keep up with my clients and all," replied Mac.

Jay said, "I need to see you. I have some work for you."

Jay felt a suspicious silence. Then Mac said, "Now it's your turn, huh? Okay, tomorrow, Seaport Village, outside the Mad Hatter. 2 o'clock."

Chapter 18

The next morning, Jay was sitting in his office reading his mail when Marna's voice came through the intercom. "Mr. Newman, you have a personal call on line three."

"Who is it, Marna?"

"I don't know, sir. He just said it was personal."

"Is it the same guy who called yesterday?"

"No, sir, I don't think so."

"Okay, thanks. I'll take it." He reached over to the phone and picked up the handset. "Hello, this is Jay Newman."

"Jay Newman, now that's an interesting name. This is your Friday morning wake-up call."

"Who is this?" Jay said firmly.

"Hey, man, don't get upset. It's me, Augy Romano." There was an awkward silence. Jay's heart began to pound rapidly. *Oh no*, he thought, *this is all I need.*

"Romano, Jesus Christ, I haven't heard from you in, oh, it must be 20 years."

"Actually, it's 25 years and seven months, plus or minus a few days, but who's counting."

Jay tilted his head back. He was frightened. His mind flashed to the memories of that dreadful morning in January, 1964. *What could he want? Why is he calling me now? Oh, Christ, what's going to happen to me?* Jay, attempting to compose himself, said nervously, "God! Augy, where are you? Are you still in Ohio? Do you still live in Mayfield? How did you find out where I was?"

"Slow down, Finch. I just called to say hello."

"Jesus, no one's called me that since high school. Where are you?"

Hesitating with the knowledge he was less than a mile away, Augy said, "Umm, I'm in Columbus, but I'm coming out to California for a few days and thought we could get together for a drink or something."

"Did you call me yesterday?" quizzed Jay, thinking that Romano might have been the mysterious caller.

"No, why?"

Jay began to sweat. "It's nothing, just that some guy called yesterday and mentioned...Forget it. I'd love to see you." *Why did I say that? I don't want to see him.* "Are you coming out on business or what? What do you do? Are you married?"

Recalling his years stamping out license plates, Romano said, "I'm in the metal stamping business. I sell and repair metal stamping machines."

"That sounds great. Is it your business or do you work for someone?"

"Kinda both. I'll tell you more when I see you. So I hear you're in the clothing business."

"Yeah, I am." He found himself picking up and mimicking Augy's speech pattern. He didn't like to do that because it brought back the memories of his childhood environment, the blue-collar, unsophisticated lifestyle he had worked so hard to get away from.

"Oh, shit, Aug, I just remembered. I gotta go out a town for a while. When are you arriving, and where are you going to be staying in San Diego? If I'm here then, I'll give you a call at your hotel," thinking to himself, *Don't call me, I'll call you. If I don't call him, maybe I won't have to see him.*

"I'll be there in a coupla days. I'm sure you're not going anywhere. I got your home number so I'll get a hold a ya some way, when I get in."

"What do you mean, you got my home number? How did you get my home number?"

"Your ma gave it to me. You're not in the phone book, but she is." *My mother gave him my number. Oh, shit!*

"Hey, Finch, let me ask you a question. How come you changed your name and all?"

This guy can't even speak English. "It's a long story, Augy. I'll tell you when you get here."

Jay hung up the phone then placed his forehead onto his folded arms resting on the desktop. "Oh, shit!" he said forcefully aloud. "My mother gave him my number."

***

Haunting Jay, throughout his life, was the eventual expectation of being exposed, as well as the consequences for participating in that crime. For several years in the seventies, he periodically sent cash to a church in Chardon, anonymously earmarked for the Fowler family. A friend forwarded the money. He had no choice but to wait and see what Romano was like and what he really wanted.

***

Mac O'Donnell was sitting on a bench outside of the Mad Hatter. He watched the happy faces of the children as they sat on bright colored horses moving so gracefully up and down. A circus symphony played as the carousel rotated smoothly in a circle.

Mac fit in well with the tourists at Seaport Village. His green shorts matched the colors of the surfing logo on the back of his white tee shirt. His wide-brimmed, white straw hat kept the sun from penetrating his dark sunglasses. Wearing white socks with sandals enforced the perceived assumption of his being a tourist.

As Jay approached, he noticed Mac hunched over his spread legs while drippings from his ice cream cone fell to the concrete walkway.

"Need a napkin?" asked Jay.

"Hey, Hey, Mr. Newman. How are you? It's nice to see you again."

"I'll bet it is," answered Jay. The last time he saw Mac O'Donnell, he had handed him a briefcase with $50,000 in it. Mac stood and shook Jay's hand. As they walked toward the sea wall, Mac threw the rest of his ice cream cone in a trash barrel.

"So, so tell me, Newman, or should I say Nubaum, what, what service can I provide for you today?"

"It's Newman." Jay remembered why Mac O'Donnell always repeated the first two words of every sentence. The last time he dealt with Mac, he was told that he had stuttered as a child. After years of speech therapy, he stopped stuttering but was left with an unusual word repetition at the beginning of most sentences.

The two men sat on an iron bench facing the eclectic Cape Cod and Spanish-style buildings, which make up the various gift shops and tourist traps throughout Seaport Village.

"Mac, I need to have someone followed."

"That's all you want? What, what are you looking for?"

"I just want to know this guy's routine."

"Newman, Newman, that could mean a lot of different things— where he lives, where he works, what he drives, wears, eats, etc., etc."

"I want to know who he's fucking. I want to know if he's in the sack with my ex. I want to know when and where and what they talk about. I want to know how much money he makes, how much money he has, and how much he owes. I want to know who he owes money to and why."

"I can, I can arrange for that, but I'll need a little seed." Jay reached into his coat pocket and handed Mac an envelope.

"There's two grand in there." Then he handed him a piece of paper.

"The name and address are on here. Two grand more when I'm satisfied. Maybe more if you're quick."

"It's, it's a pleasure doing business with you again." Jay stood. Mac removed his hat and sunglasses and stared directly into Jay's eyes. As he squinted from the bright sunlight, his left eye remained wide open. This was the first time Jay had noticed the glass eye. Mac's facial expression reinforced that he was not someone to fool with. Jay was fully aware that Mac was well connected. Although Jay liked to think that he was in control, he knew Mac was ultimately in charge.

"Don't, don't forget Newman. We provide a wide range of services for our clients. Following somebody is no big deal. You know what I mean?" Jay shook Mac's hand, nodded, turned, and disappeared into the crowd.

***

Andy Fowler stood with other passersby outside the karate studio and watched Serena through the thick glass. The ends of a black belt swung from her tiny waist in harmony with her blonde ponytail as she worked through a series of kicks and jumps with the other students. He wondered how she could be married to such a creep, a cold-blooded murderer, a man without a conscience. He knew he had to tell her, but how and when. Maybe she was just like her husband, cold-hearted and treacherous. Maybe she already knew about it. He had to find out. He had already followed and observed her for two days. He had to confront her. The time was imminent.

***

"Carlie, get your things together. We're going to be late for your swimming lesson."

"Is Daddy going to meet us there?"

"Daddy will be down for dinner, and we are going to stay on the boat tonight." Serena helped gather Carlie's two favorite stuffed animals, Bert and Ernie. She placed them into the large blue and red canvas tote. "Honey, don't forget your blanket, your Barney towel, and your bathing suit."

"Mommy, are we going to go sailing today?"

"I doubt it, sweetheart. Daddy won't be down until after dark. Then it will be too late. Maybe this weekend."

Serena and Carlie appeared rushed as they walked hand-in-hand out through the fifteen-foot, hand-polished, cherry-wood entry doors into the front courtyard. The sound of the water gracefully flowing from the fountain and the vivid smell of the tropical landscape were captivating. Serena stopped.

"Did we forget something, Mommy?"

"No, darling. Just close your eyes for a moment." Carlie closed her eyes, wrinkled her face, clamped her tiny teeth, and grinned.

"Listen, Carlie, listen to the sound of the water. Smell the flowers. Take a deep breath, and let it out slowly."

As her little nose twitched from side to side, she said, "Mommy, can we go now?" Jaime was almost finished drying the car as Serena and Carlie exited the courtyard and walked into the driveway.

"All ready for you ladies," he said as he opened their doors.

"Thank you, Jaime," Serena said. "We'll be at the club tonight. See you tomorrow."

"Thank you, Jaime," repeated Carlie. "I'm going swimming."

"Buenas tardes, Carlita. Have fun. You are a nice little girl."

As Serena pulled the Porsche onto Camino de La Costa, she glanced in her rear-view mirror to satisfy herself that she was not being followed. Once convinced, she wound through the streets of Lower Hermosa on La Jolla Boulevard. Serena didn't notice the two shabby looking homeless men passed out on a lawn around the corner, nor did she notice the van that began to follow her after she turned onto the boulevard.

***

"I'll be home in a few days," Andy said, as he sat on the side of the bed, speaking on the phone. With his back to the television and the sound put on mute when he dialed his mother, he didn't notice the commercial with Jay and his models. "The workshop is interesting. I haven't had time to see San Diego yet, but I plan on doing some sight-seeing before I come home. Give Grandma a kiss for me. Bye now."

Andy hung up the phone and swiveled toward the television set. Jay was embracing each beauty queen as they snuggled at his side. The advertisement was ending as he was pushing the button to activate the sound. All Andy heard was, "Count on that, or my name isn't Jay Newman."

"It isn't your name, you lyin' son of a bitch." Andy turned off the television set and dropped the clicker on the bed. "Your real name is Jacob Richard Fuckin' Nubaum, Finch, and you're a damn killer."

Chapter 19

It was 9 p.m. when Andy left his room at the Travelodge in downtown La Jolla. He switched his residency from the oceanfront to the old, two-story, L-shaped building located on the corner of Herschel Avenue and Silverado Street. $300 a night was just too much to pay. This place resembled an old apartment building, which had been converted to a motel at some point. His motel savings allowed him to rent a car.

He thought to himself, as he walked down the stairs, *"A hundred bucks a day isn't too bad considering everything else around here."* He walked over one block, turned right, and placed his hands in his pockets. Seemingly bored and out of place, he strolled down Girard toward Prospect, observing the shopkeepers closing their stores for the day. Traffic was steady. He had never seen so many fancy cars in his life. A Mercedes in La Jolla was like a Chevy or Ford back home. He had only been here a short time and had already seen three Ferraris, two Bentleys, and a Rolls Royce. Once he remembered seeing a Rolls Royce while driving through Gates Mills, but it was old and worn. *"Where does all this money come from?"* he wondered. *"No school teachers here."*

The closer he got to Prospect Street, the more lively it seemed. Friday evenings in the summer in La Jolla were jumping with mostly young couples strolling hand in hand. Families on vacation walked, holding and carrying shopping bags stuffed with souvenirs and clothing. Young children, obviously exhausted from a full day, squirmed and whined as they traipsed behind their parents on the sidewalk.

The distinct sounds of Mariachi music from a nearby cafe filled the air. Andy walked into Josey's and found an empty seat at the end of the bar. He noticed the giant portions of food being served. He ordered a Corona and watched through the mirror at the back of the bar as the crowd behind him sang and laughed. Everyone but him seemed to be enjoying a good time. Andy knew his visit to California wasn't to have a good time. It was to get even, for all the years of pain, for the years he and his mother and his grandparents suffered. It was up to him. He had the responsibility of revenge. The time was coming, soon.

The noise level in Josey's was too much to bear. He was confused and couldn't think straight with the loud music. Quickly finishing his beer, he stood up and started walking hastily out to the street.

Just as he stepped onto the sidewalk he collided with a young woman, almost knocking her down.

"Oh, my God," exclaimed Andy. "I'm really sorry. Are you okay?"

"Why don't you watch where you're walking?"

"Look, I'm really sorry. I didn't mean to walk into you."

Bystanders who had stood and watched soon went on their way. Andy, feeling much like a jerk, stood gesturing with his hands. "Look, can I make it up to you? I'm really sorry. Are you with somebody?"

"No, I'm just visiting. Are you with someone?"

"No. My name is Andy, Andy Fowler." *Shit, enough said for my Sherlock Holmes alibi.* "I'm really sorry. What's your name?"

"I'm all right. Sam, Samantha Lyons." Chuckling. "Is this the way you California guys meet women?"

Andy hesitated for a moment. The brilliant lighting from inside the cafe caused her jade-colored eyes to sparkle. He noticed the sheen on her short sandy hair and the brightness of her teeth when she spoke. Her skin was smooth and natural. Her only makeup consisted of a tiny bit of pink lipstick.

"I'm just visiting, I don't live here. How about you?"

"I'm on vacation also. Where are you visiting from?"

"Ohio, a town called Chardon. It's east of Cleveland. Where are you from?"

"Virginia. Quantico area."

"Isn't that where the FBI trains?"

"Yes, I guess it is." *Oh damn, did I blow it already?* "There are a lot of other things there besides the FBI academy."

"Yeah, I guess you're right. It's just the first thing that comes to mind. Can I buy you a drink or something?" he asked.

"Thanks. That sounds like a nice idea to me. Would you like to go in here?"

"Not in here," he said. "It's too loud for me. Do you know some place to go?"

"Why don't we walk down the street until we find something a little quieter," she suggested.

Andy was almost at a loss for words. He watched her as she strolled by his side. Sam was slim. Her legs were tan and smooth. "So who are you visiting?" asked Andy.

"Actually, I just decided to take a trip to see San Diego."

It was obvious to Andy that Sam was just as uneasy as he was. Then he said, "That looks like an interesting place over there, across the street, The Cove. Want to try it?"

"Sure," she said. "I'm game if you are."

Andy held out his hand to Sam. She moved closer and grasped his arm as they stepped off the curb and made their way through the slow-moving, bumper-to-bumper traffic to the opposite side of Prospect Street. Andy couldn't believe this was happening. He had spent most of his life as a loner. Sure, he would date once in a while. *How could he be so lucky?* he thought. He met Sam by almost knocking her down, and then ten minutes later she was holding his arm on their way to have a drink.

Once across, they were greeted and startled by a shabby-looking vagrant, leaning and partially standing at an angle, propped against a light pole. A foul, sewer-like odor spewed from his sun-darkened, crusty tan hide. His unruly beard and mustache were simply an extension of his sun-bleached hair.

"Hey, you two look like a nice couple. Could you spare a few bucks to help out a homeless vet?"

Sam's crooked facial expression was a result of her first whiff. She wanted to hold her nose as she turned her head to look at Andy. Breathing only through her mouth, she asked,

"Think he's really a vet?"

Having spent most of his life in a liberal academic environment, Andy's exposure to homeless people was extremely limited. He knew that whenever one showed up in his neighborhood, the police would load him into a squad car and transport him back to Cleveland. He wasn't sure how to react.

"I don't care if he is a vet or not," replied Andy as he looked at the man's filthy legs and feet. "This guy desperately needs some hygienic attention." Andy removed Sam's arm from his, reached into his front pocket, and took a ten from his makeshift, paper-clipped money clip.

Sam watched Andy pensively and didn't say anything as he reached over and handed the man the bill. "Here, this is all I can spare. Go get a bath or something."

"God Bless ya, man. God Bless ya both."

They turned and walked toward the restaurant. "I guess that's my good deed for the day."

"I guess so." Sam replied. *And they told me he was going to be dangerous.*

"Here we are. Watch your step, I don't want somebody to crash into you."

She smiled and said, "Thank you. I don't want that to happen again, either." *This guy is really nice, naive, but nice.* As he led her through the door, she took his arm again. *Step one, contact complete.*

***

Romano spent much of Saturday at Wind n Sea beach. He watched the surfers. He stared at the smooth, soft, bronze flesh of sunbathing beauties. They seemed to be everywhere, on the sand, on the rocks, and on parade, almost like a pageant, he thought, as they flaunted their bodies up and down the beach, each one more enticing than the last. The prison stories were true. The women in Southern California were beautiful, and he would soon seize his first.

During the course of the day, he strolled past Jay's house three times—once from the street and twice from the beach below. He shot several Polaroid photos of the different angles and approaches to the home. There were two pathways. One lead to a locked iron gate at the bottom of the stairs, which provided access to the expansive teak decks at the rear of Jay's house. The other pathway connected to a flight of concrete stairs from the beach up to the street. The latter provided public access to the beach area. Surfers carried their boards past the high concrete block walls on each side of the pathway. He had been there before when he picked the lock on the side door of Jay's garage.

***

A soft glow of light from the crescent moon penetrated through the open French doors of the bedroom. Roberta was lying on the bed staring at the ceiling. Her left arm was stretched behind her head resting on a pillow. In her right hand she clutched an empty vodka glass, which rested on the edge of the sheet covering her belly. As she shook the glass from side to side, the sounds of the clattering ice cubes woke David.

"Are you okay?" he said as he rolled over, grabbing the sheet to cover his naked body.

"I'm going to be just fine," she replied.

"What is that supposed to mean? You're going to be just fine."

"What I am trying to say is that you're already okay. Your divorce was simple. No one got hurt, and no one was ripped off."

Adamantly, he replied, "How can you possibly think that I wasn't hurt by my divorce? Carol left *me* for another guy. How do you think it made me feel when I found out she was fucking someone else?"

"It's not the same," said Roberta. "It's different."

"My ass, it's not the same. How is it any different?"

"Jay was screwing his young girlfriend. He lied to me. That merciless bastard waited for my father to die, then stole his business. Then he had the balls to burn it down so he could collect the insurance money." She started to weep. "Don't tell me that's not different."

After a moment of silence, David said submissively, "I'm sorry." Leaning and stretching over her body, he took the glass from her hand and placed it on the night table next to the bed.

"You're right. That is different," he said. "I didn't mean to upset you. Let's talk about something else."

Still sniffling, Roberta said, "I don't want to talk about something else. I need to get this off my che... I mean out of my system."

"Okay," said David, "but first let me pour us a fresh drink." He crawled out of the bed, put on a robe, and exited the bedroom with the two empty glasses. While standing in front of the bar, he looked into the mirror, ran his fingers through his thinning hair, and shook his head in frustration.

Roberta came into the room with a lit cigarette in one hand and an ashtray in the other. She sat at the sofa, pulled her legs up to her side, and said, "You know, I wanted to have children. He hated them."

Handing her a refreshed vodka rocks, he replied, "He told me that you were the one who didn't want kids."

She took a deep drag and exhaled heavily. The smoke was drawn upward 20 feet toward the silent, swirling bamboo blades on the Panama fan. "That's bullshit. He made me get my tubes tied before we got married. He hated the little brats."

David disregarded her remarks, walked over, and sat at the other end of the sofa. "You know, Roberta, I don't think he has two million dollars."

She looked up at the high ceiling. Illuminating the room from the fixtures attached to the tracks above were glistening gray shafts of light overflowing with hazy smoke from her cigarette. "He'll pay! That son of a bitch."

David said, "Anyway, I've been thinking. If he doesn't come up with the money, I mean. I can get in a lot of trouble and probably get disbarred."

"How do you figure?" she asked.

"First of all, I can't represent both of you, specifically, because you have your own attorney. Second, in essence, I am virtually blackmailing him."

"So," she said sarcastically, "if this backfires, and I know it won't, then I'll take the blame for the whole thing and you're off the hook. Does that make you feel any better?"

David shook his head in disbelief. "Roberta, you don't understand. This is not right."

"Listen, David, we've already been through this a dozen times. Jay's got more money than you and I will ever see. He's a scoundrel. He got rich by burning down my father's business, and he's a scoundrel because he was fucking around with and finally married his sweet young bitch, Serena."

"Okay, okay," said David. "That's enough."

"No! That's not enough." She walked to the bar, turned, and faced him again. "I can prove he burned down the store, and he knows it. I can be his royal pain in the ass for as long as he lives if I want to. All I want him to do is to give me, I mean us, the money so we can leave this place. You can sell this house for a million dollars, and then we'd have three million. Haven't you thought about what we can do with three million dollars?"

David's home was originally a wedding gift from his wealthy former in-laws. Carol deeded it to him during their divorce as a gesture of forgiveness for her being unfaithful.

Roberta lowered the tone of her voice but remained adamant. "David, darling, you make a hundred, maybe a hundred-fifty thousand dollars a year? You're a good lawyer. You care about people. Sometimes you care too much. Think about it. With three million dollars we can sit and drink futzy little umbrella-covered cocktails forever. We can watch the sunset from our own villa someplace. We can make love twenty-four hours a day. Oh David, this is our only chance."

David sat contemplating. He looked over at Roberta as she filled her glass again with fresh ice and vodka. He stood and walked over to her. "You know, you're crazy, crazy but right. Except for the twenty-four-hours-a-day thing."

She smiled and moved close to him. Her robe was open and her firm breasts rubbed against his chest as they tenderly embraced in a kiss. Stepping back, she grabbed her drink and said, "Meet you by the pool."

***

Zookey, Mac's right-hand man, depressed the send button on his cellular phone. Static joined the transmission, and he wasn't sure if Mac could hear him. "Boss," he said softly, "I don't know if you can hear me good or not. I got some really ace shit here."

"I, I can barely hear you. What, what are they doing?"

"She's a real fuckin' animal. I gotta a frickin' hard-on just watchin' 'em.

Zooky could barely hear through the static.

"Well, well just don't get caught, asshole."

"No chance of that, Boss. I think they're going out to the pool now. You sure about the sound rightness?"

"Don't, don't worry about the sound. Just, just be careful."

"Okay, see you in a few hours."

Roberta leaned over and placed her drink on the flagstone coping surrounding the pool. She stood, then let her white terry-cloth robe fall gracefully to the ground. David, freshly aroused and standing behind her, moved toward her seductive nude body. She turned and faced him. The faint glow from the moon highlighted her sensual soft curves. David removed his robe, and they embraced.

"Roberta, you are so beautiful, beautiful and wicked."

She pouted, then smiled and kissed him gently on the lips. "Why do you say I am wicked?"

"You know you drive me crazy, don't you?"

"David, don't change the subject. I'm not wicked. I just want what's mine in the first place. Once we have the money, I'll never mention his name or any of this again. I promise."

She dropped her arms to his waist and started to kneel down. Then she laughed and pushed him into the pool. She leaped in next to him.

The video was perfect. He hoped Mac was right, about the microphone's amplifier being sensitive enough to record a conversation seventy-five feet away.

Chapter 20

The white Corvette sat empty, masked by a dense mist in the small parking lot at the foot of Palomar Street. Earlier, Andy had walked Sam back to her motel and promised to call her on Saturday morning so they could go sight-seeing. After waiting for hours, he left the motel.

His Weejuns were covered with sand and water as he slowly walked south on the beach toward Newman's house. As he approached, he became distraught and anxious. The house was dark. A lone light shined through the hazy fog onto the concrete stairs at the side yard leading to the street above.

Andy paused and listened to the surf as it rushed closer to the ice plant. He jerked as the cold water engulfed his shoes and soaked his socks. He knew Jay and Serena were not at home. This was his practice run. He sloshed along the path drawing closer to the wrought-iron gate. He tugged gently. The gate was indeed locked. He cocked his head to listen as he turned from side to side. Convinced that it was just he and mother nature lurking in the spooky haze, he reached high above the gate and lifted himself up onto the lower rail on the damp deck. Rolling onto his side, he remained motionless and fearful, waiting to see if he had made too much noise.

Nightmarish thoughts flashed through his mind of the cold, wet winter morning 25 years earlier, how he had cringed and remained motionless on the wet floor of the open truck. "Down! Get down!" he remembered his father saying as he covered him with an old army blanket. Andy remembered hearing the shots and watching the blood trickle under the front seat toward his face. His father and uncle were ambushed and murdered.

Lying there, Andy now reflected upon his youth, reenacting each night, praying, and listening to his grandmother prescribe silent revenge for his demise. *Find them. Don't let them get away. You are the only one who can help.*

He stood up, grabbed the handrail, and followed it as it curved around the edge of the deck toward the spa outside the master bedroom. Tucked between his belt and shirt was an old pistol, which he brought with him from home. His hand reached slowly toward the carved wood grip. Tightly grasping the pistol with his right hand, he jerked it from his side and placed his finger next to the trigger. He firmly placed his left palm on the bottom of his right hand to stabilize his grip, just like he had seen in the movies. Then he thrust his arms straight out, locking his elbows, as he pointed at the massive glass wall of the bedroom.

Andy trembled as he said softly aloud, "You're going to pay, you son of a bitch."

He stood for a moment then slowly back stepped. A distant scream filled the air. He put the gun back and quickly catapulted over the deck rail to the wet sandy ice-plant below. Andy stood, silent, intently listening. He heard the scream again. He looked from side to side as the sand disappeared into the surf and heavy fog. The sounds from the hysterical female voice were excruciating.

"No, no, please, no!" she cried.

Andy's heart pounded. He stooped under the deck and started rushing toward the sound of the cries. It was dark as he made his way around and through the maze of concrete piers, which supported the deck above him. After walking face-first into a cobweb, he started to flail his arms in front of himself. The farther under the deck he went, the darker it got. He felt a frightening presence. He began to sweat. He stumbled on a rock and fell onto the side of a large sheet of cardboard. A huge figure arose from behind a barricade. Andy's eyes opened wide as the man pounced on him. Air exploded from Andy's lungs. Straddled over his chest, the attacker leaned forward into the sand and grabbed an empty wine bottle by the neck. He smashed it against the rock then quickly seated a jagged edge of the glass against Andy's throat. He jerked, causing the sharp glass to nick his neck.

Terrified, Andy gasped. He had no thoughts of attempting to free himself from his captor.

"No, no," the female voice sounded again.

"Hey, you motha, this is my fuckin' spot. Whatta you want?"

With agony on his face, he stared into the expressionless eyes of his attacker, wondering if he was going to die from his throat being cut or from the enormous weight on his chest. Andy struggled to inhale, then released a loud whisper, "Get off me!"

"What do ya want here?"

"Didn't you hear the scream?" Andy uttered in distress.

"I don't hear nothin'." He lifted the glass from Andy's neck but held it only inches away.

His dark wool coat reeked and seemed to weigh as much as the man inside of it.

"I'm not here for your spot." Andy spurted.

"I don't see nothin' neither."

"Let me up! I didn't know you were here. I'm just trying to help her."

"Jus' stay the fuck away from here, that's all. You got it?"

"I got it. I got it. Let me up."

The big man sat upright and dropped the glass shard. Andy stood cautiously and wrapped his arms around his aching chest. Then he reached up and touched his throat to feel the blood where the glass had cut a gash into the skin.

"Christ," he said.

The big man stepped back to the cardboard, then said, "What are you doin' here then?"

"Never mind me. I was never here, okay?" Then he scurried out from under the deck in the direction of the screams. He sloshed briskly through the sand and water toward Wind n Sea beach.

"Hey, where are you? Are you okay?" he shouted. As he approached an embankment leading up to the sidewalk, he saw the silhouette of a person running away. He reached for his gun. It was gone. He panicked and froze.

"Oh shit," he said, looking back into the haze toward the deck. "I must have dropped it back there."

He looked toward the water and spotted the naked body of a woman. "Oh, my God," he said as he leaned down to her. "Can you hear me? Are you okay?" He shook her shoulder. "Hey, are you..." He placed his fingers on her neck, trying to feel her pulse. She lay motionless and limp on the sand.

Tears sprang from Andy's eyes as he rose from her side. "Oh, my God, I have to get out of here." He fumbled in his pockets searching for his keys. "I can't be here," he said softly. Andy was in state of panic and terror. Fumbling and sloshing while running, he made his way back down the beach toward Jay's house. He ran past the deck to Jay's gate. Not aware of the public walkway, just a few feet from the gate, he again made his way over the gate and ran next to the deck up a path separating Jay's garage and the concrete wall. "Shit!" he exclaimed, "not another gate!" He made his way over the gate and fell onto the driveway. Security lights now lit the entire exterior of the home. He then ran up the street to his car. Andy closed the door, as the sound of a fast-moving car sprang from the fog. The white Corvette barely missed him.

***

A buzzing sound on an auxiliary alarm panel in the maids' quarters woke Jaime and Martha. Jaime sat up swiftly and leaped out of bed. The green flashing light on the monitor indicated a 3:30 a.m. intrusion by the south garage gate. Apprehensive, he turned on the light. Then he pushed a button activating all exterior lights that surrounded the perimeter of the residence. Scooping the key ring off of his nightstand, he hurried to the closet and pushed his clothes aside. There he grabbed the loaded shotgun, which Señor Jay had taught him to use. Martha sat up in bed and started praying in Spanish.

Fumbling with the keys, Jaime unlocked the trigger guard and dropped it on the floor as he ran out of his room toward the garage. He cocked the shotgun, chambering a shell. Then he slowly opened the door at the back of the kitchen and stooped in expectation of encountering an intruder. He reached up onto the wall and turned on the lights.

It dawned on him that the alarm was for the garage gate and not the garage door. He stood and walked into the garage. He listened carefully as he made his way toward the side exit. Maneuvering around the covered vehicle by the door, Jaime gripped and slowly twisted the doorknob. He was so frightened that sweat dripped from his forehead onto the hardwood floor. The shotgun was pointed directly in front of him. Its walnut stock was pressed against his right side and stabilized with his arm and elbow. Jaime's finger rested on the trigger. Squeezing and twisting the doorknob, he swiftly pulled the door toward him. He let out a sigh of relief as no one was there to challenge him. "Gracias, Madre de Dios," he said aloud.

Quartz floodlights shined into the heavy gray wall of fog. He poked his head out and looked around. He stood for a few minutes listening to the sounds of the surf rising from behind the house. Still somewhat frightened he was not about to walk outside or down the path to the beach. He noticed fresh fragments of ice plant and wet sand lying on the sidewalk outside the door. Then he closed and locked the door. While holding the shotgun loosely, in his left hand, he looked up, closed his eyes, and made the sign of the cross. Martha met him at the door and asked if they should call the Newmans at the boat. Jaime decided it was not best to disturb them and that he would tell them in the morning when they returned.

***

Andy parked in space sixteen and went upstairs to his room. When he entered the room, he emptied his pockets, walked into the bathroom, turned on the tub shower, and stepped inside. Warm water splashed from his head, saturating his clothes. He stood, anxious, recalling the horrifying events of the last two hours. He started to shiver as he re-experienced the terrifying murders long ago—the expression on his father's face, the blood, the cold.

Oh my god, he thought. *What the hell am I doing here? Maybe I ought to go see the police here and tell them everything. They wouldn't believe me anyway. They'd probably arrest* me *for the girl on the beach.*

After washing the sand and mud out of his clothes, he stepped out of the tub and spread his shirt and pants over the shower curtain bar. Walking from the bathroom with one towel tied around his waist and another in his hands drying his hair, he noticed the red light flashing on his phone. He thought for a second. Who knows I am here? My room was paid in advance, in cash, for a week. I can't call the desk at this hour. As he climbed into bed and shut off the light, his thoughts bellowed, the white Corvette?

Chapter 21

At seven a.m. Jay and Carlie left the Yacht Club as Serena followed in her Porsche with her top down.

"Did you sleep well on the boat, Princess?" he asked.

"It was fun, Daddy. Can we do it again today?"

"I'm afraid not, honey. Maybe next week sometime, okay?"

"Okay, 'cause I really like to play with the ducks."

Jay laughed, "The ducks, huh? Do you feed them?"

"I feed them, and I sometimes chase them. It's fun. I like to play with Bob."

"Who's Bob?"

"He's my favorite duck."

"How can you tell him apart from the others? Don't they all look the same?"

"I could tell the difference. Bob is the best one. He is the smartest one, too."

"Why do you say that? How do you know Bob is a guy duck and not a girl duck?"

"Cause girl ducks always have their babies with them, and Bob is always by himself."

"What makes him smarter than the other ducks? Just because he is a boy doesn't mean he's smarter than the girls."

"I know, but like when I feed all the ducks, Bob waits for his turn while all the other ducks jump around and splash each other trying to get the food."

Smiling, Jay said, "Okay, since you know all about ducks, I have a question for you."

"What do you want to know, Daddy?"

"Here goes. It's a tough one," he said laughing. "What's the difference between a duck?"

Smiling and throwing her hands out in front of her, she immediately responded with, "Daddy! You really don't know the answer to that?"

"No, smarty pants, I don't have a clue."

"Well, everyone knows that answer. The difference between a duck is that one leg is both the same."

"Where did you get that from?" he said quizzically.

"I don't remember, maybe at school, but everyone knows that."

Jay laughed. "Do you play with the ducks every time you come down for your swimming lesson?"

Jay adored Carlie. She was the light of his life, so innocent, so pure. Roberta hated children. He hated her for having her tubes tied before they were married. Jay was very comfortable with his new life.

"Not all the time, 'cause Mommy sometimes has to go home right away. But a lotta times I do. Pretty soon I start school again, and I won't get to see Bob much."

"I'm sure Bob will be there waiting for you." *I wasted all those years with her. Maybe it would have been different if we had kids. Probably not! A bitch is a bitch.*

"Now I have a question for you, Daddy. What happens to the ducks in the winter? Where do they go?"

"They don't go anywhere in the winter. They'll still be there for you to play with." Jay laughed as he thought of Holden Caulfield in *Catcher in the Rye* asking the New York cab driver in Central Park where the ducks go in the winter.

"Maybe Bob has a friend named Holden," he suggested with a smile.

"Bob doesn't need any other friends than me, 'specially one with a funny name like Holding."

Chuckling, Jay said, "It's Holden, and you're probably right."

Serena was smiling as she pulled next to them by the red light at the intersection of La Jolla Boulevard and Turquoise Street.

"Hi, Mommy."

"Hi, sweetheart. Are you two having a good time together?"

Jay looked over at her and with a comical expression on his face and said, "I just learned all about Bob."

Serena returned the expression and laughed. "See you two in a few minutes."

As they drove through Bird Rock, Jay asked. "Are you excited about going back to school?"

"Yep, I am. I really like school. Sarah said I are going to have a new head teacher this year."

"That sounds exciting."

"Daddy, did you go to The Children's School when you were a little boy?"

"No, Princess, they didn't have schools like that when I was little. I went to a regular school." He thought about the private schools in Ohio and how, as a kid, he dreamt of going to those schools.

"What was the name of your school?"

"Mayfield Road School."

"What's a road school?"

"It was just the name of the school. It sat next to the road." Jay began to picture the old, brown, three-story brick building—the Mayfield Golf Course, the neighborhood swimming pool, Golden Gate Estates, and Augy Romano.

"God," he said aloud, "that's all I need is Augy Romano."

"Who is Augy Minano?"

"Just someone I used to know; that's all. It's not important."

***

One San Diego police car was parked at an angle blocking the street in front of Jay's house. Several other police cars and ambulances lined both sides of the street in the direction of Wind n Sea beach. Serena had already pulled through the blockade and parked in the driveway. She was talking to Alis Brooks. Jay and Carlie pulled up to an officer on the street.

"I live here," said Jay. "What's going on?" The officer waived him through.

"Daddy, what are all the policeman doing here?"

"I don't know, sweetheart." Jay pulled into the driveway, leaned over, and opened the door for Carlie. Martha walked up to the door and took Carlie by the hand, leading her into the courtyard in front of the house.

"What's going on?" Jay asked, as he walked over to Serena and Alis.

Alis reached out and shook Jay's hand. "A jogger found two people on the beach, about 5:30 this morning. A young man and woman."

"Are they dead?" Jay asked. "Somebody killed them?"

"We're not exactly sure how they died, but it looks like the guy's neck was broken and that the woman was strangled."

"When did this happen?" asked Jay.

"Had to be sometime last night, Jay. Got pretty foggy down here again. The troops are questioning some homeless guy who apparently lives down here."

"Yeah, under my deck!"

"We're not sure as of yet, so your guess right now is as good as mine. Go on inside. I'll check back with you a little later."

Serena moved closer to Jay, put her arm around his waist, and rested her head on the side of his chest.

"Jay," frightfully, "is there *really* someone living under our deck?"

***

Rays of sunlight penetrating through the gaps of the blinds slowly crept across the bed and woke Romano. He glanced at his watch. 8 a.m. He sat up and reached for his cigarettes and lighter. Then he grabbed two pillows, placed them against the headboard, and leaned back. He lit the cigarette, crossed his legs, and placed his left arm comfortably behind his head. His thoughts reflected back to the sandy beach. He had never seen so many beautiful women in one place before. He took a drag from the cigarette and returned it to the ashtray, which sat on his chest.

Squinting and straining to visualize what he had accomplished the night before, he saw her soft skin, her smile, and her long legs. He was suddenly unable to separate her from the rest. They all seemed to blend together.

His mind flashed to childhood memories of his sister. *Her touch, her hard firm body.* He became aroused as he remembered *her wet lips and hot tongue.* Then he flashed to the night in the car when she begged him to choke her unconscious as she climaxed. She never woke up.

It was different with the lieutenant's wife. He had always been hesitant to approach women, but she pushed herself on him. She wouldn't leave him alone. She stalked him and lured him into her home when her husband was gone. He thought about *her smell, her syrupy taste.* It was her fault. She couldn't get enough. That was the only time he used a knife.

Then, the two girls in Atlanta. He followed them home from a nightclub and watched through a partially open window as they undressed each other. Entering through a rear door, like a fierce hurricane wind, he burst into their bedroom and wrapped his huge hands around their throats, watched as they squirmed. The police found the bodies two days later. That's when he left the South and went back to Ohio.

He got up and walked into the shower where he began to relive the events of the late afternoon and night before. He remembered being parked in a lot at the end of Nautilus Street, watching the sunset from the seat in his Corvette. There were small groups of people sitting on the rocks and sand, some drinking beer and others with wine. He got out of the car and paced the sidewalk, which sat above the beach. Several couples strolled hand in hand. Others picnicked on blankets as they waited for the green flash, a term he learned from surfers that referred to the instant the sun sets on the horizon.

He finally reached the end of the sidewalk by Camino de La Costa, where the beachfront homes began. As he looked onto the beach below, one couple caught his attention. She appeared young. Nice long legs, he thought. Beautiful, maybe 25. Her companion looked like a surfer, long blond hair, solid and well built, probably the same age. He recalled watching them as he sat on a worn gray wood bench above the rocks next to the sidewalk. Tan, smooth skin covered her slender frame. He could barely keep his eyes off of her tiny red bikini and unkempt golden hair.

As the sun disappeared, darkness and fog crept upon the coastline. Most others had left the area, but the couple remained. They seemed oblivious to anyone or anything around them.

Trying not to be obvious, he stood and walked the sidewalk. As he strolled past for the third time, he watched their silhouettes through the faint light as she played with him, first a kiss on his ear, then her hands rubbing his chest. Soon her lips were all over his neck and shoulders. She grabbed his hand and placed it on her chest. The seductress was in all of her glory. Her boyfriend squirmed when she reached into the front of his bathing suit.

He walked back to his car and drove the neighborhood around the beach as if he were in a void of some kind. He did this for an hour before stopping in Pacific Beach at the Boardwalk Bar and Grill. He was in awe. *More beautiful women, some with men, some by themselves or with other women, all needing punishment*, he thought.

Now standing in front of the bathroom mirror, staring into his own eyes, thoughts flashed like Super 8 movie frames as he rolled his head back and forth. Recapping, after he left the bar he returned to Wind n sea Beach. This time he parked across from the pump house on Gravilla Street and strolled through the heavy fog to the end of the sidewalk again. As he made his way down the stairs to the beach, he heard voices mixing with the sounds of the surf. He stopped and listened cautiously. His eyes opened wide as he came upon what he concluded as the same couple, whom he had watched earlier in the evening.

"We must have fallen asleep," he heard her say.

"What are you two doing down here?" he asked authoritatively as he confronted them.

Startled the young man replied, "Who the hell are you? What do you want?"

"San Diego police," Augy quickly replied. "You're not supposed to be down here after dark."

The young man rose to his feet and started walking toward Augy. "Who says we're not supposed to be down here after dark? There's no law against it."

"There is now, asshole," Augy replied as he reached out with his powerful hands and gripped the man's long hair on both sides of his head.

The young woman was bawling as she jumped onto his back. "Leave us alone. Who are you?" Twisting and turning, he tried to get loose, but Romano held him at arms' length. Her arms tugged as they wrapped around Romano's thick neck. Her feet were off the ground and kicking. Clinching his teeth, Romano twisted back and forth. The girl fell to the sand. Using all of his power, he swiftly forced the young man's chin down onto the top of his fast-rising knee. The young man's head jerked back over his shoulders. He became instantly limp. Romano snapped his head sharply to the side before he dropped him onto the sand.

The girl started running erratically up and down the beach. Romano chased and tackled her to the sand. He held his hand over her mouth as he straddled her fighting torso. "Shut up, bitch!" he warned. "Shut the fuck up, or I'll kill you!"

Tears continued to flow from her shiny eyes. Augy leaned closer. "Think you're so fuckin' smart, huh? Think you're hot shit, you little bitch?"

She shook her head as her muffled screeches penetrated through his fingers. He put more pressure on her mouth. "Be quiet, damn you, bitch! Are you going to be quiet or what?!"

She nodded. Augy slowly released his hand from her mouth. Hopelessly crying, she asked, "What do you want?"

"I've got what I want, sweet little pussy. You! How do you want it? Slow and painful or quick and dirty?"

She screamed, "No, No! Help me! Leave me alone!"

Augy heard a voice calling out. He raised his head to listen.

"Hey, where are you?" The voice shouted. "Are you okay?"

Gripping her throat tightly he leaned over and put his face an inch away from hers. He watched her eyes bulge as he squeezed harder. "So long cunt."

The intruder was getting closer. His voice advanced through the fog as he approached from behind the houses. "Hey, can you hear me?"

Romano jumped to his feet, decided not to take on the intruder, and started running to the stairs. Once on the sidewalk, he disappeared into heavy fog.

Perspiring heavily, he snapped back to the present. Grabbing a towel, he continued to stand in front of the mirror. He wiped his forehead and grinned widely as he inspected and picked at his shiny teeth. He dropped the towel, flexed several times, and admired his physique.

"No, No help me," he repeated softly as he smirked. *"They're all the fuckin' same."*

***

After a couple of hours of sleep, Andy awoke at 8:15 and called the front desk to retrieve his message from the night before.

"Just push the message button on the phone, Mr. Holmes, and you can hear your message as it was recorded." Andy was speechless. He felt stupid, thinking to himself, "How was I supposed to know it was on a tape?"

"Andy, this is Sam. I just want to thank you for a nice evening last night. It really was kind of strange, how we met and all. Anyway, sleep well. I hope we can see each other tomorrow. Good night."

He hung up the receiver, covered his face with the palms of his hands, and shook his head.

***

Jay and Serena stood at the decks edge looking up the beach. Holding each other at the waist, they watched as policemen examined the beach. Several searched through the ice plant while others stood in groups of two or three, talking to one another. Some were making notes, and others pointed toward Jay's house.

"Excuse," said Jaime, as he walked out onto the deck.

"What is it, Jaime?" replied Serena, softly.

"I must to tell you, last night when you were away, the alarm went off at the side gate. I got the big gun like you show me and went into the garage. Then I was very frightened. When I opened the side door, no one was there. The cement was wet with some icey plant from the beach. I look around careful and then I close up the door. We, how do you say, bring to an end and not call you on the boat."

"You mean decide?"

"Yes, gracias, we decide not to bother you at the boat but to wait until you arrive home this morning."

Jay said, "Jaime, you should have said something as soon as we arrived."

"You were busy, Señor. I did not want to ..."

Serena interrupted, "Jaime, did you talk to the police about this?"

"No! We decide it is important to tell you only."

Jay replied. "That's fine, Jaime. You are very loyal. What time did this happen? When did the alarm go off?"

"I remember it was 3:30"

"Did you hear anything other than the alarm? Any sounds or noises, people talking, cars or trucks?"

"No, nothing!"

Martha held Carlie's hand as they walked onto the deck from the sliding door off the kitchen.

"Mr. Broke is here to see you," said Martha.

"It's Brooks, Martha," Alis said as he walked up to Carlie and patted her on the head. "Broke means something doesn't work; it's broken." Martha smiled and looked confused.

Alis laughed. "Carlie honey, I want you to take Martha into the house and teach her my name. Teach her what broken means, okay? I need to talk with your mommy and daddy for a while."

"Okay, Uncle Alis," she said, giggling. "Sometimes Martha is silly, isn't she?"

"Sometimes she is." Carlie led Martha back into the house as Alis walked to the back of the deck.

"Was I too hard on her?" he asked.

Jay said, "No, you were almost on a roll with the broke, broken thing."

"You guys!" Serena said laughingly.

"So what's going on out there?" asked Jay.

"We think someone surprised them. We're not sure exactly what happened, or what time it happened..."

Jay interrupted. "Jaime said the silent alarm went off about 3:30 last night. The side gate set it off."

"Did someone try to enter the house?" questioned Alis as he looked to Jaime for an answer.

Jaime shrugged and looked to Jay for an answer.

"No!" responded Jay. "Perimeter alarms are silent. If someone attempts to enter the house through any opening, then the bells and whistles go off."

"So what does that mean?"

"It just means that someone was on the property. Jaime probably surprised him when he got to the side door. Then whoever it was went over the gate."

"Could the wind have set it off?" asked Alis.

"Not any more. It used to. We adjusted the sensitivity. The Santa Anas or storms from the sea used to set it off. That's why it's silent, so we don't bother you guys."

"Let's take a look," said Alis.

Jaime led the way and told of his experience with the shotgun, the garage door, and the wet ice plant on the walkway.

"There is a little sand and a little ice plant here. It's hard to tell if it's a shoe print." Alis reached in his back pocket and pulled out his portable two-way.

"Donny, this is Brooks. Copy?"

"Gotcha, boss."

"Come on up to the big house, in the front, by the gate next to the garage. I want you to take a look at something for me."

"Ten minutes okay with you?"

"Yeah, we'll be here."

"Jay, I'm frightened," said Serena.

"There is nothing to be frightened of. We are one hundred percent safe."

"I'm still a little worried about the white car and all."

"What white car?" asked Alis.

"The other day I was exiting 5 onto Ardath Road, and I swear I was being chased by a white car."

"Go on."

"Carlie was with me. He was right on my tail."

"What car were you in?"

"My Porsche. I lost him on North Scenic. We were so frightened. Carlie was crying, and I was shaking."

"Did you report this?"

Serena looked agitated. "I didn't think it was important then. I didn't want a bunch of policemen walking through my home thinking I was neurotic or something."

"Serena," said Alis, "are you sure it was a him?"

"It had to be a man." she paused. "Well, I didn't actually see the driver."

"You could have at least called me."

"And what could you have done? Put out some kind of bulletin to watch for a white car following people? Come on, Alis, you know there is nothing you could have done."

Although he knew she was right, he asked sarcastically, "Anything else strange happening that I should know about, or do you want to wait around a few days until you decide it's important enough?"

Serena's eyebrows raised. Then she shrugged and said, "Touché!"

Donny knocked on the gate. "Anybody there?" he called out. Jay pressed a few numbers on a stainless steel keypad next to the garage door, and the electric latch released the gate.

"Donny, this is Mr. and Mrs. Newman and their house man, Jaime."

"Is there any way you can determine if this is a footprint?" asked Brooks." I know there's not much to go on, but if anyone can piece this together you can."

"Thanks for the confidence."

"Jaime here scared away an intruder by this gate this morning about 3:30 or so."

"It's definitely a shoe print," Donny said. "The ice plant here looks compressed, like it belongs with the print. Jaime, did you walk out here? Could this be from your shoes?"

"No! I only open the door and look out."

"Okay, leave me alone for a while. I'll let you know."

"Thanks ,Donny! We'll be inside."

***

"I ain't seen nothing. I ain't done nothing," repeated the homeless vagrant as he sat alone handcuffed in the back seat of a patrol car.

Detective Scott Kirby was thirty-four years old and an assistant to Alis Brooks. He did most of Brooks' grunt work. He knew he was next in line for Brooks' job as chief of the homicide division, so he worked long hours and did anything Brooks asked him to do. He was one of the few who ignored the socioeconomic difference between Brooks and everybody else on the force. His Master's degree in criminology helped him rise quickly to his position in homicide. He wasn't wealthy like Brooks, but dressed expensively and did everything he could to emulate him.

Kirby walked up to the sidewalk from the sand. His pencil sat sideways in his mouth, gripped with his teeth. He carried a clipboard in his right hand and a large plastic Zip Lock bag in his left. Walking over to the officer who was guarding the patrol car where the vagrant sat, he said, "Okay, tell me what you know about him."

"Sir," said the patrolman, "his name is Jeffrey, and he's a regular. Hangs out all around the Village usually hitting on the regulars and tourists for change. He's not completely harmless.

Once in a while when he's not taken his meds he flips out, gets loud, and causes a little trouble. Not a known molester or anything like that."

"Does he have a sheet?"

"Petty stuff, booze, harassment, disturbing the peace, you know. Nothing big." Then he smiled and said, "Definitely what we call one of La Jolla's finest."

Kirby moved closer to the officer and said, "Careful what you say about La Jolla."

"I'm sorry, sir. I didn't mea..."

"It doesn't matter to me, but you'll be sorry if Brooks hears you. Now tell me what he said."

"Nothing at all. He just keeps repeating that he didn't see or do anything. Over and over again, that's all he says."

Kirby was the only detective dressed in a suit. He placed the clipboard and the plastic bag through the open window on the driver's seat of the patrol car. He looked at Jeffrey through the bars separating the front and rear compartments of the car. He loosened his tie, opened the driver's door, removed his jacket, and placed it along with his 9 mm Sig Sauer on the seat.

"What are you doing, sir?"

"I'm going in to visit our Buddy Jeffrey for a few minutes."

"I don't think you ought to do that, sir."

"Move over, Jeffrey," Kirby said as he entered the vehicle and sat next to him.

Kirby's face and nose twisted as he got his first whiff of Jeffery. "Christ! When was the last time you took a bath?"

"I didn't invite you in here," Jeffery said nervously as his right leg jerked up and down.

"Sorry, no offense," Kirby said. "I need to ask you a few questions."

"Like I said, I ain't seen nothin', and I ain't done nothin'."

"Just calm down, stop shaking, and stop repeating yourself. No one is accusing you of doing anything. My name is Scott. You can call me Scott. You like Jeffrey or Jeff?"

"I didn't do shit to nobody."

"I'll just call you Jeff. How's that?"

"Call me whatever, man. I ain't sayin' nothin'."

"Look, Jeff, all we have on you now is a misdemeanor for vagrancy. No one is accusing you of anything. I just need to know what went on here last night, and I think you might be able to tell me. What do you say? I'll even spring for a bath and a shave. How's that?"

"I got enough for my own bath and shave if I want to. I don't want nothin' from you."

"I understand that, Jeff..."

"Jeffrey. My name is Jeffrey."

"Okay, Jeffrey it is. Now, Jeffrey, the way I see it right now is that you can either talk to me here about last night, or we can formally arrest you, take you to the station, and charge you with a double homicide. If we do tha..."

"I only heard one scream after that guy..."

"Hold it for a second, Jeffrey. Let's go back to the beginning."

***

Local news stations provided continuous television coverage of the crime throughout the morning hours. Although the hotel was one mile from the scene, police and news helicopters could be heard as they circled and periodically hovered through and around the beach areas and village of La Jolla. Andy sat pensively on the side of his bed watching the screen. Cameras from both ground and air panned the beach and surrounding neighborhood.

"Again, to recap this morning's apparent double murder in La Jolla, police state that two bodies were found on the beach early this morning. The bodies were discovered just before sunrise by a jogger on the beach. We've been told little since arriving at the scene three hours ago. Our overnight assignment editor first heard the police dispatcher about 6:30 this morning. When we arrived at seven, the area was swarming with police cars. We were asked to move back here to the pump house in order to keep the area clear. Police investigators and detectives have been arriving all morning. This footage was shot when we arrived and before we were moved back. You can clearly see, as the camera zooms in, the covered bodies of two people. Again, we don't know if this was a murder, a suicide, or an accident of some kind. Our camera is now zooming to a police car at the end of the street where the police earlier handcuffed someone and placed him in the back seat. I'm not sure if we can get a good look at him but it appears that someone has just entered the back of the vehicle with him. No, we can't see anything definite."

As the news camera zoomed to the police car, Andy's eyes opened wide. "My god," he thought. "That's the guy from under the deck." He stood up, walked over to the window, opened the blinds, and watched the noisy helicopter hovering over the coastline. The television was still on.

"The police have advised us to tell everyone to stay away from the area. Wind n Sea beach and Camino de La Costa have been cordoned off by local investigators. This normally quiet millionaires' row, better known to locals as The Street of Dreams, has had another nightmare. Reporting live from La Jolla, this is Paul Stone. We return now to our studio."

***

Augy parked the Corvette two blocks from the beach and walked down to the pump station at the end of Gravilla where the news vans were set up like an RV park. He mingled with the crowd as he watched and listened. He moved closer to the yellow taped barricade. He accidently brushed against a young woman standing with a group of her friends. He smiled at her as she turned to him.

"I'm sorry, just curious. What happened?" he asked.

"Like, some jogger found, like, two people dead on the beach."

"Jesus," he said, "how ... when did it happen?"

"My roommate and me, like, we were sleeping when we heard the sirens. Then all kinds of, like, police cars and ambulances were all over the place. So, like, didn't you hear anything?"

"No, I'm not from around here, just visiting." He couldn't stand her repeating the word like. It seemed that every young person he met in California says "like" twenty times in every conversation.

"I could tell."

"What do you mean, you can tell?"

"Well, like, you... just don't look like a local." She smiled as her eyes perused his physique.

"What's a local supposed to look like?" *Ha*, he thought to himself, *I said it, too.* "I'm sorry, I didn't mean anything."

Augy stared at her firm body, as she broke from the crowd and walked away. Her smooth, tan skin extended from her bare feet up her long legs and into her thin black silk shorts. Her tee shirt, silkscreened with the slogan (There's no life east of I 5) didn't quite reach her waist. Her soft, short dark hair glistened as she disappeared through the crowd.

He laughed to himself as he remembered his prison mate talking about the Valley Girls in California. *Maybe, like, that was, like, one of them?*

***

Scotty stood in the courtyard admiring its plush greens as he waited for someone to respond to his ring. Martha opened the door and invited him in. "No, thank you," he said. "I would like to see Alis Brooks, please."

Brooks arrived at the door with Jay and Serena. He said teasingly, "Scotty, don't you ever go anywhere without a suit?"

Scotty ignored his statement as he stared at Serena, and then replied, "Sir, I need to talk with you."

"Scotty, you remember the Newmans, don't you?"

"Yes, sorry to meet again under these circumstances."

"Won't you come in?" Serena asked.

"No, no thank you, another time maybe." He looked at Alis. "Sir!"

Alis turned to Jay and Serena and excused himself. "I'll call you later."

The two men walked out into the courtyard and sat on a bench. As they were talking, Scotty opened the zip-lock bag and showed Brooks the gun he had found under Jay's deck. They talked for several minutes and decided to meet in Alis's office after lunch.

***

David Goldman stood at the big window in his office, mesmerized by a sense of poetic harmony with which the boating traffic moved back and forth from downtown and the Embarcadero to the channel leaving Point Loma. His office was rarely open on Saturday mornings, but he had an early appointment with a potential client who couldn't meet during the week. After waiting two hours and paying his secretary overtime for this meeting, the client called and cancelled.

His suspenders, unfittingly twisted, formed an X at the small of his back. Heavy starch kept his white shirt from wrinkling, and his gray suit pants were perfectly pressed, revealing a sharp vertical crease, which traveled upward from his cuffs. He removed his hands from his side pockets. One held some quarters and dimes and the other a silver money clip containing about $200 in mostly tens and twentys. Glancing at the money caused him to think about Roberta and the two million dollars.

Could this possibly be happening, he wondered. What if he doesn't have two million dollars? What if he just tells us to kiss off? What, ah, shit, there are too many whats, and what if she's right? *We could go away forever. I wonder if he really burned the old place down*. Proof, she said she has proof. Then why didn't she say something before? *I hate this. My practice is worth shit. My life is all screwed up so I like to drink. A lot of lawyers drink. I should have been a doctor. Well, maybe not. Losing a case is better than tying someone's liver to their asshole. My father used to say, "The definition of a Jewish lawyer is a Jewish boy who couldn't stand the sight of blood." Where did I go wrong?*

"Mr. Goldman, line one is for you. It's Mrs. Newman."

"Roberta," he said sharply, "I told you to call on my private line, not the office line."

Ignoring him, she said, "David, have you seen the TV today, or listened to the news?"

"No, why?"

"Jesus Christ, it's on every channel, on all the news."

"What is?"

"Two people were murdered behind Jay's house, on the beach."

"Right behind his house? Did they identify them? It wasn't Jay and Serena, was...?"

"No, not them. Not yet. We don't want anything to happen to him until he pays."

"What do you mean, not yet? Are you planning...?"

"No, no, I just want..."

"I know, the money."

"That's right, just the money. Why don't you call him and find out what happened. Then call me back."

"I'm really busy right now. I've got 15 minutes until my lunch appointment shows up, and I'm in the middle of..."

"You can't fool me, darling, I know you too well. You're probably standing with your hands in your pockets staring out the window. Just call him."

David hung up the phone, reached into his desk drawer, and pulled out a bottle of Stoli. After a swallow, he turned again to the window and thought, *what if, well, if I got possession of the money and I left. Just me. I could start a new life somewhere. I wouldn't have to leave the country, like she wants. I certainly wouldn't say anything to anyone.* He downed another swig. *She's the one with the big mouth. Then how do I get rid of her? Hmmm, I wonder.*

He gripped the bottle with two hands as he held it in front of his face. He spoke, confidingly, to the vodka bottle. "You're all the lunch date I need."

Chapter 22

Brooks was sitting at his desk typing when Scotty poked his head through the door.

The Northern Division of the San Diego Police Department encompasses more than forty-one miles and has among its many jurisdictions the community of La Jolla. The facility is not as busy or as formal as the main police headquarters in downtown San Diego, but it does have a rank and file of its own. Most days detectives sit around the office, drinking coffee and pretending they are busy. It is not unusual for someone assigned to an investigation to drag his feet. Most discussions center on sports, kids, wives, and projects around the house. When the brass is out of the office, talk turns to bad-mouthing anyone who isn't present.

This day was different. Brooks had assigned all of the detectives to the double homicide at Wind n Sea. Phones were busy, papers were being shuffled on desktops, and no lunch breaks were taken.

Scotty poked his head through the open doorway. Brooks was sitting at his desk, leaning forward with both elbows propped on the shiny, oak-wood top of his custom-made desk. He was reading reports submitted by the uniformed officers who had first arrived on the scene that morning.

Scotty admired Brooks' taste in clothing. He actually admired everything about Brooks, his position on the force, his home, his cars, his club memberships, and his family. Brooks was wearing a brown tweed coat, white shirt, and silk tie.

"Come on in, Scotty."

"Yes sir, thank you," he replied as he entered.

Scotty often wondered if the Chief's office was as well decorated as Brooks' office. The room looked like it was copied from a photograph in one of those designer magazines: thick plush carpeting, polished oak furniture, dark chocolate-brown walls accented with brass picture frames and photos of his family. Brass floor and table lamps with black shades as well as many other expensive accessories filled the room.

"This place is jumping. I don't ever remember seeing so many people working at the same time, especially on a Saturday. It's kind of nice, for change, huh?"

Brooks raised his eyebrows. "It's about time, don't you think? Can't let the cattle graze too long." Brooks liked Scotty. He liked the fact that he was well educated and qualified for Homicide. He admired his positive attitude and desire to do a good job. He knew Scotty was an ally and trusted him. Besides, the kid dressed well.

Some made cynical remarks behind his back; others spouted rumors about his wife's fortune coming from illegal drug cartels somewhere in South America. They despised his affluence and lifestyle. Scotty, it seemed, was always there to stand up for him. "What do you have Scotty?"

Kirby closed the door behind him, then placed his files on top of Brooks' desk. He stood at Brooks' side as he thumbed through the papers in the file.

"At this point I think we are dealing with some young lovers who were interrupted by our killer. Simply wrong place, wrong time. The M.E. said the guy was first. Neck snap. Somebody knew what he was doing."

"What about the girl?"

"The chick was choked, strangled. No rape. Hard to tell about footprints in the sand and ice plant. Donny said the print at the side of Newman's house was indistinguishable. My guess, the guy put up a fight and lost. Then Cinderella was chased and tackled."

"Did anyone hear anything? See anything?" Brooks asked.

Scotty straightened up, stepped back, put his hands in his pockets, and leaned against the wall. "We picked up an H.P. who is living under the Newman's deck. Said he's been there about three weeks. Says it's quiet and safe."

"Jay mentioned him to me. Is it Jeffrey?"

"Yeah, how'd you know?"

"How do I know? I know all of La Jolla's finest. I live there, remember?"

Scotty grinned, "I didn't know you knew they were called..."

"La Jolla's finest. You think I live in a cocoon?"

"No, sir, I don't. You must have eyes behind your head."

"And ears as well. You're going to need them one day. Better start practicing. What do you have on Jeffery?"

"We've got nothing on him."

"What did he say about the guy under the deck? What time was that?"

"He wasn't sure, but I figure around three or so. Said he thinks he saw the guy on Prospect earlier in the evening."

"What did you do with the pistol?"

"I sent it to the lab. Actually got a few prints. Ran a Cal ID, nothing. The serial number is gone, and it doesn't belong to the H.P., I mean Jeffrey. It wasn't used on our victims, although it might have belonged to the Unsub. They're running it through NCIC now."

"Good work, Scotty. Keep me informed. By the way, nice tie."

"Thanks, sir."

***

Andy spent most of the day walking the quaint village of La Jolla. He had a sandwich for lunch at the Coffee Cup. Sitting on a stool, at the end of the old formica counter allowed him to hear the many conversations about the incident at the beach. Jay Newman's name must have been mentioned a dozen times.

God, he thought, *everyone knows this guy. They talk about him as if he was a saint or something. Maybe it wasn't him. He gives money to charity, sponsors fund-raisers, and even helps the homeless. He even lets them sleep under his deck. Why would a killer do all this?*

He did find out that he stops in for coffee almost every weekday morning. *That's it. I'll join him Monday for coffee.*

***

"Why pay department-store prices for fine-quality men's clothing when you can get everything you need..."

Augy stared at the television. "Finch," he said aloud with envy, "you son of a bitch. Look at that sweet thing hanging on your side."

"Well, not necessarily everything, but everything you need in the way of a quality wardrobe. You're the professional. You be the judge."

"Goddamn, Finch. I don't wanna hear the word judge. What a great scam. Sell clothes using half-naked models. That's my pal, same old Finch. I wonder what else he has up his sleeve."

As the commercial ended the news continued, "Just a warning, San Diego. The meteorologists at NOAA are telling us that a powerful storm will most likely hit us soon. Pretty unusual for this time of the year. More about the storm later."

Augy heard enough about the story of the day and the weather alert. He shut off the TV set, grabbed a beer, opened the door of his room, and lit a cigarette. He stared at the Corvette sitting outside his room. I *wonder what it would be like to be able to actually own one of those. But I mean really pay for one, like most people do. I wonder. I think it's time for Finch to have some company. Maybe Monday morning.*

***

Heavy fog engulfed Shelter Island as the restaurants were closing. An occasional car pulled into the hotel parking lot. The sidewalk was deserted, and most room lights had been turned off at the Marina Inn. It was time.

Dressed in black and caring a nylon tote bag, the sleek-framed body walked speedily past the vending machines, which sat outside the lobby, then down the paved asphalt driveway to the dimly lit gate leading to the boat slips. A look in both directions satisfied the prowler—no security guard. The gate was locked. Up and over the chain link fence and to the opposite side of the gate, down the ramp and disappearing onto a dock filled with yachts, the determined trespasser knew exactly where to go.

The wind blew gently as the dingy made its way across and down the foggy channel toward the San Diego Yacht Club. Soft, silent ripples spread as the oars gently touched the water. Lines and cables clanging on masts filled the air with musical notes.

Maneuvering past one stern after another, the dingy slid peacefully toward the huge target yacht. A periodic blast from a foghorn swept through the stillness. On and off in a matter of minutes, the explosive device was set, in the aft swim locker under a towel. The dingy moved swiftly from the Yacht Club into the channel, then to the deserted Chevron gas dock. The dark shadow disappeared up the ramp and onto Shelter Island Drive.

***

On Sunday morning, Jay was sipping a cup of coffee as he sat patiently in his den waiting for Mac to call. It was 6:30. His message said he would call at 6. He's probably been out all night. *Those guys do most of their work at night,* he said to himself.

Jay answered the phone before the first ring ended.

"Hello."

Silence.

"Hello."

"Just, just making sure it was you, Newman."

"I've been waiting since 6 o'clock!"

"It, it won't hurt you to wait once in a while. A big shot like you expects everyone to jump for you, right now, quick, quick. It's, it's my turn."

"What's so important that it couldn't wait until later?"

"Hey, hey, now. Did I pull you away from your little sister?"

"Okay, enough of that shit. What's up that couldn't wait?"

"Not, not so fast. What the hell went on at your place Friday night? I, I seen it on the news. Some pervert canceled two tickets to the ball right in your backyard."

"You know as much as I do. Two kids, sleeping on the beach. Pissed somebody off. Whata ya got?" *There I go again*, he thought, *talking just like him.*

"You, you wanna know about this lawyer buddy of yours and your ex-wife?"

"Go on."

"Well, seems like this guy Goldman is pokin' your ex-princess."

"You're kidding! He's sleeping with her?"

"That ain't all. I got some film at eleven that I could sell as X-rated." Jay didn't reply but shook his head in disbelief. "You, you still there?"

"Yeah, I'm ...sorry. Go ahead."

"So she's in his house in Del Mar, talking about you and what a prick you are, how *you* burned down her old man's store and sold it for the bucks to start your new business and all. But you and me really know what happened, don't we! She's a real tiger. I, I sure hope you got a better deal with the new one."

"Enough of that shit, Mac. Back to the subject."

"This guy, your lawyer doesn't make too much money. He doesn't have a lot a clients. Likes his Stoli. Drives a nice car with a big lease payment. He's two months behind on his office rent. Wears cardboard shirts and cheap suits, which he probably bought from you, right? You don't have to answer that. Gotta free and clear house worth about two mil. His ex-wife gave it to him."

"How long has he been seeing Bobby?"

"I don't know about seeing her, but he's not doin' her."

"What does that mean?"

"She's doin' him."

"What do you mean?"

"You, you listening to me, Newman? She's doing him. I'm surprised he can keep it up so long. He's a dumb ass. Sounds like all she's got to do is wave her twang in front of him and he turns into a little puppy dog. You want to see the film?"

"No, I believe you. I've got to go now. I'll meet you at the Carousel at three on Monday."

***

Andy and Sam spent the weekend touring San Diego. They went to the world famous Zoo, to the Wild Animal Park, to Sea World, to Old Towne, and to Seaport Village. Sam attempted to get Andy to say why he was really in San Diego, but she didn't press him. He was normally a pretty shy person, but the two of them seemed to hit it off. They talked about their college days, books they read, and shared a general interest in baseball and football. They didn't go into detail about their families.

At seven a.m. on Monday, Andy sat on the black, cast-iron bench across from Ronda's Flower Shoppe on the corner of Herschel and Wall Street. Downtown La Jolla was filled with food service vehicles making deliveries to restaurants, mail trucks being loaded and unloaded at the post office, and various workers on their way into office buildings. The locals were out, preparing for another day in paradise. Tourists were not yet up and around.

Caddy-corner and across the street from the flower shop was an open patio area where several people sat chatting, drinking coffee, and reading the morning paper. A workman was cleaning the empty brass fountain. Andy watched as the man scooped up the money thrown in the day before by dreamers and wish-makers. *I wonder if he gets to keep that money.* Smiling, he acknowledged the two girls who arrived to open the flower shop. Cute, he thought. They don't look like that back home.

Andy had made plans, the night before, to meet Sam at eight for breakfast at the Coffee Cup. He was anxious to see her again, and because he was uncertain how he would react to being in the same room with Jay Newman, he felt she would be a good buffer between them.

He had spent much of his adult life looking for this person, despising him, and waiting to get revenge. Now 25 years later he was uncertain and confused. He wondered if this was the real criminal.

After sitting in the Coffee Shop Saturday and hearing about all the good this guy Newman does for the community, Andy began to have second thoughts. *Maybe it's not him. Maybe it's someone else. Maybe Finch wasn't what I heard, after all. Christ, I was just a little boy.*

The Coffee Cup, located next to the flower shop, had had a steady flow of traffic since it opened at 6:30. Andy watched as at least a dozen people had breakfast, read the paper, or gathered for informal breakfast meetings. He crossed Wall Street and paced the sidewalk across from the Coffee Cup. He glanced a few times toward the large glass window wondering if Jay Newman was already inside. He saw four men sitting at a table between the window booths and the stools at the counter. He tried not to be conspicuous. The eight o'clock hour drew closer, and the village was awake. More people filled the sidewalks, and steady traffic passed by.

Andy was walking back toward the bench by the flower shop when he spotted Sam walking down Herschel toward him. She wore navy shorts and a red blouse. Her sunglasses were the same color as her shorts. The white purse and sandals matched perfectly. As she drew closer, she seemed to be almost bouncing. Her hair, tied with a scarf, swung from side to side.

Kiddingly, "Hi stranger," she said as she approached. "I hope I'm not late."

"You're right on time."

Sam smiled and took his arm. "What about breakfast? You said you wanted to have breakfast."

"Yeah, if you want. There is a little coffee shop right here next to the florist." They had started walking toward the Coffee Cup when a black Porsche zipped around the corner and pulled into a space in front of the newspaper machines. Jay exited the car and walked to the door of the coffee shop. He held the door for Sam and Andy. Andy and Sam walked to the back of the small dining room and sat at a booth.

Jay pulled out a chair and sat with the other men at the table.

"Hey, look at Newman. What's this, a white linen suit?" asked Mobley.

"You know, Carl," said Jay, "You wouldn't know good taste if it hit you on the head."

"Good taste, huh? Is this the latest fashion craze, or what?"

Jay shook his head, looked to the others for help, and laughed. "Will you guys please tell him to leave me alone? He picks on me every day."

Doc said, "You know, Newman, I had one of those suits about a hundred years ago when I got out of medical school. I think my mother made it for me. Always looked like I had slept in the thing. Couldn't keep the wrinkles out of the son of a bitch."

"Take a closer look, boys. No wrinkles. It's the newest thing from..."

Andy and Sam sat in their booth as the loud table in the middle of the dining room continued to entertain everyone.

Sam asked, "Who are those guys?"

"Just locals who meet here every day for coffee and breakfast," said Andy.

"How do you know that?" asked Sam.

"I was in here for lunch the other day and heard people talking about them."

"Hi, I'm Quanny. Would you like some coffee?"

"Yes," Sam replied, "that's a good start. How about you, Andy?"

"Ummm, I'll have some orange juice, please. I'm sorry. I was just listening to those guys over there. Who are they, anyway?"

Leaning toward them, Quanny said, "The one guy is a stockbroker, the one who made fun of the guy who just came in. The guy in jeans is a real-estate broker. The older hippie man with the thin long white hair, well, he's the doc."

"Who is the one with the white suit on?"

"Oh, that's Jay Newman. He owns some clothing stores, and the other guys always make fun of him, the way he dresses and all."

"Hey, my boy!" said Doc. "What the hell did you do to those people down on the beach the other day?"

"You know the value of your house just went down about a hundred grand!" laughed Carl.

"Where the hell is Brooks this morning? I'll bet he'll know something," said Doc.

Andy looked into Sam's eyes. She stared back with a puzzled look on her face. "What!" she said. "What are you looking at?"

"You know, you have really pretty eyes," he said.

"Come on, Andy; that's not what you were thinking. You were squinting when you looked at me, like you were looking through me."

Andy tensed. His face showed no expression. He sat, motionless as if a heavy weight had just been placed on his shoulders. His heartbeat increased, just as it did every time he remembered. *Twenty-five years ago*, he thought. *Twenty-five years. Look at him. Finally! Tough guy! Fancy clothes. Big house. Rich bastard! That son of a bitch. He still likes sports cars, too. I'll bet he doesn't even remember me. How could he? He never saw me. He had to have read the papers then. He really thinks he got away with it.*

"Andy, are you all right?" she whispered across the table. He stared past her, through her.

She tried again. "Andy, are you okay?"

His eyes moved to hers. He said nothing. His hands tightly clasped, knuckles white, rested on the tabletop. Reaching over the table, she placed her hands on his and smiled reassuringly. His hands were wet and cold. She felt his anxiety, his passion.

"It's okay," she reassured.

He remembered his mother, holding him. *"It's okay," she would say. "Everything will be okay. We're going to be fine. It just takes time."*

Andy turned his head slowly and looked at Newman as he sat laughing with his friends.

Jay said, "Okay, you idiots, I have the answer to the riddle, or the question, from the other day."

"Which riddle is that?" asked the Doc.

"The one about the duck?" replied Mobley.

"Yes, that one," Carl added.

Doc laughed. "Tell me again; what was the riddle?"

Jay said, "The question was, what's the difference between a duck?"

"Yeah," said Belle from across the counter. "That was a really stupid question! Go on; what's the answer, big shot?"

Jay, smirking, said, "The difference between a duck is that one leg is both the same."

The hisses and boos resembled the responses to a bad vaudeville act, when they put a big looped cane around the entertainer and pull him off stage.

Andy tried to listen, but it was all a blur. Drifting back, he saw himself, as a little boy, cold and frightened, sitting in a chair at the sheriff's office waiting for his mother. Voices were a blur then, too. The sheriff, his secretary, and even Fred Masters spoke to him, but he couldn't make out the words.

Andy thought his father was playing a game when he told him to hide under the blanket. *"Get down, Andy. Get under the blanket. Don't move 'til I tell ya."* It was no game. If he knew something was wrong or threatening, why didn't we just turn around? *He never had the chance to tell me anything. Why would they shoot him? What did they do to him? They didn't even know each other. For twenty-five years I lived without my father, without my uncle, because this guy, Jay Newman, and some other guy decided to shoot them. No reason, just for fun. All the nights my mother cried. Look at him, laughing. He doesn't care. What kind of person can live without a conscience?*

He moved here, changed his name, and got rich. Maybe he was rich back then. He had a father. I didn't. He took mine away. What if I took his away? What if I take his kid away? What if I just kill him and his kid has to grow up, like me, without a father? You prick! Who was with you? I remember two people, you and one of your buddies. Do you have any idea how I felt in school? All my friends' fathers going to their games. Sure, my grandpa came most of the time, but it wasn't the same. He was old. How 'bout on holidays? I only knew one other kid growing up without his dad. That's because he was killed in Vietnam. But his mom got remarried, and he had other brothers and sisters. Somehow this doesn't seem fair. You kill someone, two someones, then move to California, change your name, and become rich. I don't understand. I grow up without a father, having to live with my grandparents in their house with barely any money, all because of you. How can you sit there laughing? Don't you ever think about your past? I feel the cold. I see my mother rushing into the sheriff's office, crying. I was crying. We never stopped crying. I remember now. Someone kept repeating your name, excitingly. Finch this! Finch that! Something about a code. The code, the code. Someone kept repeating the code, the code! What the hell does that mean? Code what? Some kind of secret code among killers?

"Andy, Andy!" Sam whispered. "You're shaking." She rubbed his cold hands. His eyes blinked; tears ran down his cheeks. He returned from his trance.

Andy's eyes focused on Sam's. "I'm sorry. Oh, God!" he said as he wiped his tears and eyes with his napkin. "I didn't mean to..."

"It's okay, Andy," she interrupted. "You want to get out of here?"

"Yeah, maybe we better."

Just then, in walked Augy Romano, sporting white slacks, a black silk shirt, and white bucks. He glanced around the dining room and saw Jay at the table with his friends. He stood for a second, walked over to the table, and put his hand on Jay's shoulder.

Augy held out his hand to shake Jay's hand and said, "Finch! It's been a long time."

Jay turned and looked at him as if the devil had arrived. Jay stood up. His eyes opened wide. He knew this day would eventually come.

"Augy Romano, Jesus, I haven't seen you since the 60s."

"Actually, since January, 1964, to be exact," Augy replied.

Andy and Sam stared at the two of them. "Oh, my God," said Andy aloud.

"What is it?" asked Sam. "Who are these guys?"

"Oh, my God," he said again.

Andy grabbed Sam's arm and pulled her up and out of the booth. He placed two dollars on the table and said, "Come on, let's go for a walk."

As they were nervously sidestepping past the crowded table, Doc said loudly, "Now there's a smart couple. Come in here, sit a while, check the place out, then decide to go someplace else. Don't 'spose it's the food, or the soap in the cup, do ya?" Laughter erupted as the door swung closed behind them.

Jay was shocked to see Augy. He introduced him to the group as an old childhood and school friend. Then he excused himself from the table and escorted Augy to another table in back of the dining room.

Andy and Sam strolled to the bench in front of the florist shop and sat. Andy stared down the sidewalk toward Jay's Porsche. He thought about what had just taken place in the coffee shop. He finally got to see Finch, and when he heard him speak he began to feel tense and anxious, but when Augy walked in and addressed Jay as Finch, and mentioned January, 1964, the puzzle began to instantly come together.

Being with Sam distracted him. It was almost as if she knew what he was feeling. *"God, it's almost as if she could read my mind."* "I'm sorry, Sam. I don't know what came over me back there. It's really none of your business"

"That's okay. I'm here if you want to talk about it." *"Andy,"* she said to herself. *"I don't know how I'm going to tell you this, but it is my business!"*

***

After sitting for a few minutes, Jay and Augy got up and left the coffee shop. As they strolled toward Jay's office, Augy said, "So Finch, how ya doin'? I didn't mean to take you away from your pals, and all."

Jay seemed nervous as he and Augy walked through the lobby door of his offices. Jay hesitated as he could feel his staff curiously staring at the two of them. As Jay escorted him through to his office, the staff rolled their eyes.

"Come on back. It sure has been a long time. You want some coffee?"

They entered the door to Jay's office when Augy said, "Long time, huh, Finch?"

"Long time, yeah!" said Jay. *Holy shit! This is all I need.*

"Come on over here and give me a big brother hug for old time's sake. It's been a lot a years, man." Augy approached Jay and quickly consumed him with the big solid hug, the kind that tells you who is in charge, the kind that doesn't seem to let go, the kind some Mafia guy in the movies would give to someone just before he killed him, that says, hey, motherfucker, your time has come.

Jay was known for being a self-confident leader. He was used to being in charge, the boss, the hero, the head of his family, someone everyone looked up to, Mr. San Diego, twice, a strong, powerful, and successful businessman not afraid of anything or anyone, until now.

Romano stood as a giant. His white teeth matched his slacks. His black silk shirt matched his shiny hair. Augy's yellow sport jacket and white shoes didn't belong in this environment. *Neither did the two of them*, thought Jay.

"Good to see ya, Augy."

The two men sat on the sofa for an hour reminiscing. Hey, what happened to so and so? Did you hear about this, and did you hear about that? Both occasionally laughed just like two kids.

Jay got up and moved to his chair behind his desk. "So, Romano, what are you doing for a living?"

Augy, a little taken aback by Jay's move from the sofa, said, "Like I told you on the phone the other day, I work with metal stamping machines. I sell parts. I do repairs." He had planned to tell Jay the truth, to come clean and share his shitty life, but now he saw a businessman, a successful executive, someone he didn't know anymore.

"Is it your company?"

"Not really. Not yet. I been thinking about branching out on my own, ya know, doing my own thing and all."

"That sounds entrepreneurial."

"What's that supposed to mean?" remarked Romano.

Sensing that Augy didn't know what an entrepreneur was, he said," It doesn't mean anything bad." Jay moved closer to his desk, placed his elbows on the desktop, and gestured with open hands. "Just that you'll be a businessman, like people who take risks, inventors, investors, people who put everything on the line for their futures. It's like craps. Put it on the come line. Sometimes you roll the snake, sometimes the seven, and sometimes you just lose."

"Yeah, like you, huh?"

"Well, maybe not exactly like me, but close. Hey, I wish you a lot of luck. Business is not as easy as some would think."

"Looks like you been rollin' some good dice, huh, Finch? You finally joined The Hunt Club. Is that your family in that picture?"

"Yes, it is. My wife, Serena, and our little pride and joy, Carlie."

"How old is she?"

"Six."

"Not the kid, your wife?"

"What do you mean?" Jay answered defensively.

"Oh, nothing, just kidding. She seems a little young to be married to you. Does she know how old you really are?"

"What do you mean, how old I really am? I'm not so old. I'm the same as you."

"She looks at least ten years younger than you."

"She is. What difference does that make?"

"So, the kid, is she smart like you? Is that your boat in that picture over there? You must live in a big house, huh?"

Catching himself and trying not to come off as a snob, Jay said. "It's not mine. It belongs to the company. I get to use it, but technically, it's not mine."

"Well, it's your company, right? I mean, like you're the president, the boss, the big kahuna, El jefe, ya know!" Augy was firing on all eight cylinders. "So maybe you and me could take some of those cute little things for a boat ride or something? What do you think?"

"What cute little things?"

"Your little models in the commercials I've been watching those little things."

"Give me a break, Augy. Business is business." Jay nervously repositioned himself in his chair. "There is a board of directors and others who have a say-so as to what goes on around here. I don't have free rein."

"I don't know what rain has to do with anything. You lost me back there. I do know you are the boss. I seen your commercials on the tube. What's that picture?" Pointing. "Your cabin in the woods?" He laughed aloud.

Trying not to seem as if he was playing defense, he fired back, "Actually, it is, my little hideout in the woods. Sometimes I go up there to just relax and think."

"You still hunt? I mean shoot little critters and such?"

"No. It's just a place to relax, read, hike, and ride."

"Whatta you mean, ride? You have a bike or something there?"

"No, I have two motor scooters in my shed. It's fun to ride the paths and streets around there. Kind of reminds me of the past. You know? Mayfield, Gates Mills, Chardon…"

"You still think of those days, Finch? I mean, when we were kids and all? Do you think of all the good times we had, the shit we did?"

"Oh yes Augy, I do think of the shit, as you call it, the shit we did. You ever think about that? The *shit* we did? Huh? Is that why you're here? Tell me. Why are you here, exactly? You need money?"

"No, no, man. I don't need anything from you. I just decided to come visit an old friend."

Jay sat upright in his chair, put his arms out over his desktop, and said. "That's bullshit! Somehow I just don't believe you. I haven't heard from you in over twenty years, and all of a sudden you show up on my doorstep."

Augy stretched back and made himself comfortable. "You're right, but it was just about twenty-five years ago when we last saw each other, not twenty. Remember that day Finch, the freezing cold, your little shit car, the woods..."

"Oh, I remember it well. I think about it all the time. That's why I moved out here, to get away from that lifetime."

"Finch, you can never get away from it. It'll always be with you. I'll always be with you."

"What the hell does that mean? You'll always be with me?"

"You think by movin' out here that your past is behind you? That just doesn't happen!"

"What do you mean, that doesn't happen? What are you saying? You going to blackmail me? You going to tell all? Remember, you have just as much to lose as I do."

"I'm not blackmailing you. I'm not going to tell anyone about anything. You say you think about it all the time. Well, I don't think about it at all. How's that grab you? I don't give a fuck about blowing those guys away at all. I don't give a fuck about hurting anybody. I never do!"

"You saying you have no conscience? You don't think we did anything wrong? Jesus, Augy, what kind of person are you?"

"Listen, Finch..."

Jay stood, clasped his fists, and looked deep into Augy's face. "Don't call me Finch! I'm not Finch anymore. I have a legitimate business, a family, and a good life. You want me to pay for that in some way?" He turned toward the window and looked at his reflection in the glass. "Believe me, I have paid for all of this."

"What do you want me to call you, Mr. Newman? What the hell is that all about? You want me to call you Jake or Jay? Tell me."

"Just call me Jay, like everybody else."

Augy stood, "Ok, Jay, I want to be your friend, not some threat, not some stranger that you have to worry about. I'm here because I wanted to see how you were doing. That's all. Just came to visit, ok?"

Obviously flustered, Jay said, "Look, Augy, my wife and I are very happy. I was married to a real bitch, for a long time. This was her father's business, not mine. She's still a pain in the ass. What else do you want to know? You act like this is twenty questions, and then I have no time to answer. Slow down. Give me a fuckin' break."

"Cool it, Finch, er, Jay. I'm just trying to catch up. I didn't mean to pry or nothin'!"

"I'm sorry," said Jay. "I am a little sensitive. I don't mean to come off as some kinda big shot." Trying to calm the discussion and take Augy away from his mind set, Jay said, "We do go back a long way. I just don't want to jeopardize my family or what I have."

Both men stood silent for a minute. Then Jay turned toward the door and suggested they go to lunch.

"You sure you want to go to lunch with me? I mean, I'm not the average La Jolla guy. It's ok if you're seen with me and all?"

"I wouldn't have suggested it if I wasn't ok with it. Let's go have a drink and a sandwich. You like steak sandwiches?"

"I'd rather have some drinks, but a steak sandwich sounds good to me."

As they passed the reception area, Jay rolled his eyes and said they were going to George's and that he would be back later.

Chapter 23

Bobby wiped her mouth as she stood from her kneeling position in front of David. He sat on the sofa, relaxed, pants down around his ankles. "So are you going to call him, today?" she asked.

"Yes, I'll call him," he replied calmly.

"David, darling, we don't have a lot of time. You need to put some pressure on him. You need to say something that will cause him to get the money."

"What do you want me to say to him? Jay I'm, ah… Your ex-wife and me… Ah, well, Bobby and I are fucking our brains out and would like two million dollars so we can leave together!"

"Come on, David!" she said as she rinsed out her mouth at the kitchen sink.

"I mean really, Roberta, what am I supposed to tell him? What do I say? He probably knows about us anyway! 'Jay. Roberta says she won't report you to the cops for burning down her father's store if you give her two million dollars.' Give me a break! He's not stupid. The first thing he's going say is, 'Why now? Why didn't she report me when it happened? Why did she wait so long?' He knows you're full of shit." He shook his head in disgust.

"Thanks for the confidence, David," she said sarcastically as she walked over to the bar.

"What are you talking about, confidence? You want his attention, you blow up his fucking house, or his boat. That will get his attention. You do something. Confidence, shit! That doesn't make any fucking sense. You lived with him, you must have something on him."

"How does he know about the boat?" she said to herself.

David continued, "I've been thinking about that. You're right about the fire and all. I put a little bait out on the line the other day at lunch. I said some things, some personal things that will surely make him think."

"What kind of things? What are you talking about?"

"I said a few things about the IRS and the fire. I pretended to be a little too intoxicated. I know it puts pressure on him. You'll see. Then he will be happy to negotiate."

"I can prove he screwed with the IRS. I did the books, remember?"

"Roberta, you need to watch what you say, especially about the IRS. That's a pretty heavy subject. You're just as guilty as he is. You can go to jail, too."

She was silent for a second. "I know where I can get proof. Just threaten him! Tell him I have proof. Tell him if he doesn't pay, I will turn him in. Remind him that I did the books for him. I know how much he stole. Tell him I am willing to go to jail with him. Tell him I don't give a shit. Tell him I'll call Mac."

"Who the hell is Mac?"

"Nevermind! Jay knows who he is." She paused for a moment, then asked, "You want a drink, dear?"

David stood, fastening his belt. "Sure, why not!" *I wonder if she swallows it.*

***

Jay rarely returned to the office after lunch. However, after spending the morning and his lunch hour with Augy Romano, he needed to get some work done. He didn't want to go to lunch with him, but he couldn't just slough him off. He knew too much.

Jay entered the lobby to his offices, and saw Alis talking to Marna.

"What's so funny?" he asked.

"Hi, Jay, sorry to barge in like this," replied Alis.

"It's not a big deal. You're actually lucky I'm here. What's so funny?"

"Nothing really. We're just having a father-daughter discussion."

"You dirty old man, she already has a father."

"Actually, we were discussing your old high-school buddy's clothes."

"Unbelievable huh?" replied Jay.

"I need to talk to you for a minute?" said Alis.

"Sure, what is it?"

"Let's go in your office, ok?"

Jay's heart started to pound.

Alis closed the door to Jay's office. "Sit down, Jay."

Jay ignored him and walked over to the window. A gentle sea breeze filled the sail of a small wind surfer and propelled it toward the cove. Gulls soared in the bright sunny sky. His mind flashed back to the snow-covered meadow in Chardon. It was so clear now that Augy Romano reminded him of all the gruesome details. He felt cold and scared. He remembered the emptiness in his stomach as the news broadcasts begged for information about the murders. The weeks and months had passed, then a year. Then two. The fear never left. Finch, Jacob Nubaum, or Jay Newman, it didn't matter; they would all have to face the eventual consequences.

Oh shit, Jay thought. *Augy Romano is here for one fuckin' day, and the cops know about everything.*

"What's the matter?" Jay asked. "Did something happen to..."

"No, no Jay, nothing happened. I just want to know something, off the record."

"Off what record?" Jay replied.

"No, I mean, just you and me."

"What are you talking about?" *It's all over now! On or off the record, it's my ass.*

Francesca was at a luncheon meeting the other day, at the beach and Tennis Club."

"So?"

"Well, Roberta, Bobby, was also there. She got a little juiced."

Jay replied, "She always gets a little juiced. What happened?"

"She may have gone a little too far this time."

"What does that mean, too far?"

"She got pretty loud. She talked about you, your business, your marriage."

"What else is new? Why is this off the record?"

"She talked about income-tax evasion. She talked about the fire. She talked about..."

"Who was she talking to, exactly?"

"Not to anyone that matters, but rumors start that way. La Jolla is still a small town, especially with that group of women."

"So what can I do about it? I can't stop her from talking. She's a drunk. Who is going to listen to a drunk?"

"You'd be surprised how many women in that group are in AA or should be in AA. You know the old saying. It takes one to..."

"Yeah, I know. Alis, I didn't arrange for that fire. I hope you believe me. Are we still off the record?"

"Of course we are. Why did you ask me if were still off the record? Are you fooling with the IRS?" asked Alis.

"No, no. Not that! Anyway, you know more about my money than anyone else. You're my friend first, a cop second, and you of all people are not the fucking IRS!"

Wrinkling his brow, "What then?"

"You know the guy that was here this morning? My old high-school friend?"

"Yeah, what about him?"

"Could you, ah, are you able to find out about someone?"

"Sure, if he's got a sheet. I mean, if he's Mr. Good Guy, then I probably won't find much of anything. Give me his name again."

Jay scribbled Romano's name on a piece of paper. "Thanks, Alis, for the information on Bobby. There's not much I can do about her mouth. I appreciate you letting me know."

Alis stood and put his arm around Jay's shoulder, reassuring his friendship. "I'll talk to you later. Go home. You don't like to work in the afternoon, anyway."

"Remember, this is all off the record."

"I know. Just go home."

Chapter 24

Jay approached the carousel at Sea Port Village. Mac sat on a bench, pretending again to look like a tourist—straw hat, dark sunglasses, tan khaki shorts, red, yellow, and blue argyle socks, and white bucks. *I guess it's my day for white shoes.*

"Hey, hey, if it isn't peeping Tom," chuckled Jay.

"That's, that's not funny, Newman."

"Sorry Mac, I couldn't help myself."

"You, you, can call me peeping fuckin' Tom all you want, but but don't fuck with the way I talk. Ya got it?"

Jay nodded as he sat. "So I guess she is having a good time with my attorney."

"Yep, you wanted to know, so I got it all. Now what?"

Jay sat silent for a moment watching the carousel spin. Mac leaned back, crossed his legs, and stretched his arms out along the top rail of the backrest.

"She called me, Newman," Mac said.

Jay turned and looked at Mac. "Who called you? Bobbie? She called you? Why?"

"Hold on, Newman. Don't get your little things in an uproar. Yes, she called me. I don't..."

"Why did she call you?"

"Will, will you let me finish, please?"

"Go on. I want to hear this!"

"I, I don't usually work both sides of an altercation unless it's petty shit. But this is definitely not petty."

"Why did she call you?"

"Well, well, she was inquiring about your finances, wanted to know if I could spread some snoop."

"What are you talking about, snoop?"

"She, she, didn't get specific, but I think she wants to fry your ass with your Uncle Sam. You get the picture?"

"Why are you telling me this? Why didn't you just do what she wants you to do?"

"Like I said, I don't like playin' both sides. At, at least not at the same time."

"Can she afford you, Mac?"

"Well, let's just say money isn't necessarily the motivation here."

"What do you mean? You trying to say you have feelings, you have a heart?"

"I, I wouldn't go that far, Newman,"

"Then what? Why don't you take her on as a client? She knew you first. Her old man was a client of yours. How many other fires did she hire you for? She's spreading rumors that I started the fire, trying to pin it on me. The whole goddamn thing was her idea. I was..."

"Enough! Enough already. Jesus Christ! You're making me sick."

Jay wiped his wet forehead with his hankie. He stared at the carousel again.

"Mac," Jay said, as he appeared mesmerized by the turning horses. "She wants two million dollars."

"Yeah, yeah. I know about that."

"How do you know? Did she tell you that?"

"I, I...got it on tape, the tape you don't want to see."

Jay closed his eyes and lowered his head. "I can just imagine. Shamu and her lover," he said sarcastically.

"There's no whale in this flick. When's the last time you saw her? We're talkin' serious sex. I could sell this kind of film. Just pure raw, hot..."

Jay interrupted as he ignored Mac's description of his ex-wife and his attorney having sex on the tape. Jay looked up at Mac. "I don't have two million dollars to give her."

"Two million is a lot of money, Newman. You got at least that much equity in your house, no?"

"Sure I have equity in my house, but if I use two million dollars of it..." He stopped, wiped his forehead again, then continued. "I can't do that. That's not an option."

"If it was anyone else, Newman. I, I...could arrange for something unfortunate to happen. I don't like her, either, never did. Even as a kid she was a little brat. But outta respect to her old man, ya know what I'm sayin'?"

"I don't want to hurt her, either. I just want her out of my life."

Mac stood up and stretched. "Let me think about it. Anything else you want to talk about today?"

Jay stood, handing Mac a folded paper with the name Augy Romano written on it. "Actually, there is something. A guy I went to high school with, he's in town and I would like to know exactly why."

As Jay reached out to shake Mac's hand, Mac substituted a paper bag for the handshake. "Here, take the tape. Pop it in some time when you're alone. Shamu is now a pretty mermaid."

Jay held the bag at his side as he watched Mac O'Donnell light a cigar and disappear into the crowd.

***

Scott Kirby pulled the unmarked police cruiser off the alley and into the parking lot behind the Ursula Younie Real Estate Company.

He looked back over the seat and watched Jeffrey's eyes as they moved pensively back and forth while he gathered his things.

"Thanks, Jeffrey. Take this. He handed him five 20-dollar bills.

"I don't need your money, remember?"

"Just consider it a present, a gift. A thank-you gift for all your help yesterday and today."

Jeffrey looked at the money, then at Scott holding it folded in his fingers. "Thanks!" he said as he took it, folded it once more, and placed it in the pocket of his clean red-flannel shirt.

While in lock-up the night before, Scott had arranged to have all of Jeffrey's clothes, including his overcoat, either washed or dry-cleaned. "No one should live like that," he thought. "Dirt is one thing, stench is another. At least the police car won't need to be fumigated after I bring it back from La Jolla."

Jeffrey fumbled for a few minutes while Scott got out of the car and opened the rear door. Jeffrey was a large man. Scott listened to him huff and puff as he maneuvered his torso back and forth struggling to get out of the car.

"You need to get in shape, Jeffrey," remarked Scotty.

Jeffrey looked at the young, strong, physically fit detective and said, "Think they'd let me come to your gym and work out?" He smiled for the first time since Scott had met him.

Scott stared him in the eyes and said firmly, "Any time you're ready to get off the street, you let me know."

Jeffrey grimaced and nodded his head. Then he turned and started walking up the alley toward the motel on the corner of Herschel and Silverado.

Scott drove slowly up the alley and watched as Jeffrey sat on the bus-stop bench across from the motel. Scotty's watch chimed, reminding him that it was 6 p.m. He turned the corner and drove off.

An hour later, Jeffrey's eyes opened wide as he saw Andy and Sam, across the street, coming down the steps from Andy's room at the motel.

Holy shit, he thought. *That's him, that's the guy from the other night, and the girl, too. I gotta call Scott.*

Chapter 25

Jay's heart was again pounding heavily as he held Serena's hand and led her down the stairs to his office. His hands were cold and clammy. Serena sensed something was wrong. She was nervous. "What's going on, Jay?" she asked. "Are we in some kind of trouble?"

Jay pressed the button, and the heavy door opened. He led Serena to the sofa. "Jay, you're scaring me. What's wrong?"

Jay stood in front of the fireplace and looked into her fearful eyes. Shivering, he ran his fingers through his hair. Serena stood up and hugged him. He placed his arms around her shoulders and held tight. "Jay, you need to tell me what's wrong. I'm always here for you, and you know that. Did you do something? Are we in trouble? Is it the business?" Jay stood silent.

"Talk to me," she begged.

"I never thought it would come to this. I never wanted to hurt you."

"What do you mean, you never wanted to hurt me?" Her heart sank as she confronted him. "Are you having an affair?"

"Jesus Christ, no! I'm not having an affair. Why would you ask me that?"

"Then tell me. What the hell is going on here? You're scaring me."

They sat on the sofa. "I never told you about certain things, when I was a kid, a teenager."

Serena's anxiety lessened. She didn't know much about Jay's childhood, other than what she had been told by him and his mother—a non-religious, hard-working, blue-collar family living in the suburbs of Cleveland, public schools, cold winters, and hot humid summers. Jay had told her of his youthful days playing in the woods, fishing at some river, and working as a lifeguard at the community pool. Serena had pictured his youth as a "Leave it to Beaver" kind of boyish adventure with his older brother being Wally.

"Jay, how serious can this be?" she asked.

"Serious enough. I never told you this before. I never told anyone before."

"It's okay. What happened?"

"Do you believe someone can change, I mean, be a certain kind of person and then be someone else?"

"What are you talking about being someone else? Are you saying you are someone other than the person I know?"

"Not now, but I was someone else for a long time, and I did some bad things, really bad things. I was never caught."

Serena's heart began to sink again. Her voice wavered. "What did you do? How bad is bad?"

"I'm not the same as I used to be. I've tried to be a nice guy, a good husband and father to you and Carlie."

"Jay, you are a good husband and father. What did you do?"

Oh God, he thought, *I'm really in trouble. I have to tell her. What is she going to think? Is she going to leave? I've been living with this too long. I love her so much. I have no choices. I have to tell her. This could ruin everything. What is she going to think of me? I'm not him anymore.*

"Jay, what did you do? What are you talking about?"

"Promise me you won't leave me. Promise you'll try to understand."

"You were a child. How bad can this be? Did you hurt someone?"

"Remember, I used to tell you about a guy who lived behind me, named Augy Romano?"

Searching her memory, she said. "Vaguely. What about him?"

"He's here, in La Jolla. He came to see me."

"About what?" She tried to reassure him. "Darling, I love you. What happened? What does he want?"

"When I was a kid, we did things together. We spent a lot of time together." Jay paused, then said, "I'm not asking for your sympathy, I just need to tell you..."

Serena spoke with a soft curious voice. "Go on."

Jay took a deep breath. "We broke into houses together, into stores. We stole things."

Serena's stare was intense. "I don't understand what you're saying. Are you telling me you're a criminal, a thief?"

"No I'm not now. But I was."

"Jay, that was a long time ago. You were young, just a child! Whose idea was it to do those things? This guy Romano? Did he come here to blackmail you? How can he blackmail you for things you did as a minor? Jay, don't let the son of a bitch scare or threaten you. You can't be held responsible. If he decides to tell the police, he'll be incriminating himself as well. He has just as much to lose as you do." She paused and gathered her thoughts for a moment. "Actually, not! But I bet Alis would know what to do."

"Alis," he said, "We can't tell Alis."

"I'm sure anything you did is well beyond the statute of any limitations."

Jay wiped his forehead and looked into Serena's eyes. He paused for a second and then said, "There is no statute of limitations for murder."

Serena slumped back against the cushions, her mouth dropped. She sat in shock.

"We shot two men. We ambushed and killed them." Silence engulfed the room.

"Who were the two men? Was it self-defense? Were they after you for something you guys did?"

"January second, 1964. Our last day together! We were out in the woods. It happened so fast. It was horrible. We were frightened. We ran away." Jay continued, and his words brought to life the vivid memories of his childhood and the murderous event in Chardon.

He paced the floor in front of the sofa. Then spoke of how he and Augy went their separate ways, how he had learned through the media of a young boy, fatherless because of him. He explained how, for years, via their church, he made anonymous contributions to the boy and his mother. "I've been living with this all my life."

Serena paced the room, shaking. "I don't know if I want to hear any more. I don't know if I can take any more."

"Serena," Jay tried to interject.

She continued, "Were those donations sent from La Jolla? Postmarked, La Jolla?"

"No, no, I sent the cash to an old college friend, who lives in Indiana, and he forwarded the packages to the church."

"This college friend. Does he know about this?"

"No! I sent the money in sealed packages, and then he sent them. I told him it was..."

"Jay, who are you? Are you wanted by the police? Is that why you changed your name? How could you do such a thing?" Jay put his arms on the mantel and hung his head. Emotionally drained, she wiped the tears from her cheeks. Her voice filled with anguish. "How much does he want?"

"He didn't say exactly how much, but at lunch he hinted around 250,000."

"If we give him the money will he go away?"

"I'm frightened, Serena. I always knew this day would come. For years, I wanted to turn myself in, pay the price. But it just got harder as time went by. I almost did it before I met Bobby. Then her father gave me an opportunity with the store. Just after he died and when the store burned, I was going to turn myself in. The insurance money gave me another chance. The business grew. Everyone got to know me. My life changed. Then I met you. I couldn't live without you then, and I don't know what I would do without you and Carlie now." He paused for a second, then said, "I don't know what to do."

"Jay," she said, "wouldn't he suffer the same consequences as you?"

"I don't know him anymore. I don't think it would matter to him. If he is anything like he was before, then no, it wouldn't make a difference. He'd probably come after us."

Jay thought about Romano's remarks concerning Serena and Carlie in the office picture. *I'll kill the son of a bitch if he ever touches either one of them.*

"I'd give him the money to go away, but now that he knows where we are and what we've got... I'm not sure he would stay away."

Still on the sofa, Serena reached behind her head, clasped her hands around her ponytail. "I think we should talk to Alis. He's a true friend first and a cop second."

"Serena, don't you understand? Anything we tell Alis Brookes could be incriminating."

"I'm sorry. You're wrong. Alis is a friend. There is such a thing of privileged information, you know, confidential."

Right, privileged and confidential, he thought, picturing David jumping Bobby's bones.

He started again, "Serena, I'm so sorry. I never wanted anyone to know. That was a different life, a different time. I'm not the same person I was."

"Jay, I don't know who you are, who I married! I don't know how much of this I can take."

Jay stepped closer, attempting to hug her. "Serena, I am really sorry for what I..."

Abruptly pulling away, she said, "Forget it! I can't listen to you anymore. I'm taking Carlie and going to the boat. Don't follow us or come down there. I need to get away from here. I need to be alone, without you. I need to think."

"Look! I'll go. I'll go to the boat. You stay here."

"No!" she commanded. She cupped her hand over her mouth and her eyes filled with bulging tears. "I don't want to be here. I just want to go! Leave us alone, please! I need to think."

She walked to the elevator door, depressed the button, and waited. He followed her. She turned and ran up the stairs. Jay stood alone. The door opened and then slid closed. *Look what I've done now,* he thought, as he walked over to his desk. "Goddamn it, Romano, you son of a bitch! Why did you have to show up?" *I knew this would fucking happen someday. No secrets! That was the deal when I married her. God, I am an asshole. See where it got me. She's pissed. I don't blame her, either. Look what she married. I should have paid for this a long time ago. I didn't only screw up my life, but look what I've done to them.*

As he sat in his chair, he pictured Carlie growing up. *So where is your father, little girl? Oh, he's in jail for killing someone. Shit, now what the fuck am I supposed to do?*

I need a plan, a serious plan.

He pushed some buttons on the concealed wall and unlocked the drawers, removed all of the $750,000.00, and stacked it in piles on the top of his desk. Then he removed the revolver and spun the chambers. He held the gun with two hands and pointed it at the money. "Here, you son of a bitch," he said aloud. "You want the fuckin' money? Come on. I'll give it to you!"

Later Jay stood on the deck outside of his bedroom, holding a yellow legal pad in one hand and a gin rocks in the other. He had spent the last two hours attempting to produce a business plan for

Augy Romano. The pad was blank, the glass half empty. A cool breeze whisked past his face as he stared aloof at the iridescent wave caps. It was time to make a decision, he thought. *Pack up, leave, and hide for the rest of my life. Then what? I would never see Serena or Carlie again. If I turn myself in, I won't see them anyway. I couldn't ask her to go with me. Maybe I should just pay him and hope he doesn't come back.* He finished the drink, looked at the glass, and said quietly aloud, "Maybe I should just kill the bastard."

Chapter 26

The phone rang. "This better be good for two o'clock in the morning."

"Mr. Newman, is this Mr. Newman?" the voice trembled.

"Who is this? What do you want?"

"Mr. Newman, sir, you told me to call you if..."

"I never told anyone to call me at two in the morning! Who are you?"

"This is Craig at the yacht club, Mr. Newman. You better come down right away. There's been a fire."

***

His thoughts were terror-ridden. "No, no, God, no!" he continually repeated out loud.

"Oh my God! Look what I've done now."

The light turned red as he entered the intersection. The smell of burning rubber engulfed the air as he slammed on the brakes and slid half way across the street. *What the hell am I doing! There's no one out here in the middle of the night.* He jammed first gear and shot through the intersection. Jay didn't notice the police cruiser parked in the lot by the roller coaster. *Romano, Romano is the reason for all of this.*

"Oh God, please! No, no!"

As he raced past Quivira Basin, flashing lights filled his rear view mirror. *Screw him*, he thought. He pictured Carlie's smile and felt Serena's anguish. *If it weren't for me, none of this would have happened. Maybe she's right. Maybe we need to talk to Alis.*

It took Jay only sixteen minutes from his house to the yacht club gate. Under normal circumstances, it would take thirty to forty minutes. Convinced that Serena and Carlie had been hurt or maybe even killed, he was sobbing as the Porsche screeched to a stop next to the swimming pool. Smoke filled the night air as flashing red reflections bounced through the palm trees and into the fog. He flung open his door and was immediately restrained by a San Diego police officer. Two more patrol cars sped through the gate and screeched to a stop.

"Get down now!" an officer yelled.

Panicked, Jay tried to explain. "You don't understand."

"Get down on the ground. Get down." Jay began to kneel. His arms were raised above his head. The officer walked behind him and with his boot shoved Jay to the asphalt.

"Goddamn it!" shouted Jay. "That's my boat on fire down there. My family is on board. Call Alis Brooks. Tell him you have Jay Newman. He'll tell you who I am."

The officer stepped back and holstered his firearm. "You could have killed yourself or someone else back there. You were doing at least ninety on Mission Boulevard."

Jay stood up and realized the officer was backing down. "Then leave me a fuckin' ticket. I gotta go." He started toward the docks and turned to the officer. "Call Alis Brooks. Tell him to get down here. I desperately need to talk with him."

Jay ran over the grass to the back of the clubhouse where he spotted two Coast Guard fire boats. One was floating alone in the water, and the other sat adjacent to the burned-out hull of a forty-five-foot sailboat. A dozen onlookers, some employees, and some live-aboards stood by the guest dock watching the devastating event.

Craig intercepted him as he rushed toward the dock. "Mr. Newman, I'm sorry. I tried to call you back, but..."

"Where are they?" he shouted. Then he spotted Serena and Carlie running toward him.

"Mr. Newman, I didn't know you moved your boat."

Speechless and tearful, they clutched one another tightly. Then Serena looked into Jay's eyes. "I'm sorry, Jay. I shouldn't have just walked out."

"No, no!" Jay comforted her. "It's me. I'm sorry. I love you both so much..."

"Jay, we're in this together. We'll figure something out."

"I sent for Alis, it's time for me to face the truth."

***

It was dawn and too early for the dining room to be open. A large container of hot brewed coffee sat next to three dozen fresh donuts, the club's contribution to the early morning coffee clutches. Most of the spectators had left.

Carlie ate half of a jelly donut before she fell asleep in her chair. Jay and Serena sat silent, opposite of each other, holding hands on top of the round, white linen-covered table.

"This is the time of day to get here," said David as he approached. "At least I can find a place to park."

"What are you doing here?" asked Jay.

"It's all over the news. Heard it was at the San Diego Yacht club. I called you at home..."

"What the hell were *you* doing up in the middle of the night?" asked Jay. Then he said, "Never mind. I think I already know."

"I was worried. That's all. I..."

"Well, if it isn't the Newmans and their lawyer," chuckled Alis Brooks as he walked over to their table. "Jay, you gonna sue the police department because of the way you were treated last night?"

"Thanks for coming, Alis," said Serena as she scooted her chair closer to Carlie's.

"Is this a private meeting or something?" asked Brooks.

"No," said David. "I heard about the fire and thought I might be able to help or something. The guard told me that it wasn't their boat and that they were here in the dining room, so I decided to come in anyway."

"David," said Jay, "we're fine. Thanks for the concern. Go home. I'll try to call you later."

It was obvious that David began to feel out of place and uncomfortable. "Okay, then I'll talk to you guys later on."

David walked out onto the edge of the deck by the guest dock. A gentle breeze had swept away the early morning smoke. The sun's rays penetrated the horizon; gliding gulls crisscrossed the majestic masts. Leaning forward, he placed his hands on the rail and gazed over toward the channel that led to the slip of the burned-out boat. "Fuck!" he said aloud.

"Okay, I'm here as you requested," said Alis. "What do you need so desperately to tell me?"

***

"Andy, would you rub some lotion on my back?" Sam was lying flat on a large beach towel.

"Sure, I will. You trust me to do that?"

"More than you know!" she said, reaching for the lotion and handing it to him. Her trim, smooth body glowed in the warm sunlight. Andy couldn't believe he was massaging sun-tan lotion onto the back of this beautiful girl, a girl he had met by accident just days before.

Still lying flat, Sam reached with both hands, behind her back and unsnapped the top of her yellow bikini.

They spent Tuesday at the Cove, rambling through the waves, sun-bathing, and talking about their lives. Both felt an attachment to each other. To Andy it seemed as if they had so much in common. He felt secure with her. He told her about his job, his college, and his family. She shared some stories as well. He spoke freely about the gruesome deaths of his father and uncle. Andy's descriptions were crisp and brought life to the photographs of the crime scene, the photographs she had reviewed before she left for California. She listened pensively to every word of Andy's detailed accounting.

Maybe, she thought, *maybe he will remember something else. Maybe he will tell me why he is really here.*

"You know," he said pausing, his slippery palms resting on the sides of her waist, "I don't know about you, but I have never felt this way about anyone in my life."

God, she thought. *This can't be happening. I'm beginning to think the same way about him. He's the first honest, down-to-earth man I've ever known. Do I keep my secret, or do I tell him?*

As she began rolling over to sit up, she held the top of her bathing suit against her chest.

"Andy, there is something you need to know about me..."

***

While perusing his notes, the phone rang. "Brooks," he answered.

"Detective Brooks, this is Special Agent Lyons from the FBI. I need to meet with you."

"I've been waiting for your call, Agent Lyons."

Taken aback, she said, "You know me? You know what this is about and why I'm here?"

"Let's just say I have been briefed. Where do you want to meet?"

Chapter 27

"I wish that damn dog next door would just shut up once in a while," remarked Roberta. "How can you stand the noise? This is Tuesday. The fucking thing hasn't shut up since Sunday. In La Jolla we don't have neighbors with barking dogs."

"La Jolla, La Jolla, that's all you think about is La Jolla. They have just as many dogs in La Jolla as they do here."

Ignoring his remark, Roberta stood staring out at the pool. She picked up her vodka and took one more sip. Her short, thin silk robe hung loosely on her shapely body. Untied and open in front, she enjoyed exposing herself to the fresh breeze as it stimulated her skin. She reached in her pocket, pulled out her hairbrush, and began stroking her hair.

David continued, "I felt like a real asshole. I told you there was no reason for me to go down there this morning."

"David, I didn't tell you to have breakfast with them. You were just there to confirm."

"Confirm what, that they burned up in their boat?"

She turned toward him and said, "They weren't supposed to be there. It was only supposed to scare them, to make it known that we mean business."

"Well, we've left him little doubt now. I know he knows about us. I felt stupid. I'm a lawyer! I'm supposed to know how to act and what to say. Jesus, Roberta," he said, flustered, "this whole thing is insane."

"I don't care about La Jolla, as you may think I do. I care about you, just you and me together gone from here with enough money to live comfortably. What's wrong with that?"

David hesitated for a moment, then walked over to her. "There's nothing wrong with that."

Roberta stood in front of David and let her robe gently slide from her shoulders onto the floor. She ran her hands over her firm breasts and gently squeezed. She stared into his eyes as he watched her mouth slowly open and her soft tongue dampen her lips.

"Oh, Jesus" he whispered, "again."

Her fingertips slid behind the elastic waist of his boxers. She began to kneel to his erection. "I wanted to feel him get big."

"Well, he has a mind of his own. I guess he couldn't wait."

"I'll bet I could make him start over," she said.

"How?"

"First, you get rid of that *fucking* barking dog next door."

David's eyes rolled as he smirked, "There he goes. You were right."

She stood up, reached for his hand, and walked him toward the bedroom. "Come on," she smiled. "I know you like to do it my way."

David awoke an hour later. Roberta was sitting next to him with her knees pulled up against her chest. She was leaning forward toward her freshly painted red toenails. As she pulled the cotton balls from between her toes, she said, "David, my dear, I think it's time to call him and make our demand. I made you a drink. It's next to you on the stand."

He rolled over to the side of the bed and picked up his drink. Then propped his back up against a couple of pillows by the wall. "Ice is melted."

"Sorry," she shrugged. "You slept a long time."

"What time is it?"

"It's time for you to figure out how you are going to ask him for the money."

David took a sip of his cocktail, then nodded. "I guess it is, isn't it?"

Roberta leaned over and kissed him on the cheek. "I gotta go out. Are you going to work today, or not?" she crawled over his body and walked to the bathroom.

David wondered, *How come she never gets out of bed from the same side she gets into it?*

***

Alis Brooks' reading glasses sat low on his nose as he sat on the sofa next to his desk. He was reviewing the results of the inquiry on Augostino Romano.

Scotty poked his head in the door. "Jay Newman is here to see you, sir. Should I show him in?"

"Please."

"Sit down Jay. Make yourself comfortable."

"How am I supposed to make myself comfortable? Serena took your advice. They're gone. They went to her parents. I don't know for how long. Then you tell me to relax."

During his early meeting at the yacht club with Brooks, Jay spent a good part of the morning placing his life on the table, describing his childhood relationship with Augy Romano. He told Brooks about how the two of them spent summers fishing at the Chagrin River, how they spooked the dogs at the Hunt Club, and how his dreams were to someday live the life as a member of something like the Hunt Club. He portrayed Romano as always being the tough guy and how he was just along for the ride. He admitted taking part in some crimes. He wasn't ready to tell him about the murders, not yet anyway.

He told Brooks that Romano was in California to ruin his life by blackmailing him for all the bad things he had done as a child. Public disclosure of his childhood, from Romano, could ruin his image, his business, and his family.

"I know this is hard for you, Jay."

"Come on. The suspense is killing me."

"Okay, first of all, when was the last time you had contact with this guy Romano before he just happened to drop in on you?"

"I already told you at the yacht club. I can't remember exactly. It was years ago, maybe twenty or twenty-five. Why?"

"Well, your old high-school buddy seems to have quite a resume."

"What does that mean?"

"It means that you were right this morning. We're gonna have some serious problems with this guy."

Jay sat back in the chair. His forehead wrinkled as he began to wonder what Alis had discovered and what was in store for the next few days.

"Jay, I need to meet with you, later, alone. I'm working on a plan."

"What kind of plan? Why can't we discuss it here, now?"

Pausing, Alis shrugged and leaned back in his chair. "Okay, did you ever know somebody named The Grip?"

"No, who is, was The Grip?"

"I'm going to tell you a story about your friend. Then we can decide on a plan to stop all of the nonsense for good. You understand what I'm saying, Jay?"

"No, not really."

"Well, let's just say I know what the two of you did. I'm torn. There are two solutions to your problem."

"What are you talking about? What did we do? How do you know about any of this?'

"I can't disclose everything to you, but you need to follow my instructions and trust me. If you do that, you just might win the game."

"Do I have a choice?"

"No, not at this point. Here's what's going to happen, unless you fuck it up in some way."

For the next half hour Alis talked and Jay listened. Then Alis told Jay to go home and wait for Augy.

Jay walked over to Alis and reached to shake his hand.

"Thanks a lot, Brooks. You better know what you're doing."

Alis sensed bitterness in Jay's voice, retracted his hand, and replied, "What the hell is that supposed to mean?"

Jay held his finger out, pointing at Brooks. "If this isn't a hundred percent..." He stopped the threat. "You just better know what the fuck you're doing. That's all!"

Brooks sat and listened to Jay's ranting. Then, he said calmly, "Just remember. You need to befriend him."

Jay got up, looked at Alis, and said, "This is what I get for spilling the beans, huh?"

Alis's pencil wobbled back and forth between his thumb and forefinger. Contemplating before he spoke, he said, "What you'll get is your family back. Now go home." Jay walked out of the office and closed the door behind him.

Alis Brooks waited a few minutes, opened his briefcase, removed a coded phone number, and dialed.

"Zucky, this is Brooks. Get hold of Mac. I need to see him ASAP. No excuses."

O'Donnell and Brooks went back a long way. They had met in the Marines during Vietnam. O'Donnell always had a scam. He could get anything for anybody. It started with cigarettes, booze, pot, and women. Brooks, as part of a special Marine Corps investigative group, was always just one step away. Several times, Brooks thought he had him, but confiscated goods would disappear, and O'Donnell was able to manipulate his way out of the various predicaments. Brooks was convinced and had proof that O'Donnell was heavy into blackmailing. He didn't expose O'Donnell for fear that the ultimate punishment would impute the careers of specific high-ranking individuals. O'Donnell, on the other hand, thought he and Brooks had played cat and mouse for so long that they actually formed a bond, a "You help me, I'll help you" kind of bond, a twisted kind respect for each other.

Brooks rarely called upon O'Donnell. The only way he was able to contact him was through his ex-con associate, Berry Zuckerman. When Brooks met with Mac O'Donnell his questions were direct. He knew O'Donnell was into many unlawful occupations, but needed a quick refresher, from an expert, on blackmail.

***

Andy and Sam sat on a bench on the bluff above the Children's Pool, staring out into the ocean.

After the awakening at the coffee shop, when Andy discovered Finch and Augy were the two men he had spent most of his adult life searching for, he was envisioning his next move.

Sam sat silent. She knew she had to tell Andy why she was there. She had tried to tell him earlier but couldn't seem to find the right words. She knew he was in California to confront or get even with Jay Newman. Once Romano entered the picture, however, the events in Andy's past pieced together like an intricate puzzle. Because she was fairly new to the FBI, she was given this assignment to observe and to report what she found, but her liking for Andy had grown into a subjective sense of affection.

Andy's primary goal was to get even for the past. When he found out about Romano, he was put into a more difficult position. He planned the invasion of Jay's home and the consequences Newman would face, but he never envisioned Newman having a family, a little girl. He botched his first visit to Newman's house and was almost killed by some freak living under the deck. Barely slithering past being involved with the murders on the beach, he now recognized and acquiesced to the fact that he was not going to be able to do what he had set out to do, and that his original plan had turned into a frightening nightmare.

Sam slid close to Andy and placed her hand on his.

"You're awfully quiet," she said as she looked into his puzzled eyes. Subtle tears engulfed the bottom of his eyelids.

"Sam, there is something I have to tell you." He turned and looked at her quizzical expression.

"I know Andy," she said remorsefully, "and there's something I have to tell you."

***

Scotty was at his desk when Alis Brooks returned from his meeting with Mac O'Donnell.

"Got a minute, Boss?" asked Scotty.

"Sure. Why?"

Scotty stood and motioned toward Brooks' office. "I might have something."

The two men entered Brook's office. Scott closed the door as Alis removed his sport coat, rolled up his sleeves, and sat in his chair.

Brooks, appearing preoccupied, gently flipped through the pink phone messages on his desk. "Why pink?" he asked. "This is the fucking police department. Who orders these hideous pads, anyway?

"Sir," Scotty interrupted.

"Go on. I'm sorry." Brooks sat back in his chair. "What do you have?"

"I got a call from our homeless friend, Jeffrey."

"What's he want, more clothes, money, or a membership at the Beach and Tennis Club?"

Scott's eyebrows rose slightly, and his forehead curled. "Maybe this isn't a good time, sir."

"I'm sorry Scott. It's been a long day. Go on."

"It seems after I dropped off Jeffrey in La Jolla, he was sitting at the bus stop across from the Travelodge. He thinks he saw the guy who was under Newman's deck."

"The guy he wrestled with?"

"Yeah, he said he saw him walking out of the parking lot with a girl."

"What else did he say?"

"He said he thinks he saw the guy with the same girl the night before on Prospect. He said the guy gave him a twenty."

"What's your plan?" asked Brooks.

"I'm going to meet him later in the alley behind the old firehouse on Herschel."

"Don't be obvious. Wear some jeans or something. Sometimes I wonder if you wear your suit to bed."

Scotty stood to leave and chuckled. "I'm just trying to follow your example, sir."

"On your salary," joked Brooks, "you need to marry it."

"Yeah I know. Like I said, just trying to follow your example."

Brooks laughed aloud. He and Scott were extremely close. No one else would dare say a thing to Brooks about his affluent lifestyle, which was a result of his wife's fortune. He liked Scott and was priming him for his job as chief of detectives. "Go on. Get out of here. I've got work to do."

Chapter 28

The sun was about to set, and as usual the low tide allowed dozens of people to stroll past on the sand. Some turned and looked at the back of the mini-mansions, which bordered the beach. Young couples sat on rocks waiting for the chance to see the green flash, a rare phenomenon when the sun drops to the horizon. Soaring Gulls swept past in the refreshing salty breeze.

Jay sat, dressed in white shorts and a navy tee shirt. Both legs stretched out on the teak ottoman in front of his deck chair. Tan leather sandals hung loosely from his feet. He slowly turned the long narrow glass stem of his martini glass as it rested in his lap. A diluted mixture of gin and ice sat melting in a small pitcher on the side table next to him. The first two drinks went down quickly and relaxed him. The third and fourth took a little longer and brought him to a somewhat moderate state of intoxication, barely dozing off.

He squinted as a teary mist filled his eyes. His thoughts wandered. *She's gone. I'm such an asshole. Why did I do this to her? What am I supposed to do now?* He pictured her walking the sandy beaches of Fiji, Hawaii, and Tahiti. His eyes closed. He saw her running playfully on the soft warm sand at Little Dicks Bay in the Virgin Islands. Her golden hair, her smile. Their private moments together. He saw Carlie. Her smile and blue eyes mirrored her mother's. He remembered her birth, her first step, and the first time she said Daddy.

Suddenly, the martini glass fell from his lap to the deck and broke. Distracted by the noise, he quickly rose and picked up the broken pieces, setting them carefully on the table. The base at the end of the thin glass stem had severed.

The sun was about to set when Martha walked out onto the deck. "Señor Jay, there is someone here to see you."

Jay sat upright blinking his eyes a few times attempting to focus on Martha. "Who is it?"

"He says his name is August, like the month. He said you are to be expecting him."

Jay stood and shook his head. He couldn't stop the house from turning. His heartbeat increased, and his chest began to ache. Holding onto the back of the chair, he wondered if he was having a heart attack. Then he said to himself, *What the hell is he doing here?* "Okay, Martha I'll take care of it. Tell him I'll be right there." She watched as he began to stagger.

"You are okay, Señor?" she asked as she moved closer to him.

"Yeah, yeah, I'm fine. Just go tell him to wait."

Jay grabbed the edges of the sliding door frame to stabilize himself. Light-headed, he gazed into the kitchen and saw Augy's mother, wearing her red checkered apron smiling and stirring something in a giant pot. Then he saw Augy, standing next to her, in a white tee shirt. The word Mayfield was stenciled across his chest in forest-green letters. Jay squinted his eyes as he leaned closer to her image. "Hey, Finch," she said, "You wanna stay for a some supper?" He watched as Augy nodded his head and motioned thumbs up, encouraging him to stay. "You go aska your mother if it's okay."

Jay shook his head. His sight was blurred. He stared back into the kitchen, attempting to focus on something. *Whoa*, he thought, *this isn't really happening.* Then he saw her again holding Augy by the neck with one hand and threatening to whack him with a long wooden spoon drenched with spaghetti sauce. "You two troublemakers are gonna be in jail together some day."

He watched himself respond to her. *No, no, it's not me. It's gonna be Augy. I didn't do anything."* Augy twisted away from her grip. *"Hey, Ma. I ain't goin to jail. Why you sayin' that? Come on, Finch. We don't have ta listen to this shit."*

Jay walked through the kitchen and down the hall to the entry expecting to see Romano waiting for him. *Where is he?* Then he noticed the door to the garage was ajar. He stood next to the door for a moment, wondering what to expect. *What the fuck is he doing in my garage?* He swung the door open and stepped inside the lighted garage.

"Hey, Augy, you in here?" Jay noticed the cover of the TR-3 was thrown onto the wood floor.

"Hey, how ya doin' Finchy, ah, sorry, Jay?"

Romano was sitting in the leather seat with his hands wrapped around the classic steering wheel. "Just thought I would take a closer look at *our* little shit car."

The side effects of Jay's alcohol consumption were rapidly wearing off. Jay wiped perspiration from his forehead, walked toward the car, and tried to gather his thoughts,

"What are you doing here? How did you know I still have *my*, not *our* car?"

"I seen it the other day, when I drove by. The garage door was open and some little spic was workin' out there."

"Jaime lives here. He's not a spic, and the car is always covered. How did you know it was there?"

Augy laughed. "The little guy's name is really Hymie? Ha, I can't believe it. A spic with a Jew name."

"Answer me, Augy. What are you doing here, and how did you know the car was here?"

He ducked his head, twisted, and slowly turned to pry himself out of the car. Romano was wearing black slacks and a partially buttoned black silk shirt. His gold chain and cross hung from his neck.

"You redone it, but it's still a shit car."

Jay couldn't help noticing how his shiny teeth matched his white shoes.

"Damn it, Augy, what are you doing here? What do you want?"

Romano, primping as he walked toward Jay, ran his hands through his hair. "You wanna know what I'm doin' here? Remember the fuckin' Hunt Club, Newbaum? I just wanna see how the other fuckin' half lives."

"What are you talking about?"

"I'm talking about you. That's what I am talkin' about." Romano stepped back. "You need a fuckin' breath mint or something. You reek like a skunk. Aren't you gonna offer me a drink or something?"

Stepping within a foot of Augy, Jay said, "Answer me! How the fuck did you know about the car?"

Augy realized Jay wasn't afraid of him. "Hey, calm down, Finch."

"Don't call me Finch. That was somebody else, a long time ago."

"Yeah, well, guess what. People don't change. You might think they do, but they don't. You know how some people were assholes in high school? Well, I'm here to tell you that they are still assholes when they are older. I remember you as Finch, the Finch which was my buddy, the Finch who woulda been probably had the shit kicked outta him a hundred times if it wasn't for me. You don't remember that, huh?"

"Yeah, I remember that. We were kids. We're not kids any more. Why did you come back here? You want money? OK, I am working on that. You're just here to blackmail me, right?"

Romano starred into Jay's eyes, and raised his hands, palms out, as if he were fending him off.

"What do ya mean, you are workin' on that? That was just something I brought up at lunch. It wasn't a for sure thing!"

Jay was pissed. "Well, motherfucker, I can't be blackmailed. My wife knows all about us."

"What do you mean, she knows all about us? Not everything, right?"

"About the shooting. I told her everything. I've got nothing to hide any more. Then she left. She took our kid and left."

"Whadda you mean, she left? Where'd she go?"

"She's gone, you bastard, so your little fucking plan isn't going to work. Nothing means more to me then the two of them."

"Hey Jakey," Augy motioned with his hands. "Take it easy, ya know. It's no big deal. All I want is a few bucks, a little start for my business."

"Well, let me tell you something, dick head, I know all about you, all about prison. Your metal-shop business was stamping out license plates. I know you've been a real shit in society, all your life."

Augy squinted, reached out, and grabbed Jay's shoulders. He squeezed and gritted his teeth. Jay felt the pressure of the strong grip.

"Listen," Romano said firmly. "I don't give a fuck that you know about me. I don't give a fuck that you told your pretty little pussy wife."

Jay became furious. He reached up through Augy's arms and clasped his hands on Romano's throat. "You fuckin' animal!"

They twisted and pushed each other over the hood of the Triumph. Both men groaned and grunted like dogs as they wrestled to the floor. Augy cut his lip on the bumper's edge.

"Don't fuck with me Jakey," he said as bloody saliva dripped from the side of his mouth. His strong hands shoved and pushed and held Jay's head against the sidewall of the Michelin.

Jay looked up at him through blurry eyes. He tried to talk, but Augy's grip tightened. "Listen, you asshole. Two hundred and fifty grand. That's not a lot of money for you. That's all I want." Augy hesitated for a minute, wondering if there was something else he could use. "That's it. The money... and the shit car."

The cold steel barrel of the shotgun touched the back of Augy's neck. "Señor, Mes," Jaime said. "I think maybe it is a good thing if you don't make me pull the trigger, no?"

Jaime backed away keeping his aim just below Romano's shoulder blades.

Romano loosened his grip on Jay's head. Then he slowly put his hands up as if he were being arrested. "I'm not afraid of you, you little spic."

"Señor, how you say? I will be very pleased to blow your fucking *cabeza* off unless you get up now."

Augy immediately responded by easing himself off of Jay. Jay raised himself to a sitting position and held the sides of his head. Blood dripped from his right ear. Augy turned slowly to face Jaime.

"Señor, I beg you do not move, or I will have to shoot you."

Augy looked at Jay sitting on the garage floor. "Is this guy for real?"

"Is it worth your life to find out?"

"Now what?" Augy asked.

Jaime looked to Jay for an answer. Jay reached into his back pocket for his handkerchief. Then he placed it against his ear. "You know, asshole, if you would have just come to me like an old friend, like a man, I would have given you a chance, not because of what we did but because of friendship, because I used to think of you often, where you were, what happened to you and your family. You could have leveled with me about hard times, about prison."

He stood and looked into Augy's eyes, waiting for a response.

"Finch, I mean Jake, or Jay. Hey, I never knew what happened to you, neither. I always felt bad that I was inside and you were out in the world someplace." He turned his head slowly toward Jaime. "Can I put my hands down now?"

Jay nodded and Jaime stepped back with the gun still pointed at Romano.

"All you had to do was come to me."

"Jake, Jay, I didn't think you would want me around and all, you know, the things that happened and..."

Jay said, "You're right. Now that I know you, I don't want you around."

"How much did you really tell your wife? I mean, did you tell her about…"

"Jaime, it's okay now," he interrupted. "You go back into the house. On *reserva*, stand by, but out of sight. I'm not sure I can trust him. *Gracias, mi amigo.*"

Jaime lowered the shotgun and backed out of the garage. When the door closed, Augy said, "That's one hell of a sad lookin' bodyguard."

Jay ran his hands through his hair, "You trying to tell me you weren't worried?"

"I guess you got a point there."

"Listen to me, Augy. I am a respectable citizen. I'm not who I was. A long time passed since we were kids. I have a life, a family, and a business. I don't want anything to ruin that. Do you understand?"

"Yeah I know, but you were always the lucky one. You were always smart, too."

Jay walked toward the door. "Come on, let's get out of the garage. You want something to drink?"

Following Jay down the hall to the kitchen Augy asked, "You got any beer?"

They paused in the kitchen as Romano stared in awe. "This place looks like a kitchen in a restaurant." Augy slid his hand over the shiny counter top. "Is this marble?"

"No, it's granite. Beer should be in the refrigerator. Help yourself, and come out onto the deck."

Augy turned and faced the stainless steel wall behind him. *Four giant stainless steel doors to choose from. Eenie, meeney, miney, and moe. Which one is the refer? Okay, moe, don't disappoint me.*

The giant door opened, and Augy stared at packed shelves of frozen foods. He opened the next door and saw the same thing. Then he looked out toward the deck where Jay stood watching him through the window. Jay motioned with his finger for him to open the last door. *Do I feel stupid or what? It better be in here.*

"I've never seen anything like that in my life," he said as he walked out through the door holding his beer in one hand and reaching into his pocket for his cigarettes.

"We don't smoke. Don't light that cigarette. Have a seat."

Puzzled, Augy asked, "How do you drink without having a cigarette?"

"We just don't smoke, that's all. End of subject."

Dissatisfied, Augy placed his cigarettes back into his pocket.

"So tell me, now that you're here. What am I supposed to do with you?"

"What do you mean? What are *you* supposed to do with me? I just came out to see you, to visit. That's all."

"Demanding money is just coming out to see me? That's a hell of a reason for a visit, don't you think?"

"I'm sorry I came on so strong. I didn't think..."

Jay reached over and picked up the stem of the broken martini glass. He spun it in his fingers, then pointed the sharp tip toward Augy's face. "That's right. You don't think. You never did. Just remember one thing. I'm the last person you ever want to fuck with."

Augy sat rigid as he tried to hide being nervous. He stared into Jay's eyes. "What's that supposed to mean? Am I supposed to be afraid of you, because you're rich and I'm not?"

"It's not me you should fear."

As Augy swiftly reached for the glass stem, Jay pulled away, cutting Augy's wrist.

Augy blurted, "Ow! Goddamn it. That hurt."

"Here, asshole," Jay said as he handed him his bloody handkerchief. "It's just a small cut. You act like a baby."

Augy placed the handkerchief over his wound and applied pressure. "I can't stand the sight of blood, especially mine."

Remembering where the conversation left off, Augy went on, "Who then? If I'm not to fear you, then who? The cops? Don't forget, you got more to lose than me, man."

Jay said calmly but with a firm tone in his voice, "Let's just say I'm well connected, and believe me, *Augostino, you've* got more to lose than I do."

"Why are we gettin' into this?" Augy said, backing off. "I said I didn't think. I said I was sorry for comin' on like an asshole. I didn't know what to expect from you. Okay, sometimes ... I'm fuckin' sorry. You know, I lived a different life than you. I was always in some kind of trouble, even when we were kids. I was the one who got caught. I was the one who took the fall, so I'm not smart like you. Jesus Christ, how many times I gotta say I'm sorry? I just wanna be fuckin' friends."

Jay sat silent as Augy, gesturing with his hands, pleaded for a response. "When I first called you, you were just tryin' to get rid of me. I could tell by your voice. Then I seen you on TV and all...I thought you were some big ass hotshot. I figured there was no way you were gonna welcome me into your life and all, so I thought I would scare ya, get a few bucks, and disappear. I'm sorry!"

After a moment of silence, Jay stood and held out his hand. Augy looked at the curved scar between Jay's left thumb and forefinger. He glanced at the bloody handkerchief and his own scar, remembering when they had become blood brothers. Augy's grip was firm, reassuring himself that he had made amends for his actions.

Jay clasped his other hand around Augy's and said, "The Code, right?"

"Right," replied Augy. "I will always honor The Code." They both nodded. "So did you really tell your wife?"

Smiling, Jay said, "No, not really."

"I didn't think so."

"Just one question before you go, did you have anything to do with what went on here, on the beach the other night?"

Smiling back, Augy said, "No, not really."

Chapter 29

The unmarked brown detective cruiser slowly approached from the south. This was Scotty's forth pass in thirty minutes. The white Corvette seemed to have a pretentious personality of its own as it sat straddling two striped spaces in a tightly packed parking lot.

"Asshole," he said aloud as he pulled to a stop. *It's not even his car. What does he care if it gets scratched or dented? I hate people like that. He's got to be an asshole.*

He took his Mont Blanc from his shirt pocket, opened his note pad, and scribbled: 2 a.m., Wednesday, August sixteenth. Made several passes. Two backups on the way. He glanced up and saw a shadow pass through a dim back light in Romano's room. *He's probably gonna take a piss. I'd love to get him while he's...*

His thoughts were interrupted as two black and whites approached. The one from Pacific Beach pulled behind him and parked. The other was dispatched from La Jolla Shores and faced south as it paused at the curb across the street. Scott and the officer who parked behind him exited their vehicles and scurried across to the patrolman in the other cruiser. All three men stood on the sidewalk next to a giant bird of paradise, which blocked the view to the motel.

After a brief exchange of hellos, Scott advised the officers that he did not personally know the subject. He told them Alis Brooks wanted him in for questioning. He did warn them that Romano had done time in Ohio and that he was considered to be tough and unpredictable. "Just be alert," he said.

Both officers looked at each other, simultaneously readied their weapons, and accompanied Scott across the parking lot to the motel-room door.

Scott carefully gripped the door handle and felt resistance as he twisted. Then he knocked lightly on the door. "Mr. Romano, this is the desk manager," he said as he paused.

He could hear Romano moving inside the room. "What do you want? It's two o'clock in the fuckin' morning."

"I'm sorry, sir. It's just that your car is taking two..."

"Jesus Christ," Romano bickered as he swiftly opened the door. Both officers then swung through the door with their guns drawn and pointing. Romano quickly raised his hands, his car keys dangled from his fingertips.

He stood, wearing white boxers. His gold cross hung from its chain on the outside of his black sleeveless tee shirt. Multicolored and faded, the globe tattoo with the inscription USMC stretched across the bicep of his left arm. "Hold on, goddamn it. You got the wrong guy. I didn't do..."

"Mr. Romano, you're not under arrest. We need to bring you to the station for some questioning."

"Questioning, for what? Who the fuck do you think you...?"

Reaching for the keys, Scott said. "We know who we are and so do you. Get dressed," he commanded.

"If I'm not under arrest, then you can't take me anywhere."

Reminiscent of the last time he was arrested in Ohio, Romano recalled how the police broke down the door in his apartment. His head quickly filled with vivid pictures and horrific sounds, the same pictures and sounds that rewound and played over and over again while he was in prison. The sixteen-year-old was his captive. He watched her convulse as the police cut her free from the thin plastic wire ties that secured her nude body to the bed. Ear-piercing screeches and cries filled the room when they took the duct tape off her mouth.

"If you resist, then we will put you under arrest."

"For what? I'm on vacation. That's all. Is it a crime to be on vacation? Fuckin' California!"

"It all depends what you do or what you plan to do while you're on vacation."

"Can I at least put my pants on?"

"Hurry up."

With both hands still positioned over his head, Romano walked to the closet. "I didn't do anything, man!"

While dressing, Romano's feverish stare at Scott and the two gun-toting officers was overshadowed by his memories of how he had last been taken to jail. The police wrapped the girl in blankets. He was literally dragged through the snow, naked and bound by the police. Every time he looked at the scars on his legs, he remembered the razor-sharp gravel protruding from the ice, first gouging, then slicing and bloodying his legs and feet.

He put on white slacks and a black silk shirt. His bare feet slipped into a pair of black suede ankle-high boots. Having secured the laces, he then stood and repositioned his hands above his head.

"Listen, you little dick head," scoffed Romano. "You don't have the right to..."

Reaching under his suit jacket toward his back and bringing foreword his handcuffs, Scott replied, "I sense you're familiar with the process, huh?"

The officers continued to hold Romano at gunpoint while Scott pulled one of Romano's hands downward and placed the metal cuff onto his wrist. Routinely, Romano slowly dropped and folded the other behind his back.

Scott held the car keys in his fist in front of Augy's face. "Who's the dick head now?"

The officers led Romano out of the room. Scotty followed, and when he reached the Corvette he called out to get Romano's attention. "Hey, dick head!"

Romano turned his head to observe as Scotty first flashed the car key in the air. Then he watched as he deliberately placed the tip of the key on the hood and began walking around the Corvette etching a deep scratch into the finish. "One parking spot, asshole! You don't need more than one spot."

***

The fifteen-minute drive to the Northern Division of the San Diego Police Department was uneventful as Romano sat silently in the back seat of the squad car observing clusters of well lighted, upscale condominiums and apartment complexes. As the cruiser turned off of Regents Road, he noticed a long, single-story, contemporary concrete and stucco building. Beams from floodlights illuminated the sandblasted placard, which read The Jacob and Serena Newman Community Center. *And he said he didn't have any money.*

With cuffs removed, Romano sat, expressionless, at the end of a long gray metal table in the interrogation room. He knew he was being observed through the two-way mirror in front of him. *Assholes! What do they think I'm going to say to the California cops! A bunch a sun-baked surfers and hippies. That little detective is gonna pay dearly for what he did. I know they can't connect me to those two on the beach. I oughta toss them the finger in the mirror. Nope, I'm just not gonna say shit. A lawyer, that's it. I'll just tell 'em I want to see a lawyer, a female lawyer, one with a tan, a blonde, nice shape, about twenty-five to three years old, one that says 'like' a lot. Fuckin' Californians! The guys were right.*

"Mr. Romano, I'm Detective Brooks. You've already met my associate Scott here."

Alis retracted his handshake when Romano didn't respond. He gazed toward Scott for a second to see his reaction. Scott, standing in the corner, nodded. Then Brooks positioned himself in a seat across the table from Augy.

"You're probably wondering why we sent for you this evening."

He waited for an answer, but Romano sat silent, nervously squinting as he focused on Scott, smirking and leaning against the wall in the corner.

"You're not under arrest for anything. There is no reason not to talk to me. We just invited you in for a brief overview on how we do things here in San Diego."

No reaction!

Clasping his hands on the table and leaning forward, Alis said, "Mr. Romano, I'm trying my best to be nice to you. I would appreciate some cooperation."

After a brief pause, Augy said, "You didn't invite me here. Your fuckin' associate, as you call him, forced his way into my room, in the middle of the fuckin' night, handcuffed me, and brought me here. No one asked me shit. You make this sound like this was a fuckin' invitation, so don't pretend that you're some kind of party host or somethin'."

Scott approached, leaned toward Romano, and placed his palms on the table top next to him. "Mr. Romano, you need to be careful with your description of how we met. No one forced you to do anything until you started to smart-mouth with us."

"Fuck off, piss ant. You barged in on me, remember?"

Still leaning, Scott said, "This is exactly what I'm talking about."

Brooks sat back in his chair and folded his arms. "Okay! Enough is enough. There's obviously a personality conflict between you two."

Scott appeared agitated as he stood and walked behind Romano. Then he leaned over and whispered in his ear. "Don't fuck with me, scumbag!"

Augy stretched his arms out across the table, fists tightly clinched. "Better get your *associate* out of here, before I do something I might regret."

Brooks motioned to Scotty. "Go on, take a break."

Romano's sneer riled Scott as he left the room.

"Cigarette?" Brooks offered.

"Thanks."

"Hey, I'm really sorry about Scott. He's a young detective and all. He's just trying too hard."

Exhaling, Augy said, "You don't need to play this good cop, bad cop shit with me. I've been around, man. What do you want with me?"

"I'll get to the point, Augy. Do you mind if I call you Augy?"

"What do you want, man? I haven't done anything wrong. I just came to San Diego on a vacation. If I gotta call you Detective Rooks or Brooks or whatever, then you can address me with respect and call me Mr. Romano. We're not relatives or buddies."

"Okay, I know you're just visiting. I also know about your past. I know about the Marine Corps. I know you are an ex-con. I know where you did time and why you did it. I just don't want any repeats here, if you know what I mean."

"My past is history. I did the time. I'm just visiting."

He stood, walked over toward Augy, and slid into the chair next to him. "I don't want any problems while you're here. Jay Newman is a personal friend of mine."

Staring into his eyes, Augy said, "So that's what this is about. Newman is a friend of mine as well, and I've known him a lot longer than you. I know him a lot better then you, too. Did he ask you to bring me in here?"

"No! In fact, he has no idea that your here with me."

"What did Newman say about me? I'm just an old friend from high school. We grew up together. I was coming to California on vacation, and I knew he was here. I just looked him up for old time's sake."

"Mr. Newman, or Jay, as we both know him, is just concerned."

"Concerned about what, that I know too much about him? Well, I do know about him, a lot about him. That's our business, between me and him, not you, unless you know what I know, but I doubt it."

"Augy, ah, Mr. Romano, he's a good friend. I don't want to see him hurt, not in any way. I know a lot more than I should, and I'll do just about anything to protect him. Do you understand that?"

Augy's face tensed as he rubbed his chin. "Yeah, I understand."

Brooks sat back in his chair. "That's it. Oh, one more thing. Did you have anything to do with the murders on the beach last Friday night, early Saturday morning, the ones near Jay Newman's house?"

"I don't know anything about any murders, anywhere."

"Can you remember where you were exactly?"

"Yeah, I was probably asleep in my room."

"Well, then, that's all I have. I said what I wanted to say."

Romano's left leg moved nervously up and down, as he sat pensively staring at the mirror in front of him. Confused, he asked, "You sure this was your idea and not his?"

"That's what I said."

"Hah," he grunted, wondering if Jay did in fact tell everything.

"I assume we understand each other, right?"

"I think so."

Brooks stood. "Well, Mr. Romano, sorry for the inconvenience. You'll be able to go in a few minutes. I'll find an officer who will take you back to your motel."

Augy rose from the chair. "Yeah, thanks."

Just as Alis was about to leave the room, he turned and asked, "Oh, yeah, when do you think it will be over--your vacation? Do you know when you might be leaving? I'm a little curious why you only bought a one-way ticket to San Diego. I'd be happy to pay for your return flight if you want me to."

Staring at the mirror, Augy said, "I don't need your help! I'll be leaving when I'm ready." Hesitating for a moment, he went on, "Soon, I guess, pretty soon."

Alis nodded, expressing his approval. "That's all I have. Enjoy the rest of your holiday." Brooks closed the door. He entered the adjacent observation room. Scott was leaning against the wall scrutinizing Augy through the mirror. "So what do you think?" asked Alis.

Scott unfolded his arms, unbuttoned his cuffs, and rolled up his sleeves. Placing his hands in his pockets, he began to slowly pace the room. "The guy's a real creep, a sleazy creep."

"That he is my boy, that he is."

"Tell me, boss. Did you ever wonder about something, or someone from your past coming back to haunt you?"

"Haunt me? What do you mean by haunt me?"

"Well, you know what I mean, someone from your past, an earlier time of your life."

Scott motioned toward Romano smoking in the next room. "Someone weird, like this guy, you know, the weird kid in high school, or a perp from 20 years ago, someone you would least likely expect to show up at your doorstep."

"Don't dwell on this guy, Scott. He's just another charming member of society."

"Charming, right! Boss, you definitely have a way with words. You refer to him as charming, and I call him fucked. You say Mr. Romano is a charming individual. I say Mr. Romano is a genuine fucked psychotic, preying on society."

Alis patiently listened to Scott carry on. "So what exactly does this guy have on Jay Newman? Why is he here? What do you know that I don't know? Does Newman have something to hide? It sure sounds like you both know something I should know."

The conversation was interrupted as they watched an officer enter the interrogation room.

"Ready when you are, Mr. Romano." Augy eyed his half-smoked cigarette and glanced at the ashtray on the table. Then he grinned at the two-way mirror and dropped the butt on the floor. He smothered it with the sole of his boot as he stepped toward the door. The officer looked at the mirror, shook his head in disgust, then leaned over, picked up the butt, and put it in the ashtray. He followed Romano out the door. "Okay, Alis, what do you call that?"

"And you're the one with a Master's in psychology," Alis said. "Don't be so gruff?"

"Gruff," he responded. "There's another one of your personality descriptions."

Brooks grinned, then glanced at his wristwatch. "You're going to miss your plane."

"Oh, shit, you're right. Is this Wednesday already? I almost forgot. The plane leaves at 6:30." Scott moved expeditiously toward the door. "Good thing I only live a few blocks from here. I've got little more than two hours to clean up, pack, and get to the airport. Maybe I'll nap on the plane. I'll tell you, I'm not looking forward to a week of forensics in the windy city."

Chapter 30

Gulls soared overhead while steam rose from his coffee cup. Jay stood barefoot on his deck watching the early morning surfers paddle out to catch a wave. His loosely tied black silk robe puffed in the gentle breeze. While sipping, his thoughts turned toward his ten o'clock meeting with Mac O'Donnell. He always knew O'Donnell was well connected, but two million dollars was a lot of money. He wondered if the money was O'Donnell's or if it was from the Mafia. Maybe it's drug money. He pictured transients standing on street corners and in alleys transacting deals, shooting up, and sniffing white powder. How does someone raise that kind of money so quickly? He knew he could repay Mack. He had a good portion of that packed in a worn leather suitcase sitting in his den. The rest, he knew, could be accessed from his hidden stash outside of the country, but that would take a while to get.

As usual, Mac was already waiting for Jay when he arrived at the fountain in Balboa Park. Rainbow-colored rays penetrated through the fine mist surrounding the fountain.

"Morning, morning, Newman," said Mac as he stood from the bench to shake his hand.

Jay acknowledged the handshake and both men sat facing the spouting geyser-like fountain.

"You bring the money?" Jay asked as he glanced at the shabby buckskin carrycase sitting next to Mac.

"It's, it's right here. You sure you want to do this?" asked Mac in a tone that would allow Jay to retract his request.

"Yeah, I'm sure. I thought about it for a long time."

Mac gestured with open hands. "Okay, it's yours. But it's not all here. My investor needs you to contribute to the fund."

"What does that mean?"

"It just means you need to contribute half of the money. Where you get it from is your business. You probably have that much in a hidden stash somewhere. You need to suffer a little setback as well."

"Where am I supposed to get a million bucks?"

"We both know you're not as dumb as you'd like us to think. You know how to raise the cash. Yours or not, you know what I mean?"

Jay sat and listened carefully as Mac placed the burden of the additional cash outlay on him. No way was he going to use his money or stash as Mac called it. He had other plans for that money.

"That's it, huh? No strings? How do you know I won't pay you back? How do you know I'm not going to just take the money and disappear?"

"I'm not worried about that, Newman. But just in case, my investor has requested you sign a small promissory note."

Jay looked pensively into Mac's sunglasses. "What kind of note? You didn't tell me about any note."

"Just, just a precaution." The one-eyed bandit reached into his pocket for a pen. Pointing, he said, "Open, open the top flap and take out the agreement."

Jay pulled an envelope from the backpack, unfolded the document inside, and began to read it. After a moment of silence, he said. "Who is the ABMO partnership? You don't know the first thing about the clothing business."

"You're right, Newman, and we don't want to, either, or is it neither? All's we want is for you to know you got something to lose if you, well, if you, you know, can't pay us back."

"You didn't tell me this before. I thought..."

"You thought, you thought, what did you think? This kind of fuckin' money doesn't fall off a goddamn plastic manikin. Jesus Christ! You, you want it or not? You, you don't have to take it, you know!"

He leaned back, resting on the bench, and wrapped his hands around the back of his head. Squinting pensively into the foggy mist, Jay's confidence heightened. With elbows raised, spread, and motionless, he resembled an osprey ready to attack. He had plans for all three of them—Romano, Bobbie, and David. "Give me the pen. I'll take the money."

***

Jay drove home and immediately went down to his den. He sat with his pad of paper and started to reconstruct the outline of his business plan. Sitting with $1,750,000 at his side was only the beginning of the scheme. He needed to raise another million dollars. That would give him enough to pay off David, Bobbie, and Augy. He had plans for the remaining $500,000.

The step-by-step execution provided multiple consequences. The crucial outcome was to rid himself of Bobby, David, and Romano. He had no one to trust but himself. He knew he could get Romano to do anything he wanted.

Chapter 31

Jay spent much of Wednesday in the Copley Press Library, reviewing articles on trust deed scams. Bits and pieces from various sources educated him. Carl had discussed and outlined the scam in the Coffee Shop several times. The goal was to get a loan on a house that wasn't his.

He learned who the local hard-money lenders were, who did business in La Jolla, their greedy tactics, and the way they preyed on wealthy homeowners who needed confidential financial help for one reason or another, help they couldn't reveal much about or get from a bank. Many were rich guys who needed to keep up with flamboyant and extravagant life-styles, and others were the quiet, old-money, reserved blue-bloods whose assets were dwindling.

Many hard-money guys secretly hoped for a default by their borrowers. This way they either moved into the properties or just sold them off for a profit. Loan amounts never exceeded fifty percent of the value. The loans had lofty interest rates, excessive usurious costs, and were never written for more than two years. As the months passed, all due and payable clauses became a threatening reality that life-styles were about to drastically change.

Jay had the keys to the house next door. Dominic Ferruccio, the Italian mobster, was away in jail again for two more months. He was sure he could pull off his scheme and cautiously planned the caper.

He met with Augy and decided that he would give him a chance to prove his loyalty, which he continuously spoke of when they were together. He believed, if he made it worthwhile, he could trust his old friend, at least one more time.

In theory, the plan was going to be easy, simple, and quick. Augy would pose as Jay's neighbor. After all, he thought, they looked alike. Nobody in La Jolla really knew Dominic Ferruccio. They heard about him once in a while, but Dom was a recluse when he was in town.

Jay researched public records and discovered that Dominic owed no money on his beachfront estate. It was assessed at $3,000,000, and a loan of a million five would be very attractive to the leeches. Worst consequence, they would cut the loan to a half a million bucks.

Augy listened and liked the plan. His cut would be $250,000 if he could pull this off and memorize the tutorial Jay made for him. Jay soon arranged an expensive "no questions asked" meeting with Mac, producing proper IDs for his friend.

Chapter 32

Andy pushed the drapes open and stood with his right foot resting on the top of the heating and air-conditioning unit built into the wall in his motel room. He stared over the parking lot toward the Union Bank building a block away where he watched two people, bundled together in heavy clothing, resting on the bench at the bus stop. Their shopping carts were undoubtedly full of treasures. "I wonder if they're married," he whispered aloud.

Both eyes opened slowly as she turned onto her side readjusting her head on the soft pillow. Content, Samantha admired Andy's physique. His newly acquired reddish tint was quickly turning bronze and was accentuated by his white boxer shorts.

"If who is married?" she said, resting her head on her palm.

Startled, he turned and walked toward the bed. "No one. I was just staring out at some street people, homeless people, whatever they're called, sitting over there on a bench."

"Why did you wonder if they were married?

"They look as if they are oblivious to everything, life, work, kids, house payments. Two shopping carts full of trash, junk, but to them, probably worth everything. I wonder if they were together before, before they were forced—or maybe they weren't forced—to go out on the street. Maybe they met out there, found each other, you know? Maybe they just…" He paused, sat on the side of the bed, and leaned toward her. "Maybe they just trust each other. What do you think of that concept, trusting each other?"

Looking deep into his eyes, she started to tear. "I trust you, Andy."

He ran his palm gently across her soft, moist cheek. "I know you do, but why? You don't really know me."

Reaching out and clasping his hand, she said, "I do know you, Andy. I know you better than you think I do. Andy, it's me. I'm the one who shouldn't be trusted."

Guardedly, he pulled his hand away from hers. "I don't understand." He stood, slipping on his clothes. "What do you mean by that?"

Keeping her chest covered as she pulled the sheet with her, she rose to a sitting position. "Andy, I'm not..."

"You're not what? You're not on vacation? Not..."

"Andy, I know why you're here!"

"You know who I am? Why I'm here? Well, who the hell are you? A cop or something?"

Hesitating, she said, "Yes, I am! I'm with the FBI."

Andy froze.

"I was the reason your plane was delayed in Dallas. I was the last person to board the flight. I was sent here to watch you, to see what you know. I didn't expect to..."

"To what? You didn't expect to what? Stalk me, deceive me?"

"No! To fall in love with you."

Pacing at the side of the bed, he blurted out, "That's bullshit! I don't believe you. I don't even know who you really are. What's your real name? What do you mean, to see what I really know?"

Shamefully, Sam said, "You already know my real name. Andy, I'm sorry I lied to you. I didn't mean to deceive you. I didn't expect to fall in love with you, either. I was sent to investigate the murders of your father and uncle, the discovery of this guy Finch. Jay Newman is the first real break in the case. I followed you here to observe and report back to my office. The FBI seldom gets involved in cases like this, but an exception was made because of your constant, or I should say, your persistence with the Chardon, Ohio, authorities.

Andy stood staring at her as she slipped into her clothes. Standing and stepping closer to him, Sam said, "The Chardon police department notified the FBI after you left their office. I was assigned to the case. This is actually my first case. I was just promoted to field status three weeks ago."

"You lied to me!"

"Yes, and you lied to me, and because of your encounter in the coffee shop, I now know the connection with his old friend, Augy Romano. Now I want to help."

Andy stood weak and held out his hands toward Sam.

She stepped closer and put her arms around him, hugging firmly. "Let me help. We can do this together. Andy, I really care."

Pulling back, he stood for a moment, turned, and walked to the door. He opened it and said, "I have to go out for a while. You're the first woman..."

Sternly, she walked to the door, reached around him and closed it. "No, you don't have to go out for a while! Listen to me." He walked to the table and sat down. "And now, because of you, I have reasons for getting even with his friend Romano as well as Jay Newman." A musing silence filled the air.

Then he spread his arms over the tabletop, palms down, and stared into her eyes. "What are you talking about?"

Sam had taken control. Andy wasn't happy that she deceived him, but was content to allow her to proceed. She called her supervisor at Quantico and requested further information on one Augostino Romano from Ohio.

Within hours, she learned of his prison time, his tendency to do great harm to women, and the fact that he could, if provoked, be extremely dangerous. Her supervisor said he would contact the San Diego regional office and make them aware of her presence. She was instructed to call the Special Agent in charge and that he would take the lead from there.

Sam felt disillusioned, as if her case was being taken from under her. She had heard about the "brass" taking cases and then taking credit for all of the work field agents did. This did not sit well with her. She had promised Andy that all would be resolved, that Romano and Newman would pay the ultimate price for what they had done, and the right way, the only way, to "get even" would be to go through the proper channels.

After requesting information on Augostino Romano, she was being reduced to the ranks, in a way. She was beginning to have second thoughts. *So he's a dangerous guy, I graduated first in my class. I have a black belt in karate, and I'm a taekwondo instructor. Do they really think I can't take of myself?*

***

Andy sat on the wall by the La Jolla Museum of Modern Art as Sam made her way to meet him. She carried a brown bag with two sandwiches and two diet sodas.

"Well Andy, I made the call."

Reaching for his sandwich, Andy asked, "What did they say? What are they going to do now? What's the plan?"

"Hold on a minute. You want tuna or egg salad?"

"I don't care. I just want to know what they are going to do now. You get any chips?"

"We don't need chips."

"How do you eat a sandwich without chips?"

"They just said to stand by. There has to be some internal protocol to get the ball rolling. They will contact me when it's time."

Anxiously, he said, "Time, time! Jesus, Sam, it's time already!"

"Eat your sandwich. I have some ideas I'm working on. It's time to eat your lunch."

"What kind of ideas? What does that mean?"

Chapter 33

George Lowe was an old Jew from New Jersey, the owner of the company. He made his money by taking investors' money, mostly from doctors, promising them huge interest and secure payments.

This was not a Ponzie scheme. On occasion George had to borrow money from the investment pot to make these payments, something like from Peter to Paul, but in those cases from Dr. Schwartz to Dr. Goldberg.

George had made a fortune lending on and reselling homes throughout the Alpine and Saddle River communities. These communities were about thirty-five minutes apart and continually supplied him with the inventory he needed for his business returns.

He had sold the company three years ago and moved from New Jersey to La Jolla, where his son was a physician. After six months of retirement George essentially got bored.

His son knew how he was able to provide good returns on investments back east and convinced his father to open a company in La Jolla. Lowe had had no trouble finding investors, as his son introduced him to other physicians. Soon a private lending factory was born. The idea was to use money from doctors' retirement funds, invest it wisely in real estate, and promise high returns to his investors and himself, just as he had done in New Jersey.

This was part of the scam Carl had talked about in the coffee shop. The hard-money guys used money from mostly rich investors. Some were not reporting taxes on the gains they made from the loans, but that was their problem. Lowe was on the up and up.

***

On Thursday, Jay and Augy went over the plan dozens of times. He walked Augy through the house next door tutoring him as to possible answers to questions that might be asked by George Lowe. Jay removed photos of Dominic and other personal items from view.

He took photos of Augy and had a local photo finisher superimpose Augy into several ornate, expensive picture frames, which he carefully placed throughout the home. It was amazing how much the two resembled each other. The new Dominic and the real Dominic became one.

Jay told Augy not to say much. He told Augy not to tell them what he needed the money for, just to act comfortable and pretend he was in his own house. He told Augy to press the urgency of the transaction. A tour of the garage would highlight a black Ferrari, a Cadillac limousine, and other toys. The home tour needed to be as short and quick as possible.

Once Jay was satisfied with Augy's tutorial and the planned caper, he had Augy initiate a call to La Jolla Financial Express.

***

Augy invited George to his home. Within hours his Mercedes pulled up to Casa Ferruccio. Lowe had first checked and assured himself that the home was free and clear of any encumbrances. He couldn't find out anything about Dominic locally so he made a phone call to a friend in Vegas who was familiar both with the Jewish mafia and the Italian mafia.

Dominic, as it turned out, was a highly respected member of the Pascal family from Beverly Hills. His contact said he would forward a complete report on the Pascal family and Dominic in a few days. George was now eager to discuss Dominic's request.

George and his young protégé, Michael, buzzed at the gate, which Augy opened. Michael was holding a bulky camcorder and a 35 mm. Nikon camera hung from a strap from around his neck. Both George and Michael were dressed alike, navy-blue khaki slacks, loafers, and blue dress shirts. "Hello, Mr. Ferruccio. I am George Lowe and this is…"

During the tour, the camera was filming continuously; dozens of photos were taken.

As expected, George did ask why Dominic needed the money, and Augy replied that it was for personal reasons.

When they entered the garage, Michael started to ask questions about the Ferrari.

Augy, puzzled because he didn't know anything about the car, said that it belonged to his brother and he was storing it for him while he was away on business.

George knew of Dominic and his ties to the Mafia. He knew that Dominic was not someone to fool with, and he was careful asking personal questions.

Gesturing, Augy said, "Gentlemen, let's go inside and sit. We can discuss this more casually in the house."

Once seated, George began, "You are aware that this is going to be an up and up transaction, Mr. Ferruccio?"

"I understand that," replied Augy in a slight bullying Italian accent. "You understand that I cannot have anyone know about this? I can pay you back in less than six a months." He was losing his level of confidence as he began to squirm in his chair. *Be the one in charge. That's what Jay told me. Don't let them talk down to you. It's your house, not theirs.*

"You know, Mr. Ferruccio, that we record a trust deed with the County assessor's office, and the deed is public information." Augy nodded, not really understanding what he was talking about. "We don't care if you pay us back or not. If you default, you lose. You become history, and the home becomes ours. We will own it. We can keep it or sell it. It doesn't matter. I know you are well connected, but as far as this transaction goes your friends or you can't do anything about it. This is a legal debt, and there are consequences for not abiding with the terms of the loan."

"Listen, you gentlemen seem really able to help me out. But you need to understand that there are others, family members, who would jump at the opportunity to lend me this money. I just want to keep them out of this. You understand? I only need a million and a half bucks. That's not a lot of money in my circle of friends and family. I asked you here to allow you the privilege of accommodating my request because you have a reputation of funding quickly." He was quoting directly from Jay's tutoring. "This is really a no-brainer for you. The house is free and clear of any liens or loans. It's probably worth three million or more on the market. You have little to no risk." He leaned and looked directly into George's eyes. "You want to do this deal or not?"

***

The sharks slowly pulled away from Casa Ferruccio and proceeded to discuss the loan. "George, this guy is really strange. He makes me nervous. Do we really want to get into bed with the Mafia?"

"Listen, my boy, I've loaned money to the best of them, bankers, politicians, and drug dealers. They are all the same, big talkers, tough guys! I know his circle of friends. I've dealt with them before. Compared to the guys in the mob on the east coast, this guy is a real asshole. "The Italian mob is more dangerous in Vegas than in LA. I have some contacts in the Jewish mafia. I already asked around."

"But this guy doesn't seem to be as sure of himself as one would expect. Did you see how he was moving around in his chair? I thought he was beginning to sweat for a minute. Something's not right. I just don't have a good feeling about him. Why does he want cash?"

"These guys travel and live in a different world than most people. Cash is their lifeblood. Checks and money transfers can be traced. Cash gives them a sense of security."

"But what if he takes the money and disappears?"

"Then I own a three-million-dollar home on the beach. I'd like to live there myself for a while." Laughing, George said, "The grandkids would like to go surfing right from my own backyard, or I sell it off at a discount and still clean up."

"I guess you're right. I'll get the paperwork ready. How do we contact him to tell him we're ready for him to sign?"

"Never fear, he will call us later."

***

Two hours had gone by. Jay was sitting in his den, nervously waiting to talk to Augy.

"Mr. Jay," Jaime announced over the intercom, "Señor, you have a guest."

"Who is it?"

"It is Mr. Mas. He wish to see you."

"I'll be right up. Tell him to wait on the deck." Jay walked out onto the deck with a Martini for himself and a beer for Romano. "So, August, what do you think?"

Proudly, Augy said, "I think it's a done deal. Really, I was shitting in my pants for a while, but I came on strong, like you would have."

Jay was leaning on the rail on the edge of the deck. "What kind of questions did they ask you?" He leaned back and positioned his back on the rail.

"I told them you planned the whole thing and that you needed the money to pay off a debt. Just kidding."

"Come on. What did they ask you?"

"They asked questions about the furniture, the paintings, and general decorating. I didn't say much about them because I had no idea what the paintings were of. I told them the furniture wasn't part of the deal. The little guy or young guy just kept walking around with his movie camera filming everything. I told him not to take my picture. I was a little nervous when they asked me who my neighbors were."

"What did you tell them?"

"I told them that I didn't know my neighbors and that I only used the house once in a while when I wanted to get out of L.A."

"Good answer. These guys are real leeches. They prey on the rich and famous. They keep everything confidential. They have just as much to lose as the homeowner. They make their money by charging high fees and churning the money into more deals. They know that they are the winners if the loan is paid back or not."

"Are we, you, gonna pay it back?" Looking at Jay for assurance, Augy went on, "I'm sure they got my picture somewhere along the way."

Jay looked out over the water in the distance. "Fuck 'em!" The fog was starting to roll in, and the temperature dropped quickly. The storm everyone had been talking about was surely on its way.

Augy said, "It's really getting cold out here. You got a jacket or a sweater I can borrow?"

"Follow me," Jay said as he escorted Augy into the garage. He opened the trunk of his Porsche and tossed Augy his new yacht club jacket.

"It should say The Hunt Club."

"Don't start that with me again! Let's just say, if this works, you can consider yourself an honorary member." Jay motioned to Augy, and they moved toward the garage door. Jay resumed the previous conversation. "You don't need to worry about any photographs. By the time anyone finds out about this, I, we will be long gone."

"Are we going somewhere? You didn't tell me that part."

"I'll take care of you. You just follow through with the deal. They will probably expect you to call them tomorrow. If they don't call in the morning, then we, you will call them in the afternoon. I'll be with you so you don't need to be nervous or anything. Okay?"

"Okay, man, I trust you. But what happens when we get the money?"

"I have something else I need to discuss with you, Augy. It concerns my ex-wife and her lover."

"The pain in the ass, right?"

"Yes, the pains in the asses."

Reaching into his pants pocket, Augy pulled out a Zagnut Bar. "Here, I brought you a present."

"Where the heck did you get that?"

"I been carrying it around with me since I got here. Just something I found in an old candy store in Ohio. I hope you still like 'em."

"God, it's been years since I had one of those. Thanks."

"I got a bunch more if you want them." Jay quickly tore off the wrapper, put it into his mouth, and pretended he was smoking a cigar, mimicking an old comic from vaudeville.

"I'll explain my ex and her boyfriend to you later. Go now, and I will contact you at your motel later today or in the morning. Stay put! Do not go out tonight! Just be there when I call."

"Okay, but one more thing."

"What?"

"You know that asshole cop friend of yours is suspicious of me."

"Brooks? How do you know that? He's not an asshole."

"Well, he had his little buddy bring me in the other night, said he was your friend and that I need to respect that, said I shouldn't do anything to fuck up your life and all."

"I know all about that meeting. Don't worry about that at all."

"He said you didn't know about it!"

"He told me later what he did. He's just trying to protect me, just like you are helping to protect me. Understand?"

"No, but I trust you. Always have. When are we going to call them?"

Chapter 34

Later Thursday afternoon, Brooks sat in his den overlooking the Muirlands and ocean in the distance. He picked up the phone and called his office.

"Northern Division. Detective Staley here. How can I help you?"

"Staley, it's Brooks. Anything going on?"

"Nothing important, sir, except for a fax from Chicago."

"What kind of fax?"

"Well, sir, it seems Scotty never made it to his forensics seminar. They say he never registered on site and that we should have at least notified them of his absence."

"Oh, my God!" Brooks jumped up from his chair. "Get someone over to his place right away. I'll be there in fifteen minutes. He hung up the phone, ran down to his car, started the engine, and raced to Scotty's condominium.

As he approached the driveway to the project, he saw two patrol cars parked on the street with lights flashing. Orange traffic cones had been placed by the driveway gate to assure no one would enter or exit the grounds. He screeched to a stop, flung open the door, and rushed toward the officers. "What have we got?"

"An 1144 ,sir."

Oh, shit! "No, not Scotty," he said aloud while hurrying up the stairs to the second floor entry of Scotty's unit. The officer guarding the scene stood fast, blocking the door.

"Outta my way," said Brooks as he motioned to the officer to step aside.

"I can't let you in here, sir."

"Do you know who I am?" Brooks said firmly.

"I have a crime scene, sir. I can't let you in."

"Listen, you little fuck," he said, flashing his ID, "I'm Brooks. I'm the head of homicide. The victim is, was a cop. He worked with me. I'm the one who called and had your ass sent over here. Did you call the watch commander? I.A.?"

"Yes sir, but you can't..."

"Brooks, leave him alone," said the detective from Internal Affairs, flashing his ID and badge. "He's just doing his job."

"I apologize," said Brooks.

The officer moved aside as Brooks and the detective opened the door and peered into the condominium. Brooks nodded, "Okay." The two men slowly entered the condominium unit, stepping carefully not to contaminate the scene.

The living room was well kept. *No sign of a struggle in here*, he thought. Upon entering the bedroom, he spotted the body of his friend, sprawled out, back on the floor. Scotty's eyes were glazed and barely open. Dark purple-colored elbows rested on the floor beside him. Deep red on the bottom and white on the top, his hands rested just below his neck, by his throat.

Brooks had seen hundreds of crime scenes in his career, some gory as hell, some clean like this one, but never a crime scene involving someone so close to him. This was a very emotional time for Brooks. He held back his tears.

As he gazed up toward the wall next to the dresser, the neatly arranged row of framed photos caught his eye. "You okay, Brooks?"

Holding his handkerchief close to his face, because of the stench, Brooks nodded and walked toward the pictures. The walls were decorated like a storyboard. Scotty's life was visible in the photos— a picture of a little boy sitting on the lap of a policeman. Brooks heart sank deep into his chest. *I didn't know his father was a cop.* He wiped his teary face with his handkerchief. Scotty's smile filled the next photo as he was being awarded a plaque from a junior police society. His parents stood proudly in the next picture as he held his college diploma toward the camera. His graduation picture at an awards banquet from the academy hung next to an American flag with his father's badge resting in the center. Finally there was a picture of the two of them, standing, hands clasped after Scotty made detective sergeant. *He didn't want to be like me,* he thought. *I was just part of the chain. He wanted to be like his father. He never told me.*

The I.A. detective walked over to Brooks and put his arm over his shoulder. "I know. It's gotta be hard." Taking a deep breath, Brooks replied, "Yeah, it is."

"The team's here. We gotta go." As Brooks sidestepped from the room, he looked at Scotty one last time. His neck showed signs of the struggle. Body position, broken blood vessels, and skin discoloration were enough clues for Brooks.

"Romano," he said out loud.

"Who's Romano?" asked the watch commander as he walked toward the body.

* * *

Alis quickly dashed out of the unit to his car. He proceeded to call dispatch and within ten minutes five patrol cars were outside of Augy's motel in Bird Rock. The Corvette sat, straddling two spaces. Three officers with shotguns and pistols drawn sidled up to the door. The two other officers quietly evacuated the occupants of the adjoining rooms and calmly motioned to the others waiting outside of Augy's room. With precision timing, the officer in charge motioned to the others, and they simultaneously smashed through the door ready to capture Romano.

Storming into the room, the first officer tripped, and his gun went off. The bullet hit the mirror on the dresser and shattered glass all over the bed. Startled, the other two officers stumbled over him and onto the floor.

Augy watched the circus like event from a van parked across the street. *Timing is everything,* he thought. *Keystone Cops, still alive and well.* He had swiped the van on the same day he rented the

Corvette. Driving cautiously, he made his way to Camino de La Costa and parked the van in front of Casa Ferruccio.

Augy pounded hard on the massive door and shouted, "Newman, Newman! Answer the damn door." Martha was on her way to see who was furiously banging on the door when Jay intersected her in the living room. He told her to go back to doing what she was doing, that everything was okay, and that he would answer the knocking.

As Jay opened the heavy door, Augy was shaking. "The cops are all over my motel. They tried to shoot me."

"Calm down. What are you talking about?" He closed the door behind them and edged Augy into the garden patio next to the entry. He placed his hands on Augy's shoulders, attempting to stabilize him. Glancing back at the huge stained-glass picture window, he saw Martha and Jaime crouched and staring at the commotion. Jay motioned with his hand for them to step away from the window. The water flow in the fountain was gushing loud enough to block any voices from being overheard.

Pacing, Augy said, "I went back to my room, just as you said to do. I was thinking about the money guys when I decided to come back here and make the call you were talking about. Then as soon as I left the room and the parking lot, I saw a shitload of cop cars swarm the place. I sat in my van across the street and watched them. They busted into the room, shots firing. They were going to shoot me. *Fuck*!"

"What do they want with you? Did you do anything after you and Brooks met?"

The sky darkened. Thunder could be heard in the distant sea. Puzzled, Jay stood for a moment. "Okay, let's go inside."

As they stepped through the door, Martha interrupted and said "Señor Brooks is on the phone and wants to talk with you *inmediatamente*."

"Hey Alis, what's so urgent?"

"Have you seen or heard from your buddy Romano today?"

Hesitating, he looked at Augy. "No why?"

"When you see or hear from him, you call me immediately, okay."

"Shit, what did he do?"

"He's a dangerous guy Newman. He's on the loose. You call me! Understand?"

"Did you check his motel?"

"Don't ask!" he said in frustration. "Just call me!"

Jay hung up, looked at Augy, and said, "What the fuck did you do?"

Augy shrugged his shoulders and said, "I do what I need to do, that's all. *None of your business!*"

Jay walked down to the theatre room. Augy followed. Agitated, Jay ran his fingers through his hair, sat in a leather recliner, and motioned for Augy to sit.

"You're wrong. *It is my business.*" Augy sat, like a young school child, hands in his lap, brooding, waiting for instructions. Jay realized that he was at his crossroad. He stared at Augy. Was it time to turn himself in and take the consequences? Was it time to rid himself of Romano, once and for all, or was he in so deep that he just couldn't stop now? He closed his eyes, put his head back on the soft leather pillow, and sat quietly organizing his thoughts.

Augy moved to the edge of his seat. "Okay, enough of this shit, man. What do we do?"

Jay slowly opened his eyes, sat upright, reached for the black princess phone on the coffee table, and said, "Let's make the call."

***

An hour and a half later, George Lowe and a notary public left Casa Ferruccio with a stack of signed papers. Augy Romano sat in the expansive mansion, puffing on a Cuban cigar, with two cheap backpacks stuffed with a million and a half dollars. Flicking ashes on the marble floor, he stood and paced the room, thinking to himself, *Goddamn, that was easy. Newman is really smart. But I'm smarter!*

Jay entered by the side door. The two men embraced. Jay said, "How does it feel to have a million plus bucks sitting right here next to you?"

Augy, while blowing smoke rings, briskly moved the cigar between his fingers, like a card shark, and snickered, "It feels like a million bucks." After gathering all the incriminating photos, the two men grabbed the two backpacks and left the scene of the scam.

Jay finally acquiesced and took Augy into his secret room. There he gathered all of his fortune and explained to Augy that there was one more thing he wanted him to do before he got his cut. Augy asked what Jay was going to do with the rest of the money. He explained to him that the money was payment to his ex and his attorney, that they had something against him, and that the cash would rid them from his life.

Augy asked if there was something he could do to help. Jay told him that one more "something" he wanted him to do, to deliver the backpacks to his attorney's office.

"Just go inside and give him the money. If he asks who you are, just tell him you are making a delivery as requested. He will know who it's from and what it's for. Then turn and leave. Don't rush, don't draw any attention, just leave."

Knowing that Augy couldn't go back to his motel, Jay gave Augy directions to his Pine Valley cabin and told him that he would meet him there in the morning. Pine Valley is approximately fifty miles east of La Jolla. Pine Valley is a small community located in the foothills of Mount Laguna. The elevation yields four seasons. Sweltering summer heat dries out the sandy creek. Fall colors resemble the beauty of New England. In the winter this rural wilderness gathers snow, and the spring thaw supplies a steady, gentle flow of water to Pine Creek. Cabins on the eastern edge of Pine Valley off of Pine Valley Road are mostly situated on land owned by the Bureau of Land Management and sit within the boundaries of The Cleveland National Forest.

Jay had signed an inexpensive 20-year land lease. The cabin belonged to him, but the land didn't. The cabin sat at about 2,800 feet above sea level while some of Pine Valley sits at over 3,700 feet, just below the Lagunas, which are somewhere around 5,700 feet. Once every six to ten years brutal rainstorms accompany the early periodic thaw and cause the creek to overflow, inevitably damaging or destroying many of the adjacent cabins. In the summer and fall, if it storms and rains up in the Laguna Mountains the flow of water down to Pine Valley can also be fierce and treacherous, causing power outages and multiple floods.

"Once you leave his office, get into your van and go to the cabin." Augy, glad to be included in Jay's plans, nodded and picked up the money. "The keys are in a bird feeder hanging from the oak tree in the front." Jay called David and told him the delivery was on the way.

Chapter 35

Sam spent Thursday at FBI headquarters in downtown San Diego. She spoke with her supervisor in Virginia, who reiterated that she was not to proceed with her investigation without the consent of the San Diego office. After a tedious and persistent session, the Special Agent in charge felt assistance in the case might be helpful. He handed her a file, much of which she already had, containing 284 pages of various reports dating back to January, 1964. The newest entry to the file was information gathered by her once she had arrived in San Diego and had had her initial interaction with Andrew Fowler.

Sam came upon the instructions from Quantico temporarily reassigning her to the San Diego office. She was told on the phone that Romano was a bad guy, but she wasn't told that the background investigation of August Romano stated that he had been in the Marine Corps at the same time she was a young girl, that her father was the JAG prosecutor in Romano's court martial, and that due to her father's abrupt death, her continued investigation could be a conflict of interest.

She sat quietly thumbing through the documents and noted that Romano had a history of attacking women, both for pleasure and for revenge. Various photos, mostly faded, were inside the file as well. She stared again at the dozens of crime scene photos and photos of young Andy Fowler. Newly added photos of Jacob Newbaum, a.k.a. Jay Newman, his wife and daughter, his home, and the coffee shop were included in the file. A separate sleeve sat within the file. Numerous entries referring to Newman's business and a suspicious fire were the sleeve of documents.

Sam doubted if she was the sole agent engaged in the investigations. She wondered how so much information got into the file so quickly. Then she found the most recent addition to the file, a dossier of August Romano from the time he was a Marine, mug shots from his prison incarceration, and photos of him in the interrogation room of the San Diego police department.

Meeting again with the Special Agent in charge, Sam was advised of a pre-arranged conference between her and Serena Newman. The meeting was arranged by Alis Brooks and was set for three p.m. that afternoon in the Spinnaker Room at the San Diego Yacht Club.

***

At 2:45, Sam pulled up to the guardhouse at the entry to the San Diego Yacht Club. She was told that she was expected and to park anywhere she chose. The guard gave her instructions to the Spinnaker Room, which was at the side of the club deck, toward the rear of the clubhouse.

As she walked toward the clubhouse, she couldn't help but notice the impeccably maintained grounds. Tennis courts, a pool, and a stately building in front of her suggested that this was a place for the wealthy boating community of San Diego. She had been a guest at other private clubs back east, but this environment reeked of assets and possessions well beyond her imagination. She made her way toward the front entry deck and noted a small sign with an arrow pointing to the Spinnaker Room.

Sam was wearing a business suit and black heels. She carried a briefcase, the kind that lawyers used, with the opening at the top. She came upon two large teak doors with smoked glass panels, and entered the empty room. Sam glanced at her watch, noting that she was five minutes early for her meet with Serena Newman. Numerous plaques and trophies sat on shelves next to a large framed burgee hanging on the paneled wall.

Sam expected a forty-ish, stately-looking, snobby socialite with an attitude. At three p.m. exactly the doors on the other side of the room swung open and in walked a woman who appeared similar to her in age. Casually dressed in a white polo shirt with navy shorts and white Docksiders, Serena said, "I'm here to meet Ms. Lyons. Might that be you?"

Sam responded, "Are you Serena Newman? I didn't expect..."

"You didn't expect what? Yes, I am Jay Newman's wife. I've been instructed to meet with you concerning my husband and his old high-school buddy, August Romano. Have a seat, please."

Sam, obviously surprised by her miscalculation, moved toward Serena and pulled out a chair from the table next to the wall. "Is this okay with you, Mrs. Newman?"

"This is fine. Call me Serena if you would. What shall I call you?"

Slightly anxious, Sam said, "Please call me Sam. My name is Samantha, but everyone calls me Sam."

"How long have you been in the FBI, Sam? No reason to be nervous." Smiling, Serena asked her, "Is this your first interview?"

"No, no, I just expected someone much older than you, someone closer to your husband's age. I don't mean that in a bad way or anything."

"It's okay, Sam. We get that all the time. Relax. Tell me about yourself. Would you like a glass of wine or some iced tea or anything?"

"Oh, no, thank you." Sam was still somewhat amazed.

Serena continued, "Where are you from? How did you get mixed up in this thing? What do you know about us, about August Romano? What do you want to know?"

At first, Sam thought Serena was taking charge of the meeting. However, that impression changed over the next hour and a half. Sam composed herself and realized that neither one of them had control of anything.

They seemed to get along well. Sam's assignment was to get to know Serena and gain her trust, not to interrogate her. Serena was straightforward with her answers. She didn't embellish anything. When asked how she was introduced to Romano, she replied, "I haven't been introduced to him. I only know that he is someone to avoid and that he and my husband knew each other in high school. Jay told me he isn't a nice person."

"What do you suspect that means? He isn't 'nice'?"

"Just that he might cause trouble."

Sam changed the subject. She asked Serena about her life, where she grew up, what her major was in college, and how she met Jay Newman.

She and Serena had dissimilar lives. Serena was well bred, went to private schools, and travelled the world. Sam was a young girl when her father died. She and her mother had some difficult times. Vacationing consisted of short trips visiting friends and family living in the South. There were no European adventures or fancy ski trips.

The two did have something in common, however, a love for the martial arts. Both were celebrated champions in their own right.

Their conversation brought them together. It seemed as if they were becoming friends.

"Let me ask you something, Serena, off the record, if that's okay?" Serena nodded. "Did your husband tell you why Romano came to see him? Did he tell you that Romano has a tendency to hurt women, to cause great harm? Does the name Andy Fowler mean anything to you?"

Serena initially thought she was aware of everything. Alis Brooks assured her that this meeting would be a simple probe into her and Jay's lives by a heartless agent who had things on her mind other than her. She hadn't been told that Sam Lyons seemed to be sincerely interested in her, nor that Sam knew the history behind Jay and Augy. She certainly didn't know anything about Andy Fowler.

Sensing the mutual trust being formed, Sam continued to confide in her. She told her about Andy and that Andy was here in San Diego, that he had come to confront his past; that Andy had been a young boy in the back of a truck in 1964 and he remembered two things from his nightmare that winter day. She told her that Andy remembered that there were two men, and that one of their names was Finch.

Sam explained that until recently no connection had existed between her husband and Romano. That connection became a reality after eavesdropping in The Coffee Cup. She explained that she was assigned to follow, watch, and observe Andy Fowler. Andy led to her husband, and the arrival of Romano seemed to have solved the mystery.

Serena sat almost numb as she listened and learned, for the first time, about the factual history of her husband and Augy Romano. Pensively, she asked, "Sam, what would have happened if Romano hadn't shown up?"

"I'm not completely sure. Andy is a really nice guy. He couldn't hurt anyone. His life was simple. He and his mother lived with his grandparents. His obsession to find the two men who killed his father and uncle led him here." Sam waited for a reaction.

Almost meditating, Serena asked, "Are we really off the record? I mean, this is truly just between the two of us? No FBI, no cops? No reporting of what we say? Am I right?"

"I promise it's just between the two of us."

"Great," Serena said, as she stood up. "I have to have a glass of wine. Are you sure you don't want one?"

"Thanks, I'm sure."

"I'll be right back."

While Serena went to the bar in the clubhouse to fetch her wine, Sam got up and walked to the rear doors and stared out at the various yachts in the private marina. Knowing that she had breached her position as a federal agent, and obvious affluence aside, she couldn't help sensing a common bond between the two of them.

Serena returned with her Chardonnay in hand and a glass of iced tea for Sam. "Oh, thank you," Sam said.

Serena started, "Aside from not being able to really place Jay at the scene of the crime, without Augy's testimony…"

"Hold on. What are you saying?" Sam interjected.

"I'm just saying that Augy Romano seems to be the bad guy here, that maybe, just maybe my husband didn't do the shooting. Maybe he wasn't even there, or if he was there, he was just a bystander."

"We both know he was there, Serena. There is no getting around that. You're grasping at straws. Even if he didn't shoot, he's still an accomplice. He aided and abetted. He's going to pay the price one way or another."

"What price? Jesus! Help me here. We both have our personal reasons and feelings tangled up in this mess. Augy Romano needs to pay the price. Okay, Jay's not Mr. Good Guy, but we need to talk about the real perpetrator, August Romano."

Sam confided, "My research on your husband's buddy, August Romano, exposed a very painful recollection of something that happened to me. I have, as you do, personal reasons for getting even with him."

Serena reached out and took Sam's hand. "I have a proposal for you."

Chapter 36

Del Mar has a reputation as a wealthy coastal community—artsy, crafty people, a lot of well endowed, aging hippie types, and a poignant need to harass smokers. Camino Del Mar, the main north-south thoroughfare, separates much of the community. Smaller beach homes, some condominiums, and small apartment complexes line the short streets west of the highway. The east side provides a gentle upslope in topography, allowing many homes a view of the village shops that line the highway below. Views of the ocean are priceless and command phenomenal premiums on real estate prices. The community is well regarded as being safe, although some residential burglaries do occur. Most police officers will unofficially state that the majority of robberies are staged for insurance purposes. Minor traffic accidents occur when drivers don't watch the road, but rather gaze toward the sidewalks in need of recognition from friends and acquaintances. The few domestic-violence calls usually turn out to be wealthy young couples, who have had too much Chardonnay for dinner and begin arguing over who is cheating on whom or whose money belongs to whom. Once every few years, some well-known Del Mar financier would make headlines for swindling other wealthy people in some kind of Ponzi scheme

Bright beams from the Eldorado's headlights cut through the thick fog as David wound through the narrow, brick-covered, tree-lined streets of old Del Mar. His left hand gripped the leather-wrapped steering wheel while his right reached across to the passenger seat and rested on the top of the backpacks containing two million dollars. The thought of blackmailing his once best friend fueled David's emotional marathon.

Shocked that he actually had two million dollars next to him, he wondered why Jay hadn't killed him or had him killed. *Jesus Christ, look at what I've done to myself, to my life! I'm an attorney, an officer of the court.* Then he laughed aloud. *Yeah, an officer of the fuckin' court. Big fuckin' deal, like the court or anyone else gives a shit about me.*

***

The Cadillac suddenly took a sharp turn to the left, clipping its side mirror on a mailbox. David's thoughts were so penetrating he didn't flinch. *I've got a nice home, a nice car, and a worthless fuckin' law practice.* He slapped the wheel with the palm of his hand, almost hitting a tree as he swerved. Again, *no one ever really gave a shit about me. It was always, 'David do this, David do that. David's a good student, a good lawyer. David will always be successful.' Well, fuck all of you! David is fuckin' David and I'll do whatever the fuck I want. Why couldn't I ever be just Dave? That's it! Just Dave. No fuck! Ma said everyone has to call me David. I hate that fuckin' name. How about Bill or Don or John? What would my life have been if my name was Fred or Paul? It was her fault! All Mother's fault. That's right! Blame it all on my mother, be a lawyer, make a lot of money. 'People will always look up to a David, not a Dave or a Davey.' Boy, was she mistaken. She'd be proud of me now. I'm a thief, a goddamn blackmailer. But I'm driving a fancy car on my way home to a big house in Del Mar, a classy rich broad waiting for me at the door.*

His hand patted the top of the backpacks. Then he said aloud, "She's not waiting for me. She's waiting for this." Swerving again, he nearly sideswiped a small sports car parked at the edge of his driveway.

"Shit, that was close," he said as he turned sharply off the bricks and into his drive. He slammed on the brakes and skidded to a screeching stop. Seconds seemed like minutes as he waited for the power window to drop. Twisting and looking back, he watched the dark-colored Porsche as it pulled away.

***

Prior to her arrival at David's house, Bobbie had spent most of the day in La Jolla packing her things. Loose ends had been tied up. All bank accounts were closed. Her passport had been reissued weeks prior, and her new name was Susan Atwood. A sequence of airline tickets sat neatly tucked in her purse. She had plans of her own, first some champagne, a few vodkas, then dinner, which she picked up at the French Gourmet.

Bobbie's chestnut skin, accentuated by her red lace teddy and white silk robe, were sure to entice David the minute he walked in. Soft music filled the house as she waited patiently for him to arrive.

The sound of screeching tires in the driveway caused her to step out onto the deck. She watched as light beams cut through the thick fog as his car moved up the driveway. Anticipating David, she stepped back into the bedroom, closed the French doors, and put a log in the fireplace. After dimming the lights, she slipped on her red heels, looked in the mirror, fluffed her hair, and tied her robe. As she walked from the bedroom, a gentle breeze blew in through the French doors, leaving them slightly ajar.

Dashing through the front door, carrying two backpacks, David called out, "I got it. I got it all." Flickering candlelight glowed through empty crystal champagne glasses on the dining-room table. Silver knives and forks rested next to white china plates. David had taken a handful of money and thrown it wildly into the air. Hundred-dollar bills were everywhere. The table, the floor, the chairs and even the chandelier were covered with money. After a quick dinner, they followed the path of bills to the bedroom where Bobbie and David stood next to the bed. Her sensuous breasts mesmerized David as he stood with his hands on her thin waist. Her body twitched as his fingers slid beneath her teddy and gently massaged her crotch. He moved his hands to her firm buttocks and squeezed while pulling her closer to his erection. Her tongue moved slowly over her moist lips. "I want you," she said. His knees weakened as she cupped his genitals with one hand and softly stroked his erection with the other. David was barely able to stay on his feet. He braced himself by spreading his legs and holding the top of her head. First her tongue, then the pulsating pressure from her wet, warm lips as she took him deeper, each time, to the back of her throat. "Oh, God, I'm going to explode," he said.

She looked up at him. "I want you to. I want it all." She licked his erection. "We have all night. Please." She closed her eyes and took him deep.

***

The silhouette stood, watching from the deck as David pulled Bobbie onto the bed and began to make love to her. The voyeur's eyes widened as David removed her teddy and began massaging, first her soft thighs, then just below her navel. She moaned as her hips gently rose and fell. His fingertips caressed every inch of her skin from her breasts to her hairy mound. Bobbie, lying on her back, reached behind the pillows and tightly gripped the wood slats in the headboard. She crossed her legs, burying David's head from sight. It took only minutes until Bobbie's climax was signaled by a loud cry. Her quivering thighs relaxed.

Perspiration dripped from the forehead of the stalker as he watched Bobbie reach down toward David and then guide his body up and over hers. He watched as they spoke, but he couldn't hear them. Then Bobbie reached under the pillows and dangled a pair of handcuffs in front of David. She smiled as she handed them to him.

The shadow moved closer to the door, then cringed as he lasciviously watched David secure her to the bedposts.

Bobbie appeared irritated when David reached into the drawer of the nightstand and removed a long, silk scarf. She tugged and twisted to no avail as David forcibly tied the blindfold. When David raised his voice, she relented. He spent the next ten minutes slowly dripping champagne on her sensuous skin and licking it off. He massaged and fondled every inch of her body.

The shadow watched intently as she pretended to fight off her captor. She moaned and cried, but not loud enough to satisfy his furious expectations. David slid his fiery erection between her breasts, than slowly moved lower over her tight belly.

Glass panes shattered as the French doors swung inward and smashed against the walls. David turned in shock toward the door.

The masked intruder leaped toward David, throwing him off the bed and onto the floor. Fighting for his life, he punched and kicked, attempting to hold off his attacker. Tears rolled from David's eyes as he felt his muscles weakening.

Sensing David's demise, the attacker wrapped both hands around David's throat and squeezed. As his knee swiftly rose towards the side of David's head, he bellowed, "Fuckin' lawyer! This is from a buddy of yours." David was motionless.

Screeching, terror-ridden sounds filled the room as Bobbie tossed and squirmed in the bed. Her wrists bled as the steel restraints tore through her skin. "Who is it? Who the fuck are you? Take my blindfold off. I'll do whatever you want. Please, please," she cried. "Leave us alone. I have money, I can pay you."

Her snooty pleas pissed him off. Scooping several hundred-dollar bills from the floor, he started stuffing them into her mouth. She began to choke as his hand pushed harder on her face. Horrified and now dominated by him, she tightened her fists. Then her body stiffened, and she became motionless. He leaned over and whispered softly in her ear. "It's my money, bitch. You don't deserve it."

Chapter 37

Mrs. Rachael Buchanan called the police to report finding eight hundred-dollar bills in her neighbor's driveway. When the police arrived, she explained that she was on her way back from her morning walk and couldn't help but notice a crisp, new hundred-dollar bill lying at the foot of David Goldman's driveway. While glancing up the drive, she spotted another, then another until she had finally picked them all up and found herself standing on the grass just under the master bedroom deck.

She noticed the door on the deck was open and called to David. When he didn't respond, she made her way to the front door and rang the bell several times. The fact that no one answered didn't seem unusual, as she knew David usually left for his office around 9:30 or ten. The door was ajar, and music was playing. As she cautiously peeked through the doorway, she spotted dishes on the table and piles of money all over the place. She hurried down the drive and called police as soon as she arrived home.

***

Brooks pulled next to the officer standing guard at the intersection of Zuni Street and Forest Way. "Big one, huh?"

"Yes, sir," said the young officer as he lifted the fluttering wind-blown band of yellow security ribbon, allowing Brooks to pull through. He stopped his vehicle a few hundred feet from the crime scene and watched as the KUSI news van set up its satellite feed back to the station in Kearny Mesa.

Headlines, Brooks said to himself. *The biggest story of the year. Shit, in Del Mar, the biggest story ever, at least since I can remember. Who this time? Look at these people, like little bugs. Reclusive neighbors. Back and forth, back and forth. How many pairs of Birkenstocks can I count? Wondering which one of them did what to whom. Now we're going to hear how unsafe our neighborhoods are. Yeah, right, unsafe in Del Mar. Get a life, all you noisy bastards. How hard can this be? I don't even have to go inside and I already know this is an easy one for the M.E. Two people do away with each other. Money, drugs, or kids, probably all three. It happens all the time. It's just a bigger deal because of where it is. Shit, this goes on three times a week in the Heights. You don't see the news coverage down there. Sure, it's no big deal. Blow away a couple of homeboys, no one gives a rat's ass.*

Enough negative talk, Brooks. Get on with it. I gotta be in bad shape when my conscience starts talking to me.

"Okay, okay, here I go," he said out loud while exiting the car and looking to see if anyone saw him talking to himself.

Brooks walked past the camera crew and nodded as he made eye contact with Paul Stone, KUSI'S special crimes reporter. Paul waved and shrugged his shoulders as if to say his crew wasn't set up yet for an interview. Brooks liked him. He had a reputation of not distorting or sensationalizing the news. When he had something to say to the reporters, he would surely include Paul.

Brooks had never been to David Goldman's home before. As he started up the driveway, he recognized the Cadillac. He walked faster and saw Bobbie's car parked by the garage. "Oh, no!" he said aloud. "Oh, no!"

Brooks walked through the front door, motioned to an officer, and asked who was inside. The officer replied, "Dr. Frankenstein." Howard Churbuck had been the Medical Examiner for nine years. Before coming to work in San Diego, he was the assistant chief of Pathology at UCLA Medical Center. At first he toyed with forensic medicine as a hobby. Then he got famous testifying. He said he retired for a few years, but it was actually a sabbatical. He wrote some unsuccessful crime novels and decided, as he put it, to "get his hands bloody again." He was a veteran when it came to bloody investigations. Howard was a big man. At five-foot eleven he weighed 275 pounds. Nothing seemed to faze him anymore, not even his nickname. In fact, he was well known for his warped and sometimes sick personality.

Every time Brooks interacted with him, he couldn't help but recall the few occasions he and his wife tried to be social with Howard and his wife. *Christ*, he thought, remembering their last dinner together at the Beach and Tennis Club. Howard was eating squid and made an unforgettable point of describing the similarities between oozing brains and the food on his plate. He raised his glass of Cabernet for a toast, swirled it around, and remarked that the wine on the side of the glass reminded him of coagulating blood. The final step that night was when Howard lowered his nose to the top of his *crème brulée*, sniffed, and then referred to the smell and texture of the rotting skin of his latest burn victim.

"Hey, Brooks. How ya doing?" Howard said as Brooks entered the bedroom. "Long time no see."

"Frank, I mean Howard," acknowledged Brooks as he perused the room. "What happened here, big guy?"

"Not sure yet. Just got here a few minutes ago. She must have been a lousy cook." Brooks looked puzzled as he glanced at Howard stooping over David's body. "Looks like their dinner didn't agree with either one of them." Howard prodded with a tweezers. "If you can ignore the ketchup, you can see his last meal coming out all over his face."

"Jesus Doc, I know these people."

"I'm getting to know them, also. Too bad I didn't know them before."

"What do you mean?"

"I hope they're not good friends of yours, because they aren't or weren't married, at least to each other."

"No, they aren't, weren't. How do you know that?" Brooks said reluctantly, waiting to fall for one of his distasteful narratives. "Howard, what happened here?"

Howard guided Alis to the bedside. "First of all, look here. She's fastened to the bedposts. The bandana was a blindfold. Look at her eyes." Brooks squinted as he looked at Bobbie's terrified expression.

"This was a lovely piece of ass. Oh, I'm sorry. You said you know them."

Brooks shook his head in disgust. "Continue."

Pointing to her eyes, Howard said, "The victim here saw her killer. The blindfold was lifted from her forehead just before she died. The look on her face isn't from seeing the biggest prick in the world. Well, actually he, the culprit, might have been a prick, but the prick, I mean his prick isn't what she was staring at when she expired." He removed his rubber gloves, placed them in his side pockets, and poked his fingers through his thin, long gray hair, leaving it mussed and standing out at the sides. "Am I confusing you?"

Now he looks more like Einstein instead of Frankenstein.

"Hold on a second, Howard." Brooks motioned to one of his homicide detectives.

"Yes, sir, Chief," was the response as he walked past the photographer who was taking pictures of the broken French door. Turning away from Howard, Brooks placed his arm around the shoulder of the young detective. He spoke quietly, briefing him about the relationship between Newman and the dead woman. "Remember, he's not a suspect, just an ex-husband. Pick him up and take him to my office. I'll be there later." Brooks turned to Howard. "Okay, you were saying, the next question is..."

"No question. I'm just telling you what I think happened here. You can pay attention or wait until you get my report."

"Howard, I'm sorry. Don't be so temperamental. Please continue."

"Okay, let's see. The killer came through the French door, probably saw them going at it, and got pissed off, scared the shit out of her, literally. Look here. He strangled her. I don't think he fucked her, though. I mean, she was fucked, but not by him."

"How did Goldman die?"

"Goldman? You know the guy's name?"

"Yes, they were lovers."

"I could've told you that. Who is this guy Goldman?"

"She and Goldman were up to no good. I'll tell you more later. How did he die? A gunshot?"

"No, no. A gunshot didn't kill him. He was beaten to death. There was a gun in the drawer next to the bed. The killer took him out first. Looks like he pulled the guy to the floor, beat the crap out of him, and then went after the cheerleader."

Howard walked over to David's body. Brooks followed. "The guy put up a fight. Looks like his wrist is broken. Must be a bitch to defend yourself while you're naked, exposed cock and all. Embarrassing. Think about it. It's one thing to know you're going to die, but to die naked. God, the thought of everyone seeing you like that. Ugh!"

Offended by Howard's crude descriptions, Brooks asked, "If he knew he'd already killed him, why did he shoot him?"

"The gunshot was just to make sure, to satisfy him. I'd bet while the two guys were fighting, that the Goldman guy reached for the drawer and tried to grab the gun. That pissed off the executioner, because to him it wasn't a fair fight anymore so after he killed him he just shot him with his own gun. He must've really had it in for your buddy, Goldman."

"He's wasn't my buddy. Where is the gun? How do you know it was Goldman's gun?"

"Look here in the drawer, a box of shells."

"Where is the gun? Did you find it?"

Dr. Frankenstein ignored the question. "He plugged him, after. Why didn't he plug her, after? Know what I mean? Who were these people? How do you know them?"

Brooks glanced around one last time and asked again, "Where is the gun?"

"It's not here in the bedroom. Unsub might have taken it with him. I hate to be rude, but I have work to do. Can you call me later, or in a day or so?"

Brooks smiled and replied, "You hate to be rude?"

***

Brooks walked outside, and during the course of the next half hour investigators filled him in about the hundred-dollar bills and the neighbor who found them. *I hope Newman didn't have anything to do with this.*

Some locals provided their two cents to the dozen television and newspaper reporters roaming around the outside of the yellow-taped crime scene. Photographers from the police lab took pictures of everything including the tire tracks at the side of the road by David Goldman's driveway.

Brooks had just finished a marginally informing, on-air interview with Paul Stone when his beeper sounded. He walked to his car and called the number displayed on his pager.

"This is Brooks."

"Boss," The young detective responded. "I'm afraid I got some bad news."

Holding the phone to his ear, Brooks stared anxiously through the windshield. "What do you mean, bad news?"

"Well, sir, I'm at Newman's house here in La Jolla. He's not here, sir. The housekeeper and her husband said they heard him early this morning, but that they didn't see him. They said he must have left in a hurry."

"Why do you assume that's bad news? Do they know where he went?"

"No, sir, but what I mean by bad news is that I just found two hundred-dollar bills on the floor in the garage, new bills, like the ones in Del Mar."

Brooks was concerned about Newman's disappearance. He instructed the detective to first check The Coffee Cup Cafe, then Newman's office, and then The San Diego Yacht Club.

"I need someone at the airport as well. Don't make a scene, just check it out and get back with me."

Chapter 38

After Augy delivered the money to David, he doubled back to La Jolla instead of going directly to the cabin. He told Jay that it wasn't necessary to pay off his ex and David; that he could resolve the blackmail issue if he paid him an extra $250,000. He explained that Jay could have the rest of the money and that he would disappear forever. Augy was relentless and didn't know that Jay had expected him to return with demands. That was part of his plan.

He listened, and after several minutes he pretended to be persuaded. He told Augy to take his Porsche and leave the van. He provided somewhat of a comfort zone to Augy, that if he was seen driving through Del Mar in a van, that he would be noticed. The Porsche fit in, and no one would suspect anything unusual. He told Augy that if the car were to be noticed in any way, it would lead back to him and not Augy. Augy liked that idea as it assured him that Jay was looking out for him.

Chapter 39

Augy returned from Del Mar and parked crooked in Jay's driveway. It was very dark, and rain was falling hard. He hastily unloaded the money from the Porsche into the van, dropping several bills on the ground. Jay was anxiously waiting for him. Jay wore jeans and a heavy sweatshirt, which hung down over his pants, covering his pockets. The two of them drove off.

Passing through Mission Valley on Highway 8, Jay informed Augy that his plan consisted of them meeting up with his wife in La Jolla and that they would be leaving San Diego the next evening. He arranged for all of them to disappear.

Augy was anxious to meet his wife and child. Once he left Mayfield, he never had a family to call his own, and now Finch finally filled that gap in his life. He didn't ask where they were going as he was comforted in knowing that his old buddy Finch would take care of him.

Jay told Augy that the meet was going to be at midnight, that it would be quick, and that it was to occur behind the little Baptist Church on Cuvier Street in La Jolla, by the Jack in the Box. He assured Augy that because it was on a dead-end street, no one would notice them.

He said that after they connected, they were going to drive to his boat and sail to Mexico. He told him that he arranged for everything.

Heavy rain was falling. The winds blew angrily on Highway 8 as they battered through the El Cajon and Alpine communities heading east. What would normally take forty-five to fifty-five minutes took them almost two and a half hours, to reach the Descanso exit. Wind shear was a common problem for high-profile vehicles in San Diego's mountain communities. The van crawled off the freeway in Descanso, barely missing a few parked big rigs, which had pulled off the highway to wait out the storm. Rushing water overflowed in poorly constructed drainage ditches on the sides of the off-ramp.

He turned left, as the tires cut through the flooding waters, which rushed sideways across the pavement. The storm grew even more ferocious as they edged through the back country. The windshield was fogged, and Augy was barely able to navigate the curvy road.

Pounding rain beat against the metal shell of the van. In an effort to be heard, Jay shouted, "Turn on the defroster, asshole."

"Kiss off!" Augy replied as he sat hunched over the wheel, wiping part of the window with his handkerchief. Looking left, Augy rubber-necked at the round, corrugated-metal roof on the old Descanso hardware store. "Hey, Finch, look at that. Didn't think you guys had Butler buildings out here. Didn't Willy Butler's old man invent them or something?" Augy swerved, momentarily losing control of the van. Two wheels lifted off the pavement as he struggled with the steering wheel. Water rose to the base of the van's doors. Crawling, he asked, "Where do I turn off this road?"

"Turn over here," directed Jay. He guided him down Pine Creek Road to the edge of his property. Jay's cabin sat back from the road in the midst of tall pines, oaks, and thick manzanita. Turbulent water in Pine Creek rushed past the north foundation wall of the cabin carrying downed tree limbs and weathered debris. Augy struggled with the van as he pulled off the road, up the gravel drive, ultimately parking behind the cabin.

***

Once safely inside the cabin, Jay told Augy to make himself at home and excused himself as he made his way toward the bathroom. Out of Augy's sightline, he bent over, unhooked his pistol from below the pool table, and tucked it securely into his belt, concealing it with his long heavy shirt.

Augy's temperament quickly changed. He became argumentative and pushy. Surprising Jay, he whacked him on the head, slammed him onto the floor, and restrained him. The gun fell from Jay's belt. Augy kicked it away. He pulled Goldman's gun from the pocket of his recently acquired Yacht Club jacket. "I don't need your gun or your money, man!"

Augy sat on the sofa with his arms stretched behind his head. Both legs quivered nervously while extended out in front of him. He stared at Jay, helplessly duct-taped to the rocker. His voice was harsh, tough-sounding. "So who's in charge now? How's it feel when it's not you?"

"Listen, untie me. What are you doing? I can get anything you want." Twisting and turning intensely, he said, "Goddamn it, will you please untie me!"

"Will you please shut the fuck up? Can't you see I'm doing my thinking."

"Untie me, I thought you were okay with the plan. I'll give you whatever you want."

Jay froze. It wasn't supposed to be this way. *He is out of his mind. He's going to shoot me. Jesus Christ! I'll just do what he says.* "Augy, please talk to me."

"I'm gonna talk to you. I'm gonna tell you what it's like, what it's like to be me, in my world, not yours. But you're only worried about you. 'Untie me. Untie me.' That's all you can say."

"Don't untie me, that's okay. Just tell me what you want. I thought we became friends again. I trusted you."

"You just don't get it, do you? I didn't want anything." A tree limb carried by the rushing water struck the side of the cabin. The loud noise drew Augy to the window. He opened the blinds and surveyed the storm. "Jesus Christ, man, you should see all the water out there."

"Augy, we can't stay here. This place is going to fall apart."

Augy stared at the torturous storm. Thunder and lightning took him back to Vietnam. The jungle was hot, wet, and loud. He pictured his fellow warriors struggling through cascading waters. He sniffed deeply, straining to smell the napalm.

He turned and walked toward Jay swaying in the rocker. He grabbed the duct tape on the shelf by the window. Approaching Jay, he tore a strip from the roll.

"What the hell are you going to do with that?"

Augy grabbed the top of Jay's hair and pulled. *He's going to kill me*, Jay thought.

"I told you to shut up."

Jay felt hair being pulled from his scalp as Augy wrapped the tape around his head and over his mouth. "Now you can't talk. I told you not to say anything." Filled with rage, Jay's eyes bulged. His squirming caused the rocking chair to continue swaying back and forth.

Thunderous explosions turned Augy back toward the window. He rushed across the room to observe. A limb from the hundred-year-old oak tree in the front of the cabin cracked and fell into the rushing water. Water carried it fifty feet, where it jammed against the base of another tree; limbs began to gather and form a dam. The water rose quickly.

Nervously, Augy put the gun on a table and began opening and closing drawers in the kitchen. He took a large knife from the drawer, waved it in the air, and shouted, "This is for your pretty wife." Then he put it into his jacket pocket. A cigarette hung from his lips. He looked toward Jay. "You got any matches around here?"

Jay motioned with his head toward the opposite corner of the room.

"Don't look at me that way. I know what you're thinkin'. You're thinkin', who does this guy think he is. Yeah, well, I got news for you, man. I know who I am." He found a box of matches on a shelf next to one of the wood-burning stoves. "But nobody knows who you are. So what, you got a lot of money. You think that makes you better than me, or anyone else? Ha, look here." He grabbed a backpack from the sofa, reached inside, and waved a bundle of hundred dollar bills against Jay's face. "I got all the money I need, just like you."

Augy tossed the backpack across the room, then pressed his forefinger against Jay's forehead. "I should blow you away. You're not any better than me, or any con I ever knew. You never been called on the line, Finch. You never did time. You were always smarter than me, talked your way out of anything. I'll bet you still do that. I bet this plan of yours is bullshit."

Jay watched as Augy slipped back and forth from present to past. *We were kids, foolish kids. I always wondered what would happen if he showed up. I didn't expect this. I didn't know what to expect. He's crazy. He's going to kill me. How many people has he killed since... since the shooting.* He began to slip back as well; the cold winter day when they drove into the woods; the shooting; the shock of what they had done; the old rusty Triumph now covered in his garage, completely restored. *I should have gotten rid of that car years ago. Why did I keep it? Did I need a reminder? God, the nightmares. The lies. Years of cold sweats and tears.* Another crash to the side of the cabin, this time tearing siding from the wall. Augy ran to the window again. Water was building rapidly in front of the dam. "I think we're gonna be in a lotta shit here, Finch. Pretty soon."

Jay pictured Augy, holding his rifle, circling the truck. "Oh, shit, Finch! Hey, Finch, look what we did. Oh, shit! What are we gonna do now Finch?" He had relived those words a thousand times. It was like yesterday, the piercing senseless barrage of gunshots. *What did we do? Why? Why? I ruined my life. Oh, Serena, Carlie, I'm so, so sorry.* Tears rolled from his eyes as he sat rocking. *I didn't know.*

Circling Jay, Augy said, "What the hell are you crying for?" He grabbed the back of the chair and stopped it from rocking. "Afraid I'm gonna expose you to all your fancy-ass friends and all? You wanna cry? Well, cry for me. I was the one who suffered. I was the one who got shot at. I spent my time remembering, too. I remembered my brave buddy, Finch, the guy who was always there for me. I could tell you anything. I dreamed about you, Finch, about someday finding my old buddy and telling him, telling him everything, like confession. You were my hero, my smart college buddy, my best friend. I finally find you, and you won't give me the time of day. Snob. You don't want nothin' to do with me. I never told. I always believed you never told, neither. Now you got that cop buddy, the one with the girl's name. You told him, didn't you? You had him pick me up, and you told him. Why? I wasn't here for nothin' but to see how you were doing, what your life was like, meet your family, your kid. I could've been Uncle Augy. I might still become Uncle Augy. I always believed in you, Finch. You turn out like this. I never did anything to hurt you. I was always there for you. Remember, remember Concerto's grandson? I took care of him for you, you, my buddy Finch. What do I get in return?"

Jay listened intensely. *That's over thirty years ago. He never left. He still thinks we are kids.*

"Shit, wait till they find out you killed two fuckin' innocent men when you was young. Then you ran away, like a scared chicken and all, went to fuckin' college. College boy! I bet that was fun. What were you thinkin' all that time. Let ol' fuckin' August take the rap. Blood brothers, remember that, Finch? Remember when we cut ourselves? You still got the scar?" Augy grabbed Jay's left hand and held his scar next to Jay's. "Remember that day? We swore to be one. That meant something to me, man." Augy paused, turned, and walked from the rocker.

Jay stared at his scar and recalled the swift slice from the knife— first Augy, then him. He remembered standing, pressing his bleeding hand against Augy's. He told his parents that he fell from a tree in the woods. *We were just stupid kids.*

"Well, I never told. Never! Then you went and told your fuckin' cop buddy. You told him, didn't you?"

Jay shook his head. As Augy circled Jay's chair, he slapped the back of his hand on the side of Jay's head. Jay flinched, and the ruby ring on Augy's finger cut his already tender ear.

Augy stood in front of Jay, clenching a white knuckled fist an inch from his face. "You had to tell the cop, didn't you? Did you ask him to pick me up, question me?" Jay shook his head again. "Don't you fuckin' move, not even an inch. You're gonna listen to me. I could've wiped your ass all over your driveway if I wanted. I brought you here to listen, to maybe understand what my fuckin' life was like, what it's still like. While you was out getting fucked and getting rich, I was barely makin' it. I went into the Marines. I wrote you letter after frickin' letter. But no, big college man, you never wrote back. You just wanted to get rid of old August."

Leaning toward Jay angrily, he gritted his shiny teeth, shook his head, and put his face up to Jay's. "What were you thinkin'?" he said in a calm firm voice. "Maybe if you never seen or heard from me again, then the truth would all go away. On the inside we had an old saying. "If you ain't been around to hear nothing, then you ain't got nothing to fear." Augy paused again. "It goes something like that. No difference. I know you know what I mean."

He rose and began to pace, palms pressed against his forehead. "Sometimes, man, you know, since 'Nam I get my words mixed up. I forget stuff. I know what I'm thinkin', but it just doesn't come out that way. Headaches, I get these pounding headaches. The pain is un-fuckin' believable. My head goes dizzy, hazy. They called it shell shock. Crazy quacks, what the fuck do they know about shell shock? The loudest thing they ever heard was a firecracker on the fourth of July. They're a bunch a college boys, too, assholes, the lot. You ever seen your buddies filleted like fish, skin clean off? No, you didn't. You were just out layin' co-eds while the rest of us were dying and getting shot to pieces. You march? Ha, did ya? Did you fuckin' protest the war, burn the fuckin' flag, maybe? I got in trouble, blew my fuckin' lieutenant up, the prick. No one else had the balls to do it. I did. Then I spent time in a fuckin' box. Days went by. I couldn't stretch an inch. The cramps, man, I'll never forget the cramps. Fuckin' yellow slope bastards kept pokin' me, too. First thing I did when I got out was get even. Before I cut their balls off and let them bleed to death, they watched me butcher their wives and daughters. I got my share. To this day, man, I hate rice."

Jay watched as Augy paced throughout the night, becoming more irate as the hours passed. "One doc said it was if my head was a, ah, ah, oh yeah, if my head was late. No! He said my head was absent. That's it. Remember when we skipped out of school? We were absent." Giggling and gesturing by throwing open his hands, he went on, "Well, my head is still absent." He amused himself and laughed out loud. "They told me that my life was a waste. But I don't think so. I wasted other people's lives, the ones that deserved it."

A large tree limb, carried by the swift turbulent water of Pine Creek, struck the side of the cabin. It sounded like thunder. Augy stopped, lost track of his thoughts, and rushed to the window spreading the blinds. Dawn was coming.

Five cabins had been destroyed in 1981 by the furious waters carrying heavy debris down the mountain from Mt. Laguna. "Holy shit, Finch, if we don't get washed away we'll be lucky." He walked back to the sofa, sat, and began fondling the money in a back-pack. "All my life, all my life I wondered what it would be like to have this. Now I got all I need. No sense jumpin' around, I ain't gonna let you go, not yet, anyway. First you gotta hear my story."

He began chuckling. "I was gonna write a book, but I figured I'd be locked up forever if anybody read it. It would be a fuckin' confession for the whole world to hear. I even have the title. "The Half-Ass'd Life and Times of August J. Romano"—I like the J, don't you?—or I was gonna call it "The Serial Killer," but there is probably too many like that. You know, I heard some of those guys actually eat their prey, like fuckin' tigers and lions and shit." He shook his head. "No fuckin' way."

Lightning flashed, and thunder pounded simultaneously as a large limb from the old oak tree smashed through the roof. The side wall gave way, and the cabin started to break up. Augy leaped from the sofa and ran toward the back door. He fell, dropping the money next to him. Frantically reaching with both arms, he grabbed the backpacks and pulled them up against his chest. Water consumed the cabin as he watched Jay squirm in the chair as it flushed into the raging water. The floor rose and broke apart in front of him. Augy grabbed for the handle on the back door and pulled himself to a standing position. Jay's eyes appeared huge as he disappeared from Augy's view. Frightened and fearing for his own safety, Augy made his way out the door and into the miry water. He fought the muddy deluge as it came down from the hill behind him. Slipping and sliding, he made his way into the van. A thunderous blast of lightning struck the woodpile next to the van. Augy screeched as he started the engine and shifted. Sliding sideways, the van bumped into the kitchen wall. Then he shifted from drive to reverse and back again. The van slid, then cleared the side of the cabin and fishtailed down through the muck towards the road. He saw Jay, water rushing past his waist, waving his arms above his head and tangled in branches and debris from the cabin. *So long, old friend*, he said to himself as he passed. *I'm going to meet your pretty little wife.*

***

The worst of the storm damage was in San Diego's mountain communities, like Pine Valley. Emergency crews were spread out all over the East County. Utility trucks, tow trucks, and Forest Service vehicles lined the back-country roads. Main and secondary thoroughfares including the freeways morphed into torturous, oily ice sheets causing hundreds of accidents throughout the county. The old and shabby sewer system overflowed throughout the entire center city. Floods at the beach brought water into the homes and shops lining the Pacific Beach and Mission Beach areas. Lake Hodges and other reservoirs with dams were overflowing as continuous rainstorms were predicted for the next few days.

Chapter 40

Above his garage, in the old carriage house, Brooks sat in his worn, overstuffed, brown-leather chair drinking his morning cup of coffee staring out through the rain at the laced eucalyptus trees and Spanish, clay-tile rooftops in the distance. Brooks gazed at the tumultuous ocean waters just blocks from his hillside home. His view took in the mansions lining Camino de la Costa. Newman's house was partially blocked by a larger home on a terraced lot across from it.

Eighteen hours had passed since the homicides in Del Mar, eighteen hours with Jay Newman missing. Two days ago he had talked with Serena's mother and was told that she dropped off Carlie days ago and left. *What do I tell Serena? 'Your husband is missing and is a suspect in the murder of his ex-wife and his attorney.'* He closed his eyes and rested his head back in the soft leather chair. He took a deep breath and exhaled slowly. He thought about Scotty lying on the floor of his condominium. The phone rang.

"Hello."

"Brooks, this is Zookie. Boss wants to talk with you."

"Zuckerman," he replied sarcastically. Brooks disliked Zuckerman, considered him a waste to humanity, a two-bit, offshoot ex-con sucking on the apron strings of Mac O'Donnell.

"Boss wants to see you soon as possible."

Mac O'Donnell, Brooks thought, San Diego's shrew of shrews. Mr. Unscathed. There isn't a judge in town who would convict O'Donnell of anything. He loaned money and did favors for the best of them. Need money, bank says no, or it might three weeks, O'Donnell says yes, three hours. He remembered the pimp who was going to expose a judge in a prostitution sting. One call to O'Donnell and the guy disappeared. The banker, Smith, crossed Mac; his empire collapsed, and he went to jail.

"Where?" asked Brooks, knowing O'Donnell likes crowded places.

"The trolley station in Old Town. Three o'clock."

"Tell him I'll be there."

***

Earlier, Brooks had called Dr. Frankenstein and arranged to meet him. Brooks knew Howard was disgusting but needed his feedback, no matter how warped. Brooks got up, put on a yellow slicker with the word "police" stenciled on the back, walked down to his car, and drove to Goldman's house in Del Mar.

Property was cordoned off when crimes were committed. Policy required an officer to be on duty twenty-four hours a day until the scene became unrestricted. Brooks held up his badge as he drove up. The officer stationed at the foot of the driveway, also wearing a yellow slicker, waved him through.

As Brooks got out of his car, the patrolman walked toward him. "There is someone from the M.E.'s office already here to meet you, sir."

As he approached the house, he noticed Howard, puffing on a long cigar, stretched out in a lounge chair on the covered upper deck outside the master bedroom.

"Brooks," he stood and shouted, then puffed, "Up here."

Exiting his car, Brooks shook his head and laughed. There, standing on the deck above the stairs, was the semblance of a man with his head obscured in a thick foggy cloud of smoke. Laughing, he said to himself, *Howard the Headless.* "Come on up," he heard Howard declare. "The view is great."

"What view?" He chuckled, "How can you see anything?"

"You're right on time," said Howard as he greeted Alis in the living room by the front door.

Alis glanced around the room, noticing the mess. "What'd they have for dinner?" he asked.

"You mean, the last supper," Howard replied. "Chintzy broad, brought in from La Jolla, the French Gourmet. Too lazy to cook. Damn women these days."

"How do you know she brought it in?"

"In the kitchen, bags under the sink, in the trash."

Alis strolled through the house as Howard followed, occasionally puffing on the cigar.

"That thing will kill you, you know!"

"Not to worry. There's a lot of worse things I could do to myself. I don't inhale, anyway."

"I do, and it bothers me. Anyway, we're in Del Mar. No smoking in Del Mar."

"Give me a break. Arrest me," Howard said as he glanced around looking for a place to smother his cigar. He walked over to the dining table and dropped the cigar in a glass of water.

"These yups don't have anything else to do but complain about second-hand smoke. But it's okay to snort powder up their snooty noses. What a joke!" He picked up the glass and held it out toward Alis. "See, it's a goner, like your friends."

"Jesus Christ, man, you're contaminating a crime scene."

"Nah! I already checked out the water. Anyway, I'm about ready to release the place."

"They weren't my friends. I just knew them. Actually, I used to know her. She was the wife of Jay Newman. The guy was Newman's attorney."

"Jay Newman, Mr. San Diego, the guy with the clothing stores?"

Brooks looked at Howard and shrugged. "You know any other guys named Jay Newman?"

"I know Paul Newman, the actor. He smokes Havanas, has 'em smuggled in."

"Come on. Be serious will ya?"

"Okay, you got the ragman."

Brooks interrupted. "Why did you call him the ragman?"

"I'll get into that later. The ex-wife and the attorney. Was he still banging the ex? Triangle love affair. He catches her doing it with his attorney. He pretends to break in, the door was unlocked, kills 'em, and leaves. But that doesn't explain the lottery winnings."

Brooks stepped over David Goldman's chalk outline on the floor in the bedroom. "You're right. Newman's ex was involved with Goldman here," he said, pointing to the floor. "She set herself up with a new identity, had plane tickets to leave."

"Was Goldman going with her?"

"I don't think so. Newman told me that she was trying to extort money from him."

"Why? What did he do?"

"I'm not sure he did anything. She was a real pain in Newman's ass. It had to do with the business and the divorce."

"Figures. He fucked her over the coals. Isn't that what we're supposed to do?"

"He bought her a house, a car, and paid her a lot of money every month. She was jealous, didn't like the new wife."

"So Brooks, what's the difference between a housekeeper and an ex-wife?"

Alis looked at Howard. "Okay, what?"

"Nothing! They're both the same."

He waited for a response, then said, "I've seen her, the new wife, nice, like a model." He pointed toward the blood soaked bedding.

"This one wasn't too bad, either, had a lot of surgery. Oops, I mean before this. "

Brooks shook his head in response to Howard's remarks. "So she didn't like the young wife. I bet the new wife didn't like her, either."

Brooks moved out the door onto the deck. He stood looking out over the yard below. He put his hands in his pockets and turned facing Howard. "We found some more of the 'lotto jackpot' in Newman's garage and driveway."

"Too obvious," said Howard as he stood leaning with his palms resting on the wet railing and staring out toward the end of the drive.

Brooks looked puzzled. "What's too obvious?"

"There is something either seriously wrong here or amazingly simple."

"What do you mean?"

"Would you say your buddy Newman is a smart guy?"

"Yeah, he's not a rocket scientist, but he's a..."

"I'll tell you what he is. He's either really stupid or really sly."

"What makes you say that?"

"Stupid dictates that he was being blackmailed and decided to rid himself of the blackmailer or blackmailers. Sly says he had someone else do it for him. Either way, he accomplishes the same thing. What puzzles me is Newman's car was here."

"How do you know that?"

"I did a little checking on the tire treads at the apron of the driveway."

"What tire treads? You didn't say anything about tire treads."

"That's because I didn't finish my report yet."

Alis was getting impatient. He reached out and grabbed Howard by the shoulders. "What the fuck are you talking about? Tire treads!"

Pulling away, Howard said "Come on. I'll show you."

Alis followed as Howard walked down the stairs from the deck, across the lawn, and to the edge of the driveway. He motioned for the guard to take a walk. Yellow tape blocked access to a small strip of dirt, covered with a tarp, adjacent to the street and the lawn. "Look here," he said, pointing toward what was left of tire impressions in the dirt.

"What does this have to do with anything?" Brooks asked.

"I did a little checking on my own. To make a long story short, your buddy drives a Porsche, right?"

"Yeah, so? There's a lot of Porches in this neighborhood. What are you telling me?"

"Hey, don't get defensive with me."

"I'm not getting defensive. Why didn't you tell me about this before?"

"Before what? I told you I wasn't done with my report."

"Yeah, well, it sounds like you..."

"It sounds like what? I'm just doing my job, Brooks."

"It's not your job to convict someone."

Throwing his arms up in the air, Howard said, "You're the one who wanted me to meet you here. You want me to leave, or you want me to continue?" Brooks gestured for Howard to continue. "Okay. Why would he, Newman, deliver money, cash, hundred dollar bills, to them? He's a rich guy. He could just as easily write a check. He could have transferred money from one account to another. Why cash? Because whatever he was doing was illegal or incriminating, that's why. A payoff for something? And listen to this. Your buddy Newman drives a Porsche. His license plate is RAGMAN. I checked. A neighbor drove past the house about an hour before the picnic. The back plate read RAG something. She said it was a dark-colored Porsche. Newman's is dark blue, almost black."

Brooks shook his head in disappointment. "What else?"

"You sure you want to hear this?" Howard pressed.

"Go on."

"You got four different tire-tread patterns. Each wheel has a different tire. I checked with both Porsche dealers, and Alan Johnson Porsche down on Rosecrans conducts tire tests for BF Goodrich. Every sixty to ninety days, the customer brings his car in and he gets four new tires, all different tread patterns. The technician from the tire company records the wear on the tires he replaces and sends him on his way. They're all comp TAs."

"Comp TAs?" Brooks questioned.

"Those are high-performance tires. They only do this on a select number of cars. Your buddy has two Porsches in this program."

Brooks turned and paced. "That doesn't prove he was driving the car."

"No, you are absolutely right. It doesn't prove he was driving the car. In fact, it might not have been his car at all."

"What are you saying now?"

"I went to his house to check out his tires. His wife's Porsche is black. It wasn't there, but his was. Tires match."

"You sure it was...You think..."

"Sorry, Brooks. You tell me what to think. Her license plate is RAGS 2."

***

Brooks stopped home and changed clothes. Later, Mac O'Donnell was waiting for him, leaning on the side of the ticket booth of the trolley stop in Old Town. As Brooks approached, wearing a wool sweater and Levis, Mac said, "What, what, a miserable, wet afternoon this turned out to be."

Alis was somewhat annoyed by the urgency. "So what's so important?"

"I'd tell you to sit down, but I don't want to get any wetter."

"What's the problem here? I drove all the way from Del Mar to meet you. I'd rather be somewhere warm and dry."

"Look, Brooks. I've been thinking about the arrangement. I mean the money and all. I hear your friend, my client, is in deep shit. It's all over the news. No, no one knows where he is. Have you heard from him? Do you know where he is? I, I don't know shit about the clothing business. Do you? Is he going to get away with this? I, I mean, what do we do now?"

"If anybody can find someone, it's you, you, of all people, Mac. You getting scared?"

"I'm not scared. I'm concerned. This is real money, my money, your money, our money. The ABMO partnership, remember?" He moved close to Brooks and put his face to his. "You got just as much to lose as I do."

Snickering, Brooks said, "Christ, Mac, what's a million bucks between friends?"

Brooks turned to walk away. Mac reached out and grabbed his arm. "He's your friend, not mine."

***

Irrational thoughts fueled Augy's mind on his journey back to La Jolla. He blamed Serena Newman for taking her husband from him. She didn't deserve him. She was like every other attractive woman. If she was just ugly, he thought, ugly women are okay because they need people. Other women think they can do anything. They think they have some kind of power to throw around. *Bossy bitches*, he said to himself.

Augy returned to La Jolla, then parked the van on a side street by Wind n Sea beach. No one knew of the van, he thought, and he would be safe inside. He moved to the back, pulled the curtains closed, put another jacket on, over his yacht club jacket, and rested his head on the two backpacks. His last, self-imposed duty was to meet with and terminate Serena Newman at midnight.

***

Jay broke loose from the restraints, scurried through the water, and made his way up Pine Creek Road, where several utility trucks were parked. The crews were hard at work on the opposite side of the creek. He noticed a Gas and Electric pickup truck sitting with the keys in the ignition. He was soon on his way back to La Jolla.

***

Earlier in the evening Sam and Andy had had dinner at Alfonso's Mexican restaurant in downtown La Jolla. Andy was pressuring Sam for answers pertaining to her meeting with Serena Newman. Sam wasn't about to expose the fact that the two of them seemed to have much in common. Andy did, however, notice a change in her demeanor. She wasn't as upset about Jay Newman as she was about Augy Romano.

"You know, it's pretty obvious to me that you seemed to drop the idea of Jay Newman needing to pay for his crimes. It also seems to me that Augy Romano has taken priority as the main felon here."

"Why would you say that? You know I have a job to do. The job is to make sure these men pay for what they did."

Andy sipped his Corona and reached for a tortilla chip. "You seem nervous tonight. Is something going to happen? I want to help. I want to be part of whatever you are going to do."

"Andy, I can't let you be part of anything right now. So far you haven't done anything wrong. I don't want you to do anything that can get you in trouble."

Dipping his chip into the salsa bowl, he said, "Look, Sam, this whole thing was my idea in the first place. I found Newman and Romano. Without me, you wouldn't even be here. I can't compete with the FBI, but I need to see this resolved."

Sam reached across the table and grasped Andy's hand. "Trust me. I just need a little more time. In a day or so it will be all over. Then I will tell you everything. Can you trust me? Please."

He hesitated. "You know how I feel about you. Of course I trust you." He began to laugh. "Don't they have anything here other than Mexican food?"

"I heard the guacamole is really good as a starter, and the calamari is out of this world." She laughed back. "That's what the waiter said."

"I'll stick with the salsa for now. I'm not ready to eat anything green or anything I picture with multiple legs." Playing it safe, they each ordered cheese enchiladas with rice and beans. After dinner they swiftly scurried through the heavy rain, holding hands on the way back to Andy's motel.

Chapter 41

Jay was supposed to meet Serena behind the rec center between 12:15 and 12:30 in Augy's van. She was of course unaware of the nightmare in Pine Valley.

As the evening progressed, the rain and wind varied in strength with periodic lulls. The streets were flooded, and the palm trees, bent to extremes, were dropping old, weak fronds, which flew through the air like small missiles.

***

Augy never slept. He waited patiently, as he had done so many times before in his life, for the executioner to arise within him. At exactly 11:45 he sat up, made his way over the backpacks to the driver's seat, and started the engine.

The short ride through the neighborhood streets and onto La Jolla Boulevard took but minutes. He turned on Pearl Street, passing the Jack in the Box and again onto Cuvier Street, parking the van at the corner. He didn't notice the homeless people gathered together in the doorways and crannies surrounding the church.

At midnight he exited the van and walked through the flooding street toward the old church. He flipped a cigarette into his mouth and lit it. An old woman struggled past, pushing a tarp-covered grocery cart. She didn't look at him, and he ignored her. Seconds later a black cat scurried across the cul de sac to his right. His heart was hammering with anticipation as he turned his head quickly and watched the cat disappear into the drizzling darkness.

Turning his head back, he was suddenly surprised by a black shadow standing next to him. He sensed another shadow on his opposite side. A voice coming from one of the silhouettes said, "August Romano, it's your turn to pay the piper."

Augy jerked forward and twisted. The first kick in the chest pushed him back against the building. Both figures were small and dressed in black.

"Remember Jack Lyons, Augy? Remember his wife? Remember the little girl screaming on the stairway while you attacked my mother?" She guided a kick to his head, knocking him toward the other attacker.

"Romano, why did you have to show up here? After twenty-five years you decided to come make trouble for us." Augy helplessly reached out to grab either one of the women. He just needed to get his hands on one of their throats.

Another kick to his leg came from the left. The sound of his bone breaking was muffled by the sound of his nose being smashed from a leaping chop to his face from the right.

"Does the name Andy Fowler sound familiar? You killed his father and his uncle. You and your buddy!"

Serena paused, turned and pointed sternly at Sam. "This retaliation has nothing to do with my husband." Seemingly helpless and still standing, he caught them off guard and reached into his jacket pocket for the knife. Lunging toward Sam, the blade sliced through her sleeve and slashed her arm.

He continued waving the knife furiously back and forth, hoping to cut one of his attackers again. A swift kick from the left to his wrist and a simultaneous powerful blow to his arm from the opposite direction caused his arm to thrust back toward his body. The blade cut through his jacket, penetrating his side.

Augy was in extreme pain as he slouched to the ground. He had never been beaten so badly in his life. Blood seeped from his nose and mouth like a broken faucet. This wasn't a fair fight, he thought. *I always made the first move.* Excruciating pain from broken ribs and the broken leg felt unbearable. Squinting, he watched the ballerinas disappear into the haze.

***

"Units 125 John, 126 Baker."

"125 John, I copy."

"126 Baker, copy."

"Report of a 415 (disturbance) and possible 211 and 242 (robbery /battery) at the rear of the Baptist church on Pearl and Cuvier. RP (reporting party) states when he turned into the alley his headlights shined against the wall where at least one and maybe two people were beating on someone, said it looked like kickboxing or something. When his beams hit them, they turned and ran in the direction of the Jack in the Box on Pearl. No name on the RP. He hung up."

"10-4,126 John from La Jolla Scenic and Nautilus."

"126 Baker, did you copy?"

"10-4, 126 Baker, five minutes from The Farms."

Blue and red flashing lights bounced through the palm trees and off the dark, shiny, drenched pavement as the two San Diego Police cruisers entered the alley. Each officer switched on his searchlight and swung a wide beam in the direction of the sopping, bloody body.

Both officers, wearing yellow, department-issued slickers, bolted from their cars and hurried to the victim.

Stooping next to him, "Another one of La Jolla's finest, huh?" remarked the first officer.

"Is he still alive?" asked the second officer.

The back of Augy's head was braced by the wall of the church; he sat slumped in a diluted pool of blood. Unshaved, rain-soaked, with matted hair, and terrified, his swollen eyes moved rapidly from side to side.

"Hey, buddy, can you hear me? What's your name? Do you know who did this to you?"

His khaki pants were torn below the knees, and his white boat shoes were covered with mud. He wore two jackets. A dark inner jacket was zipped up to his neck. The outer was filthy and half open. Embroidered on the upper left chest area of the inside jacket was a blue and white burgee with a red star in the center, San Diego Yacht Club.

"Maybe this guy's not homeless." remarked the officer. "Maybe he was just in the wrong place at the wrong time?"

"Yeah. Look at his eyes. I'll call for an ambulance."

As 126 Baker made the call, the first officer slowly rolled the victim to the left and spotted the handle of a knife protruding from his side.

"Make that 11-41 a code 3, will ya? There's a knife sticking out of his right side."

Leaning close, the officer said, "Listen, sir, can you hear me? An ambulance is on the way. You might die. What's your name? Who did this to you? If you know who did this, you better tell me now."

The rain fell harder as the ambulance backed into the alley. While paramedics placed him on the gurney, the officer leaned closer, squeezing his hand.

"Tell me, man, what's your name. Who did this to you?"

Augy's desperate eyes penetrated the policeman's. His mind was spinning as he dreadfully uttered... "Finch, Finch! He, ah, he didn't..."

"Who is Finch? He didn't what?"

Augy knew this was the end. He could hardly breathe. His words were slow, and he was choking as he continued.

"Blanks," he mumbled. "Blanks. I put blanks in his gun. It was supposed to, to be a joke, but..."

"What are you talking about? Blanks what?"

Gurgling through, what appeared to be his last breath, Augy said, "Tell the guy with the girl's name. Tell him, tell him that Finch didn't shoot anybody. Tell him…"

***

As planned, Serena ran to the van, climbed into the back, and Jay started the engine.

"Who was that other person with you? I thought you…"

"Not now, Jay, just drive. We only have thirty minutes to get there."

***

"What, exactly, did you do?"

"I did what needed to be done," she replied as she changed her clothes. "I took care of the problem."

"Both of them?" he asked, as he nervously paced. "I only saw one."

"You weren't supposed to be there, Andy. I told you to wait here."

"Are you kidding me? How could I wait here when you left dressed like a…"

"Don't ask any more questions. The less you know the better."

"Believe me, I know what you did. I'm okay with that. I need to know you got both of them."

Pulling her sweater over her head, she boldly approached him. "We only got one of them, okay? I'll get the other one. The FBI probably has him as we speak."

"What does 'probably' mean?"

"Your taxi will be here in a few minutes. You are going home."

She put her arms around him and hugged him tightly while planting a solid kiss on the lips. "I'll contact you as soon as I can," she said, darting out the door. "I love you, Andy Fowler."

Chapter 42

The van drove north on highway 5 to Palomar Airport Road. The gate entering the airport was unlocked, as he drove through puddles and rain. Jay and Serena got out of the van with both backpacks and hurried toward the parked planes.

Standing next to an unmarked police cruiser stood Alis Brooks with an umbrella high over his head. Another person exited the police car and stood next to Alis.

Jay stopped in his tracks, put down the backpack and looked at Serena. Sadly, he said, "I guess it's all over now?"

She took his hand, faced him, and replied, "This is the only way, darling. There is nothing else we can do."

Remorsefully, he said, "I knew this day would come." He hugged her, picked up the backpacks, and they walked sluggishly toward Alis and his partner. Approaching the tarmac, he spotted the cockpit and cabin lights switch on and radiate through the windows of the Gulfstream.

"You're late," Alis said as he walked up to Jay and hugged him. "Did everything go as planned."

"Not everything, but I think it worked."

As Alis's wife, Francesca, hugged Serena, Alis handed Jay an envelope. "Everything you need is in here. Your passport, your papers, and your new identity."

"You better hurry," said Francesca. "You have a 6,000-mile trip ahead of you. Once you arrive in Buenos Aries, my father will meet you at the airport. The money you have given me over the years has accumulated to a little more than four million dollars. You will live very comfortably."

"I can't thank you enough, Francesca."

"Your new home awaits you, in Palermo Chico, near my family. You will be well cared for. You must learn to speak the dialect. Your tutor is your housekeeper. You can trust her. She has been a long-time employee of my family."

Turning toward Serena, Jay said, "I'm so sorry. Tell Carlie..."

"Don't worry about Carlie, and don't worry about me. Once this is finished we will join you as planned."

Alis leaned in. "Maybe we'll all be together again at Christmas. You gotta go now."

Jay picked up the backpacks and walked up the stairs to the cabin. He turned and waved, then entered the plane.

All three watched silently as the silver jet disappeared into the black hazy sky.

***

Serena Newman sold the house at the beach and moved in with her parents in Rancho Santa Fe. Jaime and Martha moved with them.

Augy Romano's sealed casket was sent back to a cousin in Ohio for burial.

Dominic Ferruccio returned to La Jolla two months later and met the new owner of his home, George Lowe. Soon thereafter, while George was walking in the dark alley behind his office, he fell victim of a deadly hit and run.

Andy returned home and continued to teach school. While Grandma was lying on her deathbed, he whispered in her ear, "It's all over, Grandma. It's all finished."

Sam left the FBI and reunited with Andy in Ohio. When he introduced her to his mother, he told her that she was someone special he met at the teachers' convention in California.

Mac O'Donnell received an unmarked package containing $500,000. He used the money to make ridiculous commercials for his newly acquired clothing business.

Serena, Carlie, Alis, and Francesca visited Buenos Aries at Christmas. Serena and Carlie stayed.

Two years later, while strolling home from his favorite coffee shop near his home, Jay Newman was attacked and killed in an alley. An eyewitness said that he saw someone hold a gun to his head and pull the trigger. He watched as two gunshots were fired.

Police never found bullets or evidence of any gunshots. They ruled the death as being the result of a robbery and beating. They could not determine the significance of the wrapped Zagnut Candy bar shoved into his mouth.

The End

About the Author

Bob Feinstein has always been a storyteller. Like many people, he always had the desire to write a book.

The concept for The Hunt Club began many years ago after having been inspired by a novel written by a well-known author known for his stories of cops, criminals, high-flyers and low-lifes.

Like most of us, however, years passed by and life got in the way of finishing the manuscript.

Suspense, murder, sex, love, blackmail—what else do you want in a book?

Bob's goal was to get his hooks into you and drag you along by engaging your imagination in an unconventional way. He certainly hopes you enjoy his book—he had fun writing it—and he is optimistically anxious to see the movie…